Connell
Pullman
395
12
95
Orofino
Lewiston
12
Dayton
Waitsburg
Asotin
NEZ PERCE
RESERVATION
Richland
182
Kennewick
Walla Walla
Cottonwood
82
12
Umatilla
730
Milton-Freewater
Troy
Flora
Hermiston
Wallowa-Whitman
National Forest
White Bird
84
Stanfield
Pendleton
Mission
Minam
Elgin
Eagle
Imnaha
Lucile
84
Pilot Rock
Winslow
Alder
Riggins
Prairie Creek
La Grande
395
Hot Lake
95
Umatilla
National Forest
Snake River
84
Ukiah
Dale
Halfway
Sumpter
Baker City
Richland
Council
Greenhorn
Snake River
395
84
26
Durkee
Cambridge
95

Murder of Ravens

A Gabriel Hawke Novel

Paty Jager

Windtree Press
Hillsboro, OR

This is a work of fiction, names, characters, places, and incidents either are the product of the author's imagination or are used fictitiously, and any resemblance to actual persons living or dead, business establishments, events, or locales, is entirely coincidental.
MURDER OF RAVENS

Contact Information: info@windtreepress.com

Windtree Press
Hillsboro, Oregon
http://windtreepress.com

Cover Art by Christina Keerins
CoveredbyCLKeerins

Published in the United States of America

ISBN 978-1-947983-82-3

Special Acknowledgements

I'd like to thank the Oregon State Police Fish and Wildlife division for allowing me to ride along with an officer to learn all the ins and outs of the job. Special thanks also go out to Judy Melinek, M.D. for answering my pathology questions, Dr, Lowell Euhus for explaining about the Wallowa County Coroner's job, and Lloyd Meeker for his expertise on helicopters.

Author Comments

While this book and coming books in the series are set in Wallowa County, Oregon, I have changed the town names to old forgotten towns that were in the county at one time. I also took the liberty of changing the businesses in the towns and populating the county with my own characters, none of which are in any way a representation of anyone who is or has ever lived in Wallowa County. Other than the towns, I have tried to use the real names of all the geographical locations.

Chapter One

The threat of potential poachers wouldn't spoil Hawke's day. He glanced up through the pine and fir trees at the late August summer sky to appreciate the blue sky and billowy white clouds. Half a dozen shiny black ravens circled above the trees half a mile away. So much for thinking he'd come upon the poachers before they did any damage.

He and Dog, his mid-sized, wire-haired, motley mutt, had picked up the trail of two people on horseback with a pack horse at sunrise. He'd started the pursuit after finding spent cartridge rounds at a spot where they had stopped. Only poachers would be carrying rifles during bow season and following an elk trail. From the circling birds, he feared they were too late to stop an unlawful kill.

He'd used the Bear Creek Trail to patrol Goat Mountain in the Wallowa Whitman National Forest and check bow hunters for tags.

He whistled for Dog to stop.

"Easy, Dog. We're going to go slow the rest of the way." Hawke dismounted, trailing his horse and pack mule behind him. It took longer to reach the kill site by walking, but he didn't want to chance surprising a bear, wolf, cougar, or the poachers.

He picked his way through the brush, being mindful of the scraping noises from the packsaddle being caught in the limbs of young growth pines. Any other time he wouldn't have minded. The fresh pine scent from the abuse to the limbs, filled his nostrils.

Dog's tail started whipping back and forth when they were twenty feet from the area where the birds circled.

"Don't tell me you've become friends with the bears and cougars on this mountain," Hawke whispered, easing out of the thicket and into a small clearing.

A woman was bent over what appeared to be a man's body. He noted the backpack on the ground by the woman and knew why Dog's tail wagged. Biologist Marlene Zetter. She traveled this area keeping tabs on the wolf bands that had made their way to Northeast Oregon from the Northern Rocky Mountains.

"What are you doing with a body, Marlene?"

The woman in question lunged to her feet and spun to face him. Her gaze latched onto him, skimming from his cowboy boots, jeans, denim jacket, to his face under the brim of a western hat. The panic on her face disappeared as she recognized him.

"Hawke! You nearly scared ten years off my life."

Dog bounded toward the woman.

"Dog! Sit!" ordered Hawke.

The animal flopped down on his haunches, obeying the command.

"What are you doing up here alone and leaning over a man's body?" Hawke dropped his reins and walked over to the body and woman, studying the ground and taking care to not cover any tracks.

She pointed downward. "That's what brought me here."

Hawke scanned the dusty camouflage boots, pants, jacket, orange transmitter collar around the man's neck, and unseeing eyes. He whistled. "Why does he have one of your collars?"

She shook her head. "We were doing a count in the area. Roger is up in the helicopter. He gave me quadrants for about a mile to the north, but as I worked my way that direction, I stumbled over this."

"Did you touch anything?" Hawke walked her fifteen feet back from the body.

"No. I'd just knelt beside him when you arrived." She glanced around him toward the body. "Why is he wearing a tracking collar?"

"I don't know. Stay here. I'll start my investigation." Hawke walked over to Horse, his pack mule, and retrieved a camera. "If you have radio access, notify dispatch. Tell them I have a body. We'll need the medical examiner and a retrieval team."

He didn't wait for Marlene to reply. His digital camera, radio, and cell phone were the only pieces of current technology he used when on duty as a game warden in the Eagle Cap Wilderness. Before he began documenting the area with his camera, he did a quick look for footprints. He found Marlene's. She came from a southeast direction. He noticed two sets of tracks, one of which matched the boots on the victim, that came from the northwest. The other set came to where the man lay, there were a few scuffed marks. As if the person were hesitant to view the body. A squeamish killer? He followed the set of tracks that returned to the trees and discovered the distinct shoe prints of the two saddle horses and pack horse he'd tracked all day. This was one of the men he'd been tracking.

"I didn't hear any shots. How did they get a wolf collar?" He glanced around at the ground, brush, and trees, searching for any sign of a struggle or blood.

Nothing.

Aware he'd left Marlene alone with the victim, he took photos of the impressions and hurried back to the opening.

The biologist remained in the same spot he'd left her. Her back to the victim.

"Do you know him?" Hawke asked, approaching the body and snapping pictures.

"He looks familiar, but I can't put a name to him." She held up her radio. "I contacted Roger. He's calling dispatch."

"Thanks." Hawke patted Dog on the head when he walked by. "Stay."

Once he had all the photos, he walked over to Horse and pulled evidence bags, a marker, and latex gloves from the pack. He never knew what would help in an investigation and made a thorough search around the body for anything that didn't appear to belong in the clearing. He had gathered a small collection when he crouched by the body.

A long hair clung to the victim's shoulder. It wasn't coarse like mane or tail hair. The color was close to Marlene's two-tone brown-blonde. He'd give her the benefit of the doubt that it could have fallen when she looked down, but it was evidence and went in a bag.

Hawke had come across dozens of deaths as an Oregon Fish and Wildlife State Trooper. Judging from the bulging, blood-shot eyes, red dotted face, and scratch marks on the neck where the victim had tried to take the collar off, he'd say the man had been strangled. A check of the bolts and the tightness of the collar made him wonder how someone could have wrestled with a man this size to get the collar tightened. The bolts would have had to have been in place. He mimicked the actions it would have taken to put the collar on and then tighten it. Not an easy feat on a man of the victim's size.

Yet, there was no sign of a struggle. "Accidental or on purpose?" Talking to himself was his custom from spending so many days and hours alone with his horse, mule, and dog.

"What did you say?" Marlene asked.

"Nothing."

He felt the pockets for a wallet or identification and noticed the victim's belt wasn't latched in its natural hole. It was one hole looser. Had someone else tightened his belt? Or had the belt been the murder weapon and the collar put on after the man was incapacitated? He took a photograph.

A cell phone was in the coat pocket along with a wad of tissues. These were placed in evidence bags. Rolling the body on its side, he scanned the area under the body. The ground appeared more disturbed than from a body lying on it. Tuffs of grass had been unrooted. The retrieval team would look for evidence under the body. He found a wallet in the back pocket of the man's camo pants. A quick flip revealed a driver's license. Ernest Cusack, 20456 Elm Loop, Alder, Oregon. The victim was a local.

The wallet was bagged along with coins, a pocket knife, and lip balm found in his front pockets. There didn't seem to be any other evidence to collect.

Back at the mule, he put all the evidence bags in the pack and pulled out a small tarp. He walked back to the body and placed the tarp over the victim, using rocks to hold it down.

"Now what do we do?" Marlene asked.

Hawke walked over to his horse and started unsaddling the animal. "We wait."

"You know no one is going to get up here before tomorrow." She shouldered her pack.

"Put that down. You'll have to remain until the others get here." He walked over and slipped her pack off her shoulder. "Make camp. You're staying here."

She peered up at him. "I didn't bring overnight gear."

"I'll share." He walked over to his horse.

After placing his saddle upside down on the ground under a tree and tying Jack, the horse, out on a weighted tether away from any trees, he took the pack and saddle off Horse and tethered the mule as well.

Dog settled himself on the ground between Marlene and Hawke.

"I didn't bring a lot of supplies with me." Marlene leaned her pack against a tree, using it as a backrest.

"How did you plan to get off the mountain before dark?" Hawke tossed her a package of vacuum sealed jerky. His forefathers had survived for days with pemmican, a mash of dried salmon and berries. He survived most trips on the mountain with jerky, freeze-dried meals, and granola bars.

"Roger planned to pick me up at Wade Flat." She opened the jerky. "Thanks."

"You'll have to radio him to come back for you tomorrow." Hawke studied the woman. They had met at several Fish and Wildlife public meetings where the locals voiced their concerns about the growing population of wolves in the county. Ranchers had lost cattle to the wolves, making them angry at the animal and at Fish and Wildlife.

Some had tried using the nonlethal methods biologists suggested to keep livestock safe. But the wolf was cunning. Hawke's ancestors had revered the wolf for his fur, his cunning, and how they worked as a pack to feed everyone. His ancestors also knew the consequences of too many wolves in one area. Not only did cattle get eaten, but so did deer, elk, and mountain goats, staples of the Nez Perce over a century ago.

"Roger, this is Marlene," the woman said into the large radio she held in her hand.

Garbled words crackled in the air. "Dispatch wants Hawke to call them."

"Did you hear that?" Marlene asked.

Hawke grunted and knelt by his pack. His radio was in the side with all the evidence and his forensic kit.

"Hawke won't let me leave. Meet me same time tomorrow afternoon at Wade Flat."

"Copy."

The crackling sound ended and the forest sounds

settled around them again.

Hawke glanced in the sky. With the body covered, the birds had stopped circling. The rest of the night would be spent keeping the ground scavengers from destroying the body.

He turned on his radio, listened to the crackle, and held the button down. "Hawke checking in." He raised his fingers off the button and listened.

"Is the body contained?"

"Yes. I'm holding a witness until the others arrive."

"ETA for body retrieval is ten-hundred tomorrow."

"Copy." Hawke turned the radio off, replaced it in the pack, and pulled out his filtered water bottle and a plastic bottle of water he hauled around in case he came upon a dehydrated hiker or needed it for cleaning a wound when there wasn't any water available.

"Here." He tossed the plastic bottle to Marlene. "Use this to drink. Should be a small stream to the east if you want to wash up."

"I crossed it shortly before coming into the clearing." She held up the water. "Thanks, again."

He nodded and tore into his bag of jerky. The day had been spent in the saddle with only a stop to refill his water bottles and stretch his legs. He'd hoped to catch the two he'd tracked before dark. Instead, he would watch over the victim and keep an eye on his suspect.

It would be a long night.

Chapter Two

A full moon lit up the clearing like early dawn. Grays and blacks were highlighted in golden moon glow. Good for keeping an eye on the body. Hawke waved his hand, and Dog chased away a curious coyote.

Marlene stirred under the blankets Hawke had given her, but didn't wake.

He was thankful she'd not tried to make small talk before making a bed and closing her eyes. By her furtive glances, she knew she was at the top of his suspect list. Not his list. He'd hand her and the evidence over to whoever arrived tomorrow and go after the man's partner. His best work happened out in the wilderness, not at a desk behind a computer.

Finding the second poacher would most likely find who put the collar on the victim's neck and strangled him. It was either a cold-blooded killer or a joke that went wrong. Either way, he would find the person.

Dog made several circles around the body, before returning to Hawke's side.

"Good boy." Hawke stroked the smooth hair on Dog's head and scanned the area where he'd tethered Horse and Jack. They were both munching on the grass and flicking their tails.

By the moon, he guessed it to be after midnight. If Dog stayed vigilant, he could get an hour or two of sleep.

His eyelids lowered, his mind cleared…

Howling wolves straightened his spine and raised the hair on his arms.

Dog sat up.

Hawke grabbed the animal's collar before he dashed off.

Marlene stirred. "Did I hear wolves?"

"Yes. Go back to sleep. It was several miles away." The sound had echoed in the draw. He wasn't positive they were miles away.

The howling and sharp-pitched, excited yips of the wolves sang of pursuit. He hoped in the opposite direction of them. Keeping a pack of wolves away from the body wasn't a task he wanted tonight or any night.

Marlene remained sitting up, her head cocked, listening.

The pursuit call echoed through the forest, standing his hair on end again. This time the calls were closer.

Hawke shot to his feet, grabbed the ropes dangling from Horse and Jack's halters and tied them to the highline he'd made earlier between two trees. He didn't need the animals bolting and dragging their weighted tethers or getting caught up in the long tether ropes, injuring themselves.

"They're close," Marlene said, grabbing her pack and pulling out her laptop. She tapped the keys and a faint beeping started. "I'm picking up number twenty-four-ninety-three. An alpha female." Her words came out on a rush.

The beeping grew in volume.

"She's coming toward us. And it looks like two others with her have collars."

He heard the excitement in her voice. "You aren't going after them. If they show here, I'm shooting my rifle in the air." He didn't want or need the trouble wolves and women brought.

"Don't chase them off before I can get a count." She pulled a book and flashlight out of her backpack. The sound of pages flipping was followed by accelerated beeping.

"Number twenty-four-ninety-three is from the Minam pack. They had five grown wolves last year. I hope they have pups with them." Marlene stared at her computer then into the trees on the far side of the clearing. "That's the way they're coming from."

Hawke stared into the trees on the far side of the open area. He didn't know much about what the computer could register, but the way Dog's hair bristled down his back, the wolves would be upon them soon.

Limbs cracked, hooves pounded the earth, and the tang of fear filled the air before a wild-eyed horse burst into the clearing followed by three adult wolves.

Hawke untied a lasso from his packsaddle. "Keep the horse in the clearing!" he shouted to Marlene. "Get 'em," he said to Dog.

As Dog deterred the wolves and Marlene ran along

the side of the clearing, keeping the horse from darting into the forest, Hawke swung the loop over his head, running behind the horse. He was just about out of breath when the animal darted to its right. He finally had a clear shot of the animal's head.

He let the loop fly. It landed over the horse's head and around its neck. Hawke ran to the closest tree, wrapping the lariat around once before the horse came to the end of the rope. It stood, shaking and wild eyed.

Hawke turned his attention to Dog, toying with two of the wolves.

Where had the third one gone?

"Grab this rope and try to get the horse to come to you. I'm getting rid of the wolves." He ran to the tree where he'd set up camp and picked up his firearm. Other Fish and Wildlife State Troopers packed an AR-15. Hawke relied on his trusty pump-action shotgun. He shot in the air, pumped another shell into the chamber, and shot again. The boom of a shotgun did more good when chasing critters away than the spat of an AR-15. By the second shot, Dog was at his side. All three wolves ran back across the clearing and into the trees.

Hawke glanced at the tarped body. One of the wolves had dragged the tarp a short distance.

"Hawke, I could use some help," Marlene called.

He had a feeling the wolves hadn't gone far. Not if the one had discovered the body.

The horse calmed down as Hawke crooned to it in his forefather's ancient language.

"What are you saying?" Marlene asked as she walked up with the halter he'd asked her to get from his pack.

"I'm telling him he is safe. He was a good horse to

come to us." Hawke slipped the halter on the animal's blond head. He was a nice palomino quarter horse gelding. The horse was one someone would miss in the morning when they wanted off the mountain.

"Hold your flashlight on his legs," Hawke said. There were scratches and a couple gashes on the animal's forelegs and hocks. "It's a shame. Nice animal like this."

"Did the wolves do that?" Marlene asked, her voice wobbly.

"Yes and no. The wounds were caused by running him through the brush. But had he not been chased by the wolves, it wouldn't have happened." He led the gelding over by Jack and Horse and tied him to the same highline.

"There is comfort in numbers," he mumbled to the animals.

Marlene stood by her pack, writing in her book.

He picked up his collapsible bucket and shotgun. Hawke stopped beside the biologist. "Take my shotgun. The wolves know there is an easy meal here. If they come back shoot in the air. I'm getting water to doctor the horse."

She shot a glance the direction the wolves disappeared and took the shotgun. "What about you? Will you be safe?"

He grinned and patted where his Glock rested in his shoulder harness under his jacket. "I have Dog and my side-arm with me."

Dog arrived at his side. Using his flashlight, Hawke made a direct trail to the small stream twenty yards or better to the east of camp. He took the time alone to take care of personal hygiene.

Feeling less like a cur who'd rolled in a mud puddle, he filled the bucket with water and headed back to camp. Halfway there, a gun shot rang out. "Go!" he told Dog, who took off through the trees, leaping downed logs and making faster progress than Hawke sloshing water out of the bucket and cursing the thorny bushes grabbing his pant legs.

Another shot rang out as he rushed into the clearing. Dog chased one of the wolves into the trees on the other side.

"Dog! Come!" he shouted with what little air he still had in his lungs. If Dog followed the wolf too far, all three would turn on him.

A dark shadow burst from the trees and straight toward him. Hawke's heart started beating again. He and Dog had been together too long to lose the animal from his own stupidity.

"You were right. One snuck out of the trees and then another. I waited until all three had emerged and shot." Marlene was out of breath as she hurried over to where he and Dog stood.

"Keep the shotgun until I get the horse doctored. Then Dog and I will make camp by the body." Hawke didn't like sitting practically on top of the deceased for the remainder of the night, but he wanted a body left in the morning when his associates arrived.

Chapter Three

The wolves made three more attempts to get to the body and finally gave up. Hawke sat propped against his packsaddle. Dog reclined beside him. They both gave a long, heavy sigh and peered up at the sun peeking into the clearing.

It was going to be a long day whether he went after the other person or decided to travel off the mountain.

"Coffee?" Marlene called.

He sniffed. The aroma of his dark roast coffee overrode the gases brewing in the deceased. Hawke stood and grabbed his packsaddle, hauling it back to the edge of the trees. "I see you helped yourself to my coffee."

"You were sleeping. I didn't want to wake you to ask your permission. I pulled the pot and grounds out of your pack." The smile tugging up the corners of her chapped lips revealed she perceived she'd outsmarted him.

He was a tired master tracker, not a ninja.

Hawke opened the flap on his pack and plucked out two tin cups. "Since you're sharing my coffee with me, I could share a cup with you."

She laughed and used the corner of a horse blanket to grab the coffee pot off the small fire she'd made to brew the coffee. "I don't suppose you have any eggs or bacon in there." She nodded toward his pack.

"I have dehydrated scrambled eggs with bacon bits you can make."

"That's better than an empty stomach."

He placed the cup of coffee on the ground and dug out two packets of dried eggs, a small aluminum pot, and a spoon.

Marlene took the packets from him, read the directions, and poured water into the pan. When the water came to a boil, she poured some into each packet and stirred.

She picked up her cup of coffee. "Do you have another spoon?"

He shook his head. "But I do have a fork." He dug into his pack. "You use the spoon, I'll use the fork."

Marlene didn't object. She handed him one packet and dug into hers.

He finished his food, drank the rest of his coffee, and poured another cup.

"Will they contact you when they are on the way up?" Marlene asked, refilling her cup and settling on the blankets.

"If I had the radio on." He left the radio off between uses to conserve the battery. Hawke set his cup down and dug through his pack. Turning on the radio, he placed it next to the pack, and reclined against his canvas back rest. There were several hours before the retrieval team would arrive.

The coffee tasted better than he made. Same grounds, same pot. He glanced over at Marlene. What did she do to make it taste better?

The horses nickered. He finished off the coffee and grabbed the pan and utensils. "I'll wash these while the horses are getting a drink."

"Do you need help?" she asked.

"No. Dog and I can handle it." He whistled for Dog, who still slept by the body.

The animal's head jerked up and he glanced around. With his gaze on Hawke, he stood, stretched each leg and his back, and trotted over.

Hawke had Horse and Jack untied. He handed Jack's lead rope to Dog and untied the runaway horse. With the mule on one side and the new horse on the other, Hawke led them to the stream. Dog followed behind leading Jack. He'd bought Jack the same year he'd rescued Dog, as a pup. They had become friends. Having taught Dog how to lead Jack was a good thing. It helped when Horse was having a mule day.

At the stream, he crouched between Horse and the palomino to wash the dishes. Dog stopped on the other side of Horse and Jack drank. The slurping and gulping of the animals accented the gurgling of the stream over smooth rocks. Even after the dishes were clean and the horses stood, drooling water back into the stream, he sat on his haunches, breathing in the musty forest floor, earthy horse, and tang of pine.

He understood why his ancestors were angered when this land, their home, had been taken from them. His father's family had been part of the treaty Nez

Perce, the bands that had moved to the reservation. His mother's family had been with the non-treaty Nez Perce who had refused to sign the treaty taking away their land and followed Looking Glass, Young Joseph, and White Bird, to Montana.

His great-grandfather had managed to get away the night before Joseph surrendered at Bear Paw. He wasn't welcomed at the reservation by his own people and had moved in with the Walla Walla at the Umatilla Reservation. But his grandfather told the stories that had been passed down to him from his father.

"Hawke! Hawke!" Marlene called.

He stood, leading the horse and mule back to camp. A glance over his shoulder, caught sight of Dog and Jack following.

Marlene met him part way into the trees with his radio. "They want to talk to you."

He plucked the radio from her hands and handed the two lead ropes to the biologist.

Static crackled. He pressed the button and said, "Hawke," and fell in step behind Jack's back end.

Static and popping then a voice said, "The retrieval team left the bottom at six. A helicopter should be hovering soon."

As if the announcement conjured up the aircraft, he heard the soft thump, thump, thump of the blades cutting through the air.

"Visual," Hawke said.

"Copy." Static crackled.

Being a master tracker, his gaze constantly scanned his surroundings. But it was the familiar print on the forest floor that grabbed his attention. He stopped, crouched, and stared at one set of tracks. The horse they'd saved was one of the three he'd followed yesterday. Did it get away from the other person or was it set free on purpose? Either way, he had a fresh, easy to follow set of tracks.

Hawke made sure the horses and mule were all tied tight as the sound of the copter grew louder and the tops of the trees danced from the blade airstream.

In the clearing, he peered up into the cockpit of the helicopter. He hid the smile that started to tip his lips. Dani Singer. The niece of his old friend Charlie Singer. She'd taken over Charlie's hunting lodge when he'd passed eighteen months ago. Hawke had met Dani on two occasions. The first time when he'd been called to the lodge to investigate a death. They'd gotten off on shaky ground because he was mad he hadn't been told about Charlie's death and mad that some smartass Air Force pilot thought she knew enough to run the lodge. And the second when he'd needed to spend the night at the lodge. They'd agreed to a mutual truce, and that evening they'd played cards and had a pleasant visit.

He waved.

She waved back and pantomimed if she could land. Knowing she'd flown copters for the Air Force, he figured she could land anywhere that was flat and open enough. He directed her to the widest area between the trees. If the body hadn't been in the middle of the clearing, it would have been easy for her to drop in.

She gave him an okay and hovered over the area, slowly lowering the aircraft.

Hawke held his cowboy hat on his head as the wind from the blades whipped the tarp off the body and started the extra horse panicking.

The blades gradually eased along with the wind.

He hurried to replace the tarp on the body before meeting Dani.

"I'm surprised to see you," he said, keeping his tone neutral, unsure if she was still mad over his believing her a suspect or if their night of playing cards had made her forget.

"I've contracted with law enforcement to help out with Eagle Cap search and rescues. I can get here quicker than Dunten in Baker City." She nodded to the tarp. "Hiker get lost?"

"No. I believe it's a murder." He walked toward Marlene.

"Up here?" The skepticism in her voice made him remember why he shouldn't get friendly with the woman. She thought she knew everything because she had been an officer in the Air Force.

"It can happen anywhere." He strode over to the horses, calming the extra one and checking its wounds.

The two women greeted each other like friends before putting their heads together, sending furtive glances his way as if discussing him.

His pride wanted to think they liked what they saw, but his gut said they were talking about how he was crazy to think a man was murdered in the wilderness. Without a word, he picked up the water bucket, whistled to Dog, and headed to the creek for water to wash the horse's wounds and reapply salve.

Blocking the women from his sight and mind, he focused on the fact the extra horse had been part of the group he'd followed to the dead man. It was one sick person who murdered a man and left his horse loose for wild animals to kill and eat.

The more he thought about it, the angrier he

became. He'd catch the person if he had to track them for a month. Which would be good. Snow would hit the high areas by then and aid his tracking.

With his hawk eyes and the knowledge he'd soaked up as a child from his father and grandfather, he could track just about anything anywhere. There were more than marks in the dirt that showed where something had been. He paid attention to his surroundings and what was out of place.

He dipped the bucket and headed back to the horses.

The women now stood by the body.

Damn! He ran toward them, sloshing water on his leg. "Get away. You both know better."

Hawke stepped between the women and the body with the tarp flopped back.

"I know him," Dani said.

"How?" Hawke asked, flipping the tarp back in place.

"He owns the Firelight Restaurant in Alder. He purchases truckloads of food from suppliers. I was told to go to him to get all my staples in bulk." Dani shook her head. "Why would someone put a wolf tracking collar on him?"

"That's something that doesn't go any further than this mountain." Hawke glared at both women to emphasize his statement.

"Loud and clear," Dani said, glaring back at him.

Marlene nodded, but he could see she was thinking something.

"Is there a way to find out where that collar came from?" he asked.

"It's not one that was on a wolf. It would have

registered on my computer. Unless the tape wasn't pulled on the battery. If the battery isn't activated, the tracking device doesn't work. When they take it off, I can check the serial number and check the battery. If it was from our supplies that's all we'll know. But your suspect list will be slim it if came from our supplies. Only employees of the ODFW building have access to the collars. They are too expensive to leave laying around." Marlene jammed her hands on her hips as if she were ready to go a round with whoever stole the collar.

While they were talking, he'd moved them back to the trees. He wished the others would arrive and he could get tracking.

"Did they plan on you taking the body out?" Hawke set the bucket down and refilled his coffee cup, watching Dani.

She glanced at his cup. "I'm not sure. They asked me to find you and radio your coordinates."

He grinned behind the cup. These days everyone relied on GPS. He could find any spot in the Eagle Caps by a brief description.

Marlene picked up her coffee cup. "I'll wash this, and you can have some coffee." The biologist disappeared into the woods in the direction of the creek.

"Do you think Marlene killed him?" Dani asked.

He didn't see any reason to not tell her the facts. It would surprise him if Marlene hadn't already told Dani why she was here. "Don't know. She was over the body when I arrived and that's a wolf collar on his neck."

"She said she was following coordinates Roger gave her for a sighting." Dani studied him.

He shrugged. He wasn't giving up any more than

the facts. "On your way here, did you happen to see a person with two horses?" It would make his tracking easier to know which direction the suspect was headed.

"There wasn't anyone between here and the lodge." Dani nodded toward the horses. "Marlene said wolves chased that horse through here last night. Think it belongs to the victim?"

"I'll know when I catch up to the dead man's partner." Hawke took his coffee and bucket of water over to the horses. He set the cup on a mushroom growing on the trunk of a dying pine five feet from one of the trees that he'd tied a tree saver strap around for the highline.

"I'm here to help you," he said softly to the nervous horse.

The animal blew out air and watched him with round eyes. He spoke to it again with words he remembered his grandfather using when calming an animal. He wasn't clear what all the words meant, but he'd learned to copy the sounds.

Using the same rag he'd used the night before, he washed away the salve and dried scab from the horse's worst wounds.

Soft footsteps approached. He ignored the woman that had been on his mind too much since their first meeting.

"You have gentle hands." Dani stopped close enough that if he stood, he'd have to look her in the eye.

He ignored her and kept on cleaning the wounds. When he finished, she handed him the salve he'd left in the crook of the tree where he'd placed his coffee.

Grunting a thank you, he grasped the tube and

worked it into the gashes on the hind legs and chest of the animal.

"You're good with animals. Why did you decide to be a game warden and not a veterinarian?" she asked.

He wiped his hands on the rag and walked over to his cup of coffee. "Less schooling." The coffee had grown cold, but he drank it down. He told few people about his struggles in school. It wasn't his lack of trying. It was his lack of someone who thought schooling was more important than helping keep food on the table.

She nodded. "I can see where that might have been a struggle."

Hawke glared at her. It was one thing for him to demean himself, but she had no right. "I'm not a person who couldn't pass tests."

"I didn't mean you struggled with the schooling." She stared at him. "I know about life on the Rez. I may not have lived there, but we visited family."

He still found it hard to remember she was half Nez Perce. Her father had been the son of Charlie's brother. Her mother was the daughter of an ex-congressman. That was how Dani made it into the Air Force Academy. That and her grades.

Hawke nodded but didn't feel the need to continue the conversation.

Dog barked in the direction the retrieval team would use to get here.

Dani walked back to Marlene.

Hawke stepped away from the horses, peering into the trees to the northeast. The sound of hooves and horses snorting carried out of the trees along with the creak of leather and jangle of bits.

Within minutes, Wallowa County Sheriff Rafe Lindsey, Deputy Calvin Corcoran, State Trooper Tad Ullman, and the Medical Examiner, Dr. Gwendolyn Vance, rode single file out of the trees.

Hawke greeted them halfway between the trees and the body. "Sheriff, Calvin, Tad, Doctor." He tipped his head to the tarp. "A wolf took a couple bites out of him last night while I was catching that horse and chasing the other two wolves away."

They glanced at the horse and back at the tarp.

"You'll put all of that in your report?" Sheriff Lindsey asked, dismounting.

"Yes, sir." Hawke grasped the bridle of the horse the doctor rode. He knew from past encounters with the woman, she didn't like these trips into the mountains.

"There's a helicopter here?" were the doctor's first words.

"Dani Singer from Charlie's Lodge flew in an hour ago." Hawke offered, handing the horse over to the dismounted deputy.

"Tell me what you know," Sheriff Lindsey said, walking toward the tarp.

Hawke told how he'd spotted the birds and all the way up to the copter landing that morning.

"His death appears to be strangulation." Dr. Vance pointed to the collar. "The discoloration and petechiae are pretty good clues."

"That's what I figured," Hawke said.

Tad shook his head. "Seems to me, Marlene is the clear suspect since she was found with the body and the victim is wearing a wolf tracking collar."

Hawke shook his head. "He was with someone else. I was on their trail when I spotted the ravens." He pointed to the northwest. "The tracks of the other person came here and remounted their horse over there. If you don't need any more from me, I'd like to follow the tracks."

Sheriff Lindsey nodded. "I'd like to know who killed Ernest. We'll take the extra horse back with us. It will give Marlene something to ride."

"She's having Roger pick her up at Wade Flat," Hawke said, wondering if the sheriff planned to take the biologist in for questioning.

Lindsey stared over at the two women standing at the edge of the trees. "I'll have a talk with her."

Hawke nodded and strode over to Jack and Horse. There were too many people in the clearing for his liking.

Chapter Four

The sun had started to set, throwing darker shadows under the canopy of lodgepole pine, fir, and a scattering of spruce trees. With the drop in temperature, the tang of evergreen trees dwindled and crisp evening air enhanced the earthy scent of the forest floor.

Hawke had discovered where the extra horse had begun his flight from the wolves. It was close to what appeared to have been a failure of a fire pit. Rocks formed a small ring around green sticks, steepled in the middle, with charcoal wisps of what must have been paper underneath.

There had been tracks from all three horses. It appeared two had taken flight and one had been held onto by the person he pursued. What he didn't understand was the path the horse and rider had taken. They'd come to a crest of a ridge, walked along the top for a mile, then came back down the same side they went up and stopped. Either the rider was trying to hide their trail, or the person was lost and trying to get their bearings.

Hawke crouched, staring at the ground. The person had dismounted. From the impressions in the dirt and leaves and wet spot on the ground, he was pursuing a woman. He grinned at his other thought. Or a man with a limp dick. That would make any man mad enough to kill. Hawke chuckled at his own humor and returned to his first thought. He was following a woman.

A woman with feet the size of a man's and sufficient weight to have him thinking, up until now, the tracks had been made by a man.

He'd pictured a man putting the collar around the victim's neck but had wondered at the lack of a struggle. That a woman may have seduced him into putting the collar on, that would make sense for the lack of struggle marks. Had this been a jilted lover who'd killed the restaurant owner? There was always a mystery when coming across a body in the wilderness.

One thing he knew, the woman had to be thirsty and hungry if the other horse that had run away had been the pack horse and still saddled. Without supplies, she'd be cold and hungry tonight.

He pushed on, following the trampled grass, displaced leaves, needles, and pine cones on the forest floor, and the snapped twigs of the bushes. His stomach rumbled. He pulled a bag of jerky from his saddlebags and tossed a piece to Dog, when he'd stopped. Much longer and he'd have to pull out his flashlight to keep an eye on the trail.

Limbs snapped. Not in rapid succession as the horse fleeing the wolves the night before. This was at the speed of a creature walking. He listened.

Dog tipped his head.

"Oh, why can't you be a barn sour horse," a woman's frustrated voice said.

The loud snap of a fair-sized branch cracked the air.

"Ouch!"

Hawke reined Jack to the right. "Heel," he said softly to Dog and eased forward toward the sounds.

His horse and pack mule made snapping and scraping noises as they walked through the brush. He wondered if the woman had a gun. He'd witnessed evidence of firearms the first day he'd found their trail. Not knowing if the rifle had been lost with one of the frightened horses, he decided to make himself known. When working in the woods, he didn't wear his Kevlar vest. Up here, he dressed like all the other people hunting or packing on the mountains. It made it easier to strike up conversations and not be a target.

"Ma'am, I'm Fish and Game State Trooper Hawke. Do you need assistance?"

"Over here! Please!" she called.

Following her voice, he found a large woman atop a bedraggled looking mare. "Ma'am. Are you all right?" he asked, wanting her confidence before he asked her the questions that had been bunching up in his brain as he followed her trail.

"No! I'm not all right. I lost my husband, wolves ran off the other horses, and I'm lost." Tears trickled out of her eyes and ran down her round face. Twigs, leaves, and pine needles stuck out of her curly dark hair, coming loose from a ponytail.

"Where were you coming from?" he asked.

"We started out two days ago from Bear Creek

Trailhead. We were going bow hunting. And Ernest said it would be a good trip for us to take. We'd been apart a lot lately. My new job. Things." She rubbed the heels of her hands across her cheeks, leaving muddy streaks.

"Would you like some water?" He dismounted and walked to Horse. A dozen bottles of store-bought water sat in his pack.

"Please. The damn packhorse spooked along with Ernest's horse." She took the offered bottle and drank down half of it.

It was odd she hadn't said more about her husband than she'd lost him. He studied her boots. They were the kind that worked for riding a horse or hiking. She had on camo pants like her husband, a T-shirt, and a camo long-sleeved shirt tied around her ample waist.

"One of the horses was run toward my camp by wolves. He's safe." Hawke remounted his horse. "Follow me. Where did you lose your husband?" He watched her closely.

"I don't know. He got off his horse, told me to stay put, and he'd be back. I thought he was either taking a dump or thought he'd found the spot where we were going to camp." Her face puckered up. "I waited an hour and he didn't return. I called his name. I went the direction he'd walked, but I couldn't find him. I finally made camp but couldn't start the damn fire."

He urged Jack forward, leading Horse behind him.

"Then the wolves started making noise and the horses got nervous. I caught Star, but the others took off. I didn't know the wolves were actually chasing them." Her voice gradually lowered.

As they worked their way down the side of Goat

Mountain toward Bear Creek, Hawke wondered how to catch the woman in her lie. She knew her husband was dead. Her tracks had led up to the body and back to the horses. Did she kill him? There weren't a whole lot of other suspects. But he wouldn't mind having another look around where the body had been found.

First, he had to get Mrs. Cusack out of the mountains and closer to people who could question her.

Darkness had descended when he stopped an hour later. "We can stop here for the night or we can keep going. Which do you prefer?" he asked, wondering how the woman was holding up riding for so many hours.

She glanced around, then said, "I'm fine. I'd like to get off this mountain." Even though she shifted in her saddle as if she wasn't fine.

"Should hit Bear Creek soon. From there it's straight out to Bear Creek Guard Station and the trailhead." He mounted back up.

"Will you be able to see good enough? How late do you think it will be?" Mrs. Cusack asked. "That's where we left the pickup and horse trailer."

Hawke peered up into the sky. "If we're lucky and don't stop often, we should get there around nine or ten. Along the river it's easier to navigate at night."

She didn't say another word until they arrived at Bear Creek.

"Can I get off and wash up a bit?" she asked, when he stopped to water the horses.

"Just don't take too long."

He watched her slowly lower her feet to the ground. She winced. Riding as long as she had, there had to be sore muscles and deadened nerves.

Hawke dismounted, taking her reins.

She didn't smile or look at him. Just hobbled into the trees far enough he couldn't see her.

He didn't fear her trying to get away. It was clear from when he found her she'd been lost and had no clue which way was north, south, east, or west. She didn't act like she knew enough to follow the creek downstream.

The horses finished drinking. He dug in his pack for a couple packets of trail mix and waited.

She emerged, dangling what appeared to be a tank top. The woman didn't say a word, just knelt at the edge of the water, dunked the clothing in, and washed her face. What little makeup she had on left dark circles under her eyes.

Hawke didn't know whether to say something or let it go. Not being one to butt in on another's life, he decided not to say anything.

When she'd finished washing, he held out the packet of mix. "Thought you might be hungry."

"Thank you." She took the trail mix, ripped open the top, and dumped it into her mouth.

He hadn't thought she'd be a dainty eater, but even he didn't pour food down his throat when he was hungry. The woman was proving to be more coarse than he'd expected. However, that didn't make her a killer. Her silence about facts he knew, put her above Marlene on his list of suspects.

"Let's go." He shoved his packet into his shirt pocket and mounted his horse.

Mrs. Cusack led her mare over to a downed tree, stepped up onto the tree, and then put her foot in the stirrup, swinging her other leg over the horse's back.

That was why she'd dismounted here. She had a

way to get back on her horse. And why she'd dismounted so few times while he'd followed her.

«»«»«»

They walked out of the trees into an unloading area at the head of Bear Creek Trail. He'd parked his truck and trailer here to not take up one of the nine camping sites down the road twenty yards at Boundary Campground. Dog wearily walked over to Hawke's truck and horse trailer and laid down.

The glowing light of gas lanterns flickered through the trees that separated this area from the camping area. He continued down the road to the camping area.

It was easy to spot Mrs. Cusack's vehicle. The state police vehicle beside it and the deputy and trooper waiting by the truck and horse trailer gave it away.

He'd used their brief stop at the Bear Creek Guard Station to ask the ranger on duty to call in to dispatch that he would have the homicide victim's wife at the trailhead around nine. A quick glance at his watch said he was half an hour late.

The soft clop of hooves behind him stopped. The woman must have noticed the officers waiting for her.

Hawke twisted in his saddle. The darkness made it hard to tell what the woman was thinking. He dismounted and took hold of her horse's reins, leading her over to Deputy Novak and Trooper Shoberg.

"Did you tell her?" Shoberg asked quietly, as he walked over and took the reins from Hawke.

"No. She told me she thinks he's lost." He shook his head, to let the man know he didn't believe her.

"Mrs. Cusack, I'm Trooper Shoberg and this is Deputy Novak. We're here to escort you to the Sheriff's Office."

"Sheriff? I don't understand?" Mrs. Cusack's gaze landed everywhere but on the two officers.

Hawke held a hand up to the woman. "You might want to climb down. This is a conversation best carried on with your feet on the ground."

She glanced at his hand, the officers, and back the way they'd traveled.

"Ma'am?" Hawke placed his raised hand over the horse's mane. "You need to tell the police how you lost your husband."

She nodded. "Yes, you're right." She slowly eased her feet to the ground, wincing.

"Is there someone who can come get your horse and vehicle?" Deputy Novak asked.

The woman stared at him.

"We'll take you in one of our vehicles," Shoberg said.

"But Star needs food and water." She patted her horse.

"Is this your trailer?" Hawke asked.

She studied him before saying, "Yes."

"I'll make sure she eats, is rubbed down, and in the trailer. But you'll have to call someone to come get her." Hawke believed animals deserved the same respect he'd give a human.

"I can call my friend Margie." She patted the mare. "Do I need my purse?" she asked the officers.

"It would be a good idea," Shoberg said.

Hawke led Jack, Horse, and Star back up the road to his trailer. Dog slept by the door of the truck. He'd been keeping up with the horses all day and chasing down a few animal trails. The dog deserved a good long sleep.

Hawke twisted his neck, this way and that, as he tied the two horses and mule to the trailer. He also deserved a good night's sleep. He'd welcome the bed in the apartment over the indoor arena owned by Herb and Darlene Trembly.

"Hawke." Shoberg strode toward him. The county car was nothing but taillights as it bounced down the road.

"Yeah." He leaned an arm over Jack.

"I need your statement about finding her." Shoberg opened up a small notebook.

"Does this mean I don't have to write it up?" He knew he still had to, but he liked pulling the legs of the troopers he worked with.

Shoberg grinned. "I'm sure the lieutenant would like that as much as you. He says your reports wander."

"They don't wander. I tell the facts as they happen."

"Give me the facts about finding Mrs. Cusack." Shoberg poised his pen.

Hawke told about trailing the horses, finding the body, noticing the two sets of tracks and after the body was secured by other officers, tracking down who the other tracks belonged to.

"She said she lost her husband." Hawke stared at the trooper.

"If she lost him, why didn't she go for help? Or ask you to call in search and rescue?" Shoberg asked.

"Exactly. She knows he's dead. Whether she killed him…I don't know. There wasn't a struggle which to me means it was someone he knew and didn't fear. Or the person somehow made him immobile while putting the collar on."

"Drugs?"

Hawke studied the trooper. "Your guess is as good as mine. We'll have to wait for the forensics to come back."

"A wolf tracking collar. Do you think it was some of these hot-headed cattlemen who did it?"

Hawke shook his head. "They would have put it around a biologist or environmentalist's neck not a restaurant owner." He returned to unsaddling his horse. "But the killer had to have access to the collars."

"Yeah." Shoberg closed his book and wandered back to his vehicle.

Hawke finished unsaddling, wiping down, and graining the three animals. He yawned and thought about just spending the night here in the truck, but in less than an hour he could pull into the Trembly's, put Jack and Horse in a corral, and drop into his own bed.

He walked Star over to the Cusack trailer, loaded the mare in, and opted to leave her loose. Depending on when someone came to get the mare, he didn't want her to remain tied in one spot too long. Noticing hay in the area over the fifth wheel hitch, he grabbed an armful, dropping it on the floor for the animal. He spotted a bucket and thought it wouldn't hurt to give her some water as well since he didn't know when Mrs. Cusack's friend would get to the campground.

Something rattled in the bucket. He glanced down and stopped his hand from reaching in as a beam of moonlight through the slats of the trailer illuminated a tool with the same type of end as what the biologists used to attach the nuts and bolts on wolf collars.

Hawke placed the bucket back where he'd found it and pulled out his phone. He took a photo of the bucket in its original place, then on the floor to take a photo of the tool inside the bucket. He packed the bucket to his trailer, pulled out a latex glove and an evidence bag, and bagged the tool, placing it in his packsaddle.

He filled the bucket with water, retraced his steps to the Cusack trailer, and hung the bucket on the inside of the trailer. Before walking away, he made sure the trailer door was closed and locked.

Loading up the horses and his gear, he mulled over the fact a tool that had the same hex end for attaching the nuts to the screws on a wolf collar was found down here, in the trailer. There was no way of telling if it was the tool that had latched the collar on the victim's neck, but Mrs. Cusack couldn't have used that one and had it end up in her trailer before she even arrived back down here.

This was looking like a setup. But by whom?

Chapter Five

Hawke woke Monday morning to the buzzing of his cell phone.

He picked it up.

Sergeant Spruel, his Fish and Wildlife boss.

"Hello," he said, sitting up and scrubbing a hand over his face. The scent of brewing coffee filled the two-room apartment. He'd been awake enough when he came home last night to set his coffee pot timer.

"Hawke, heard you caught a homicide up on the mountain."

He liked Spruel. He was a man of few words.

"I did. Found something else after the deputy hauled off the victim's wife. I'll bring it to the office before I head back up Goat Mountain."

"Why are you going back up today?"

"I feel like there may be more information that I missed. Want to get back up there before the weather changes." He was also thankful that Sergeant Spruel had witnessed his tracking skills and didn't dismiss them like other law enforcement officers.

"Be sure to call in and keep us apprised of your whereabouts."

Hawke padded across the wood floor in bare feet.

Dog sat, staring at the door.

"I will." He opened the door. Dog bounced down the wooden stairs as the phone line went silent.

He hadn't been home for several days and rarely kept more than coffee, bread, and peanut butter in his cupboards. Opening the refrigerator door, his nose was assaulted by the combined odors of moldy cheese, sour milk, and two black bananas.

Looked like he'd have breakfast at the Rusty Nail in Winslow. The town was two miles farther from the Trembly's horse ranch than Alder, the county seat. But the ODFW and the State Police Office for the county resided in Winslow.

Hawke drank two cups of coffee as he checked his mail, of which, he received very little. Mostly letters from his mom and sister. His utility bills were paid with his rent. He wasn't home enough to pay for cable TV and didn't have any magazine subscriptions. His life was minimalistic. He liked it that way. His biggest bills were for his animals. Feeding, vet bills, shoeing, and boarding.

Dog barked, Jack nickered, and Horse brayed in his own unique, high-pitch staccato.

It was time to feed.

His boots tapped out a cadence as he descended the wooden stairs down to the dirt floor of the arena and stables. Others might not like the earthy aromas of dirt, horse manure, and hay, but he did. Dog stood in front of the gate to the large paddock Hawke rented for Jack, Horse, and his four-year-old appaloosa gelding, Boy. The younger gelding was making progress but wasn't ready for a trip in the mountains that lasted more than one day of riding. He was young. His back and bones needed time to rest in between long rides.

"Mornin' boys," Hawke said, rubbing each one on the forehead. They stood side by side, their heads hanging over the gate. Jack was gray with the distinctive appaloosa white rump and black dots. Boy was called a leopard appaloosa. His body was white and covered with varying sizes of brown spots. His love of the appaloosa breed came from his paternal grandfather. Horse was a bay with variegated colors in his mane and tail.

Hawke placed grain in three plastic feed troughs and hung them over the second rail on the gate.

Dog dove to the stall where the hay and feed were kept. It was his way of sneaking up on any rodents that might be snitching grain. Hawke put the rations of hay in the wheelbarrow and pushed it outside. He walked along the side of one of the stall runs, noting the other horses at the facility had been fed and cared for already.

He grinned. Darlene was a stickler for everything being done punctually. When he'd first moved in five years ago, she'd had a fit every time he didn't get up at six in the morning to take care of his horses, until she realized he may have come in at midnight or later and they had been fed then.

"Hawke!" Herb sat atop a tractor with a four by eight alfalfa bale balancing on the forks on the front of the scoop.

Knowing his landlords had their ears to the

heartbeat of the county, he made a detour, pushing the wheelbarrow over to the tractor.

"Looks like a good day to get that hay all hauled off the field," Hawke called out to the man, trying to be heard over the rumble of the tractor motor.

Herb narrowed his eyes and called back, "Heard you found a body up on Goat Mountain."

Even living and working in this area for as many years as he had, how fast information traveled in the 3,152 square miles of the county always surprised him. Especially considering the population was only around seven thousand.

"I did." There was no denying the fact.

Herb shut off the tractor motor. The rumbling died and silence filled the space between them.

"And it was Ernest Cusack. I can't say I'm surprised." His landlord spoke as if to himself, but his gaze was on Hawke.

He was curious about the victim, but he wasn't the investigating officer.

Herb studied him. "Can't say anything? Well, I can. That man was rude to his wife. That tells me what kind of a man he was."

Hawke nodded. Could be the reason Mrs. Cusack hadn't been sad about her husband's death. But why had she pretended not to find his body, unless she'd killed him. "His wife. She the vengeful type?"

Herb's eyes widened. "You think she done it?" He shook his head. "No, I can't see Ilene killing him. She was too scared of him."

The information settled in his mind. The woman had seemed to have plenty of bravado to try and set up camp and wander around the mountain alone. She was as big as her husband. He didn't see her cowering to him.

"Why do you think she was scared of him?"

"He kept a tight fist on their finances. If she didn't jump when he said jump, he withheld money."

"But she said she had been away a lot working." Hawke had heard her right. That was what she'd said.

"She did take a job that required her to travel to Portland once a month." Herb leaned on the steering wheel. "Darlene heard Josie Olson tell Merle Suther that when Ilene went to Portland, she kept the traveling money her company gave her and told Ernest she needed traveling money."

Hawke scoffed. "That doesn't sound like a reason to kill anyone."

"Max Durr has seen a car parked overnight in the Cusack's driveway when Ilene has been gone." Herb's bushy brown eyebrows rose.

"Any idea who the car belongs to?" This was more like it. An angry husband of the woman the victim was fooling around with made more sense.

"Nope. It's always a rental car." Herb started the tractor back up. "You going to be around for a couple of days?"

"I need to go back up the mountain later today. Won't be back until tomorrow most likely." He waved and pushed the wheelbarrow over to the end of the run where his horses and mule were patiently waiting. A flick of the frost-free faucet handle started water flowing into the trough in the pen. He tossed the hay over in three piles and watched the animals eat until the water trough filled up.

Rolling the wheelbarrow back to the stall, he took

the stairs two at a time to his apartment. Inside, he grabbed his hat, wallet, phone, evidence bag with the collar tool, and pickup keys.

Since he wasn't on duty yet, Hawke walked over to his blue Dodge Ram truck. Dog jumped into the back end. Hawke closed the tailgate and slid behind the wheel. This was easier than unhooking the horse trailer he'd need later today or hauling the trailer around. He opened the glove box and put the bagged tool, he'd found in the bucket, inside. He'd drop that off at the State Police and ODFW building after he had breakfast.

At Winslow, he glanced at his fuel gauge and pulled into the only gas station in the town. It was across the street from the Rusty Nail.

"Hey, Hawke. Fill it up?" Darren Finlay asked as he walked up to the vehicle.

"Yes. And give the windows a washing, too." Hawke stepped out of the vehicle to make sure the twenty-year-old didn't spill any diesel on the side of his truck. The young man, while having an affable personality, was known for forgetting what he was doing and spilling fuel.

"Sure thing." Darren started the diesel and walked over to the bucket with the long-handled window scrubber. Back at the truck, he scrubbed at the bugs on the windshield and asked, "You know anything about the guy they found on Goat Mountain?"

Hawke shook his head. "Not much."

"I was hoping you'd know something. I heard…" Darren moved to the other side of the truck, "that it was Old Man Cusack who owns the Firelight."

"You know him?" Hawke asked, hoping he sounded uninterested.

"My girl, Lonna, worked there a couple weeks last summer." Darren's grip on the handle of the scrubber tightened, whitening his knuckles.

"Only a couple weeks?"

The fuel pump clicked off. Hawke flipped the lever and withdrew the nozzle from the truck tank.

"Yeah. She didn't like working there. Said he was nice when she started but then things started happening she didn't like." Darren tossed the scrubber back in the bucket with a splash and glanced at the pump. "That'll be seventy-four-thirty-seven."

Hawke pulled out his debit card and followed Darren into the small office of the station. "What things didn't she like?"

Darren stepped behind the small counter and slid the card terminal his direction. "Lonna said he got handsy after a while. She didn't like it."

Hawke put that bit of information away for later. He waited for the card transaction to go through on the small machine and glanced around the establishment. This wasn't a mini-market. All that could be purchased here were fuel and an oil change if you made an appointment. Darren's grandfather only changed oil one day a week. He felt it was his right after working the oil rack and the station for fifty years.

Once the transaction was completed, Hawke drove behind the station and out onto the side road. He crossed the main highway and pulled through the Rusty Nail parking lot. There were quite a few vehicles in the parking lot for mid-morning on a weekday.

He continued around the building, taking the outlet to the main road, and parked in front of the café even though he could have parked in the back. Having his truck in front of the Rusty Nail, he could keep an eye on the truck and the evidence in the glove box.

Entering the café, he scanned the eight tables, noticing a number of people who should have been at work by now.

"Hawke, long time no see," Merrilee, the seventy-something owner of the café, said as she flopped a menu down on the counter in front of her in his usual spot.

"I've been busy." He held up the empty coffee cup and she filled it.

"We've heard."

He glanced around the establishment. Expectant eyes were on him. A sigh escaped. All he had on his mind was filling his aching belly. He hadn't considered all the regulars had hoped he'd show up this morning.

"I'll have my usual," he said, ignoring her implication he should tell them what he'd been doing.

She snorted and called back to the kitchen, "Two cackleberries over easy, slab of hog, and hotcakes." Her rheumy brown eyes behind thick lenses bore into him. "Heard you not only found a body, you brought Ilene Cusack down off the mountain as well."

He shrugged and sipped his coffee.

Ralph Bremmer, the owner of the gas station and towing service in Eagle, sat on the empty stool beside him. "The body you found was Ernest Cusack. Did his old lady off him?" The man always dressed as if he were a salesman instead of a gas attendant. He shoved a hand into his jacket pocket and pulled out a pack of cigarettes.

"You know you can't smoke them in here," Merrilee said, swatting her cleaning rag at the pack of cigarettes.

"There isn't a law that says I can't put an unlit one in my mouth." Ralph glared at her.

Hawke saw his breakfast appear at the window between the kitchen and café. He pointed it out to Merrilee.

She picked up the plate and slammed it down in front of him. "When you going to learn if we don't get the real story, we'll make one up?"

He chuckled. "If you don't like the truth, you make something up that is more interesting."

"That's true!" someone from the far corner shouted.

Merrilee glared at the corner then at Hawke. "You know I'm related to your boss. I can say you were in here blabbing about the murder and –"

"Who said it was a murder?" He knew the truth but wanted to keep them guessing.

The café owner peered at one of the tables near the door. "Darnell, you said it was murder. You get it wrong?"

"My wife was on duty at the hospital when they brought him in. She said he'd been strangled." The man Merrilee had her gaze on squirmed under her scrutiny.

"That's what I heard, too," a woman said.

"Who'd want to strangle the man?" Hawke asked, as if wondering to himself. His gaze wandered about the establishment, watching the dozen people at the tables and counter.

"The people who work for him," a man said. "My Shelly could only stand working at that restaurant for two weeks. She said the boss was nice at first. Telling her how he appreciated how well she worked and made the customers feel at home. Then when she decided he wasn't like the stories she'd heard and let her guard down, he wouldn't keep his hands to himself. She said if a waitress kept her distance and didn't let him touch her, he made them do all the shitty jobs."

"Joe drove the truck for the restaurant supplier. He said Ernest would decide after the truck arrived he didn't need as much of something and would send it back. You can't do that with some items that have short shelf life." The woman talking held up her coffee cup for a refill. Merrilee left her sanctuary behind the counter and limped over to the table.

"Where's Justine?" Hawke asked, realizing the morning shift waitress was missing.

"Called in sick." Merrilee said, a disapproving scowl on her face.

"She's never sick." Hawke wondered if he needed to check on the woman. She lived alone two miles north of town. When she wasn't waiting the tables at the Rusty Nail, she trained bird dogs. Her kennel had been where he'd found Dog. Only Dog hadn't been one of her prized bird dogs, he'd been a rescue from a bad situation. She had a kennel of rescue dogs as well.

Hawke finished his breakfast, paid, and walked out to his truck. He unlocked the door and slid in. He made the decision to check on Justine as he drove to the office.

Chapter Six

Hawke sat at his desk reading over the file on the body and Mrs. Cusack. He'd added his report to the file and was getting antsy to head back up the mountain. By the time he loaded the animals, drove there, and rode up to the area, it would be dark. But he had a feeling he'd missed something.

"Did you figure out any more on the collar?" he asked Sergeant Spruel.

"Trooper Shoberg is in La Grande tracking down where it came from. So far, I haven't heard much." Spruel sat on the corner of the desk where Hawke sat. "You have any ideas?"

"I don't think Mrs. Cusack killed him, but she knew he was dead. Her tracks had clearly walked up to the body and walked away. I missed something. There had to be someone else there who put that collar on him. It was too tight for him to do himself."

Spruel nodded. “I agree. From the photos, it appeared the bolts were at the back of his neck.”

“Since everyone knows I found the body, I’ve been getting a lot of chatter about possibilities.” He leaned back in the chair. Rumors were rampant in a small community but most of the time there was some truth to what was passed around. You just had to dig for it.

“What have you heard?”

“That when Mrs. Cusack was out of town there was a rental car in the Cusack driveway. He didn’t treat his employees very well, or should I say, his female employees, too well.” He raised an eyebrow, and the sergeant nodded. “And it sounds like he was having trouble with his food service delivery.”

“Lots of possibilities.” Sergeant Spruel stood. “If you’re going back up there, you better get to it.”

“I’m headed that way. Need to stop and see a friend first.” Hawke turned off the computer and left the building. He squinted at the bright August sun and walked to his truck.

Dog sat on the cab.

“Get down,” he said, waving his arm.

Dog jumped down into the truck bed and hung his head over the box.

“What were you doing up there?” Hawke asked, roughing up the dog’s hair on his head, before unlocking his door and getting in.

He pulled out of the parking lot wondering what other plausible reasons the patrons of the Rusty Nail had come up with for the victim’s death.

The short drive out River Canyon Road to Justine’s didn’t clear his thoughts. It only added more confusion. He wondered at the probability of him finding anything on the mountain that would help the case but felt compelled to take another look.

Turning into her drive, he noticed a vehicle with the logo of a car dealership from another county on the license plate frame. Had she skipped the café to work with someone who had purchased a dog?

His windows were down to soak in the clean summer air. The chorus of barking had his hand reaching for the window button. He parked behind the other vehicle and stepped out.

Dog hung over the side of the truck box whining.

"Stay."

The animal sat on his haunches in the truck bed but continued to whine. He didn't get many chances to hang out with his own kind, but Hawke didn't want to hunt for him when he was ready to leave.

Justine opened the door to her small, ranch-style home backed up to the Wallowa River. "Hawke, what brings you here? In need of another dog?" She stepped out onto the porch.

"Just checking up on you. Merrilee said you called in sick. I've never known you to miss work." He studied the forty-four-year-old. She looked as healthy and vibrant as usual. Her dark hair was pulled into a braid down her back, her brown eyes sparkled with humor.

"I'm not sick. But that's the only thing, other than a death in the family, that Merrilee gives me a day off for without saying she's going to fire me." Justine walked out from under the porch.

"You have a potential client in there?" he asked.

She studied him a moment. "It's my sister. She and her husband had a falling out. She showed up here last night and doesn't feel like seeing anyone. The way she was talking, I didn't want to leave her alone."

Hawke nodded. Growing up on reservations, he'd witnessed many people who were depressed and thought about ending their lives. There was a desperation to them, he'd never felt but understood, considering the situations many lived in.

"I'll let you go. I just wanted to make sure you were okay. Living out here by yourself, if you were too sick to call anyone…" He left it unsaid.

"I know my limits. Thanks for checking on me." She smiled and headed back to the house.

Hawke returned to his truck. He wondered where the sister lived. Funny Justine had never mentioned her.

He backed down the drive and turned around. He had the vibe Justine wouldn't mind going out on a date with him, but he'd managed to stay clear of any entanglements with women in the county. He didn't need to have his job get tangled up in a family dispute with a woman he dated. That had happened with his ex-wife. He'd arrested her brother on drug charges and she'd left him.

When he had an itch that needed scratched, he headed to Pendleton, looked up an old girlfriend, and left again. No entanglements, no commitments. That was the best way to be. He'd seen too many good men tossed on their heads by a woman. Him included.

Back at the Trembley's, he loaded up Boy and Jack. It would be a good chance to give Boy more exposure to the mountain. He only planned on spending the night and coming back for his two days off.

He put saddles on both animals and tossed his canvas pack bag that fit over a saddle in the truck along with rations, water, his bedroll, and all work-related items. When the horses were loaded up, he whistled for Dog.

«»«»«»

The drive to the Bear Creek trailhead took close to an hour. His stomach was grumbling when he pulled into his usual parking spot. On his way by Boundary Campground, he'd noted the Cusack's truck and horse trailer were gone.

He unloaded the horses, tying them to the outside of the trailer. Wandering over to the truck unloading ramp, he sat on the ramp. He ate jerky and trail mix while watching the people milling about in the campground down the road. A man had ducked into a tent when Hawke drove through the campground. He'd peeked out twice as Hawke sat eating.

While his truck gave away he was law enforcement, his jeans, T-shirt, and denim jacket didn't. He tossed his wrappers in the trash, grabbed a bottle of water, pulled his badge on a chain, out from behind his shirt to allow people to see it as he walked up, and started making the rounds of the camps. He visited with the ones who were there, asking how they were enjoying themselves and where they'd hiked. While he wasn't a chatty person, he'd learned the art of getting others to talk. He took notes as he talked with each person or group. The more contacts he could add to his log book, the better his superior liked it.

At the tent of the man who'd been watching him, he called out. "Fish and Wildlife, anyone here?"

No one answered but the tent wobbled.

"I know someone is in there. I'm visiting with everyone to learn what trails you've been on and if there have been any incidents I need to check out."

The man finally stepped halfway out of the tent.

"Afternoon, I'm Trooper Hawke. How has your experience on this trail been?"

"Fine." The man's gaze roamed around the camp area.

"What trails have you hiked?"

"None. Just got here. I'm trying to get everything set up." He started to duck back into the tent.

"This tent was here last night." Hawke remembered the tent because it had been the only one without a lantern.

The man stopped half way into the tent. "I arrived late yesterday and slept in. Now I'm setting things up."

Hawke didn't believe him but couldn't call the man a liar.

"Have a good hike," he said, and walked back to his vehicle. There was something suspicious about the man, but he had no legal way to see what was in the tent, nor the time to wait him out to see what he did.

He placed the canvas pack over Jack's saddle, made sure he had food supplies and work supplies, and mounted Boy. "Come on, Dog," he called the hound from sniffing at the tires of the nearest vehicle.

At first Boy was hesitant to take the lead up the trail. The gelding soon learned nothing would hurt him, and Jack was right behind. Hawke couldn't let his mind wander riding the younger horse. He had to pay attention to anything out of the ordinary that would cause the youngster to balk or jump sideways. Boy was more suspicious of the trail than Jack had been when he'd brought him out the first time.

As the afternoon gave way to dusk, Boy jumped at

every dark shadow and flap of a wing. By the time they arrived at the murder site, Boy was slathered with sweat and chewing on his bit. Hawke hadn't thought the horse would be this spooked by night trail riding. He'd use him as a pack horse for a while before trying to ride him as the lead horse again.

He dismounted, keeping the horses and Dog in the same area they'd stayed the night waiting for the retrieval team. He didn't want to add any new tracks to the area.

After tending to the horses and giving Boy a good rub down, Hawke rolled out his sleeping bag and laid down with Dog beside him. He chewed on some jerky and drank water before falling asleep.

«»«»«»

Sunlight flickered on Hawke's eyelids. A horse snorted, and he felt the heat and weight of Dog lift from his side.

He stretched, opened his eyes, and regretted it. The full sun beamed down into his face. It was early enough the sun was low and able to brighten the ground and trunk of the tree he slept under.

Hawke sat up, did a quick glance at the horses. They were standing with one hip cocked, relaxing. He'd tied them snug to the high line, not allowing them to eat the grass, for fear something would spook Boy and he'd hurt himself.

He walked over to the horses, untied them, and led them to the creek for water. When he returned, he tethered them out to eat grass. Using the same small fire ring Marlene had made, he heated up water, poured some in an oatmeal stir-n-eat bowl, and then dropped a coffee disk into the water and let it brew.

The oatmeal slid down his throat. He didn't care for it. The slimy substance reminded him of too many mornings when he'd had to prepare his own breakfast before school because his mother was at work and his stepfather was passed out from drinking too much the night before. He was glad his mother had been a hard-working woman who passed that on to him and his sister. That had helped them get off the reservation and see life didn't have to be depressing.

The aroma of coffee brought him back to the forest and the life he'd made for himself. He had worked hard to be accepted into the State Police and even harder to get the job of Fish and Wildlife Trooper. Thanks to his grandfather training him to track, he'd captured the job that had been his goal from the start. To preserve nature and the wilderness for the people who understood and appreciated the mountains. And for his ancestors.

He poured a cup of coffee, blew on it to chase the steam away from his face, and took a sip. Carrying his cup, he wandered out to the spot where the victim had lain.

Crouching, he scanned the area that would have been under the body. There were signs of creatures having walked through since the body was taken away. But it wasn't wildlife signs he wanted to find.

Using his pen, he separated the grass one blade at a time, lifting it and moving it from side to side. A piece of hair caught on the pen near the base. He set the pen down and returned to his pack, grabbing a kit of small evidence bags. The retrieval team would have picked up anything that had looked out of place to them. But they wouldn't have taken the time to go inch by inch through the grass.

He placed the hair in a bag and labeled it. Then began his search once more. Using the tweezers in the kit, he picked up what looked like a bead. He held it in the sunlight, studying it. This was a glass bead, but not something that could have been here for years. He bagged and labeled it.

When he was sure he'd discovered what was left, he sat on his haunches and scanned the trees and brush lining the clearing. "If I were waiting for someone to arrive and didn't want to be seen…" He knew the direction the victim had walked in from.

Hawke stood and walked toward a denser area of brush the opposite direction from where the victim had entered the clearing. His gaze on the ground in front of him, he cautiously placed each foot. Something shiny reflected the sun. He stopped, crouched, and grinned. A silver dome nut like what was on the tracking collar around the victim's neck. He used the tweezers to put it into an evidence bag. Lowering his gaze to the ground once more, he continued a foot by foot inspection of the ground all the way to the brush.

Hawke stepped through an opening in the brush and knew he'd found the killer's hiding spot. A section of the grass and vegetation about three feet by three feet appeared to have been trod upon in a back and forth motion as if the person had been nervous. He stopped as soon as he saw the trampled plants and displaced dirt. The bushes toward the clearing had small branch ends that dangled from the bark, as if they had been snapped as someone leaned into them.

This would be a good place to look for fibers, hair, anything that could have transferred to the plants.

He pulled out his phone and took a photo of the

ground, then the bushes. On his hands and knees, he searched the ground and found another silver dome nut. Whoever had brought the collar to the mountain had been careless with the means to tighten the item on the victim's neck.

The nut went into another bag. He scanned the area beneath the bush for any evidence. A gum wrapper that looked fresh. It might have DNA or prints. He placed that in a bag and labeled it.

The limbs revealed another hair and small sampling of fiber. He bagged those and turned. How had the person known this was the spot to meet the victim? And how had they arrived and left?

Were they still on the mountain?

He whistled for Dog. Within seconds, he appeared through the bushes.

"Sit." Hawke opened the bags with the hair and the fibers. He held them up to Dog's nose. "Find."

Dog sniffed the area, back and forth, over the spot where the person had paced and then trotted to a tree about ten feet farther into the woods. He sat down.

Hawke followed him and noted the disturbed plants and dirt at the base of the tree. The dimensions were the right size for a backpack.

"Good boy." Whoever killed the victim had packed in and most likely packed out.

He scanned the area and picked up the faint track of a shoe tread. He photographed the print. Following it, he noted the direction the person had headed. Down to Goat Creek. The suspect could have followed that creek to Bear Creek and walked out to the trailhead, got in a vehicle, and drove away.

It had been three days since the homicide. It would

be up to forensics and detective work to find the person now. But he could follow the trail.

He walked back to his camp. Doused the fire, spread the ashes and rock ring, saddled his horses, put the pack on Boy, and led Jack. “Come, Dog!” He returned to the tracks headed toward Goat Creek. The person had stopped many times and looked back as if he was afraid of being followed. The furtiveness of the person made Hawke wonder if he could have committed the murder. He seemed frightened and worried the way the steps stalled and he looked around.

Hawke was surprised when the tracks veered back up the mountain after a mile and became less hesitant.

As if the person realized they’d gotten away with murder.

Chapter Seven

Hawke unloaded his horses, put them up, and unhooked the trailer, before heading to the office with the evidence he'd collected. He'd hand it over, write up his report, and grab a bite to eat at the Rusty Nail. There were other places to eat in town, but he liked the relaxed atmosphere and knew Merrilee needed the money. Her husband had run off and left her with bills to pay.

He knew the feeling.

Sergeant Spruel was still in his office at seven-thirty.

"Hawke, looks like your trip was eventful."

"I found things that might be evidence in the Cusack homicide." He handed the bags over to the sergeant. The man logged it all in and Hawke signed.

"Come into my office and tell me what you found." Spruel led the way to his office. He was the only lawman in the building who had an office. The troopers' desks lined two walls.

Hawke dropped onto the seat in front of the sergeant's desk. "I found two domed cap nuts like the ones used on the collar. One twenty feet from the body and another behind the bushes where the suspect waited."

"Waited? How did they know Cusack would be there?" Spruel started asking all the same questions Hawke had been asking himself on the ride back down the mountain.

"I don't know any of that. The best I can say is he hiked down toward Goat Creek about a mile acting nervous. Then he turned back up the mountain. I lost his tracks in a clearing. The way the vegetation looked either a strong wind blew through or a helicopter had landed. It's going to be hard to find him unless the hair and fibers I found can be matched." He stood. "I have a report to write and then I've got two days off. Forensics is going to have to help you solve this one."

Hawke filed his report, left the office, and drove over to the Rusty Nail.

The café windows were dark. There was only one other option for food in Winslow this time of night.

He swung around through the Rusty Nail parking lot and headed down the main road and highway through town to the Blue Elk Tavern. Three vehicles were parked along the street in front of the tavern. Just the way he liked it. Few people, and hopefully, not locals. He'd like a nice quiet meal before going home.

The inside of the place was a typical bar atmosphere. Low lights, booths and tall tables, pool tables on one end, a juke box by a small dance floor and an old oak bar with brass legged stools. The only oddity was the mounted five-point elk head and shoulders that was dyed a bright blue. Two spot lights made sure anyone entering couldn't miss the creature.

Hawke took a stool at the bar, noticing there wasn't a barmaid tonight. He'd get served quicker by sitting close to the only person running the place.

"Hawke, long time no see," Ben Preston, the bartender and owner of the bar said, placing a paper coaster in front of him. "What'll you have?"

"I'd like a burger and a beer, but since I'm driving a state vehicle, make it a burger and a coke."

"I can do that." Ben poured him a glass of the soda and disappeared through the swinging doors into the kitchen.

Hawke sipped the drink and scanned the seven people in the place. Four had to be tourists. They were huddled together at a table, pointing to places on a map. The other three were at the pool tables.

His dinner should be uneventful.

One of the men from the pool tables walked over to the bar, carrying three empty beer bottles. Hawke nodded to be polite and sipped his drink.

The man plunked the bottles onto the bar. "Where's Ben?"

Hawke tipped his glass toward the kitchen door.

The man looked him over, his gaze studying him closer. "You're the Fish and Game guy, Hawke." He shifted his body to face Hawke. "You found Cusack's body."

Hawke groaned inwardly and nodded his head.

"It had to be some coward to catch him up in the mountains like that. If it had been me, I'd have just shot him when he walked out of his restaurant."

Hawke narrowed his gaze. "You had a grudge with

the victim?"

"Victim, hell! He deserved it."

"Why did he deserve it?"

"He was a jerk who took jobs away for no reason."

Ben returned from the kitchen. "Your burger will be up in about five minutes." He picked up the beer bottles. "Three more, Jim?"

"Yeah." The man, Jim, pulled out his wallet and plunked money on the bar. "Whoever killed him did this county a favor." He grasped the full bottles and stomped back to the pool tables.

"Don't listen to him. He's sore his wife lost her job at the restaurant." Ben wiped the bar where the empty bottles had sat.

"Do you know why she lost her job?" Every person he talked to opened the investigation to more suspects.

"She told Cusack off when he made advances." Ben glanced toward the pool tables. "From what Jim's said, he doesn't know about the advances or he chooses to not acknowledge it."

The more he heard about the man, Hawke wondered if it hadn't been Mrs. Cusack's idea to go on the hunting trip and not the victim's. Had she paid someone to kill her husband? Then went back to make sure it had happened?

"I'll get your dinner." Ben disappeared into the kitchen again. Hawke sipped his coke and wondered if the investigating officers were checking into the women who had been fired from the restaurant. And to see if Mrs. Cusack was aware of them?

Ben brought out a basket with a burger and fries.

Hawke dug into the food, letting the thoughts in his head disappear as he enjoyed every greasy, delicious bite of real food.

«»«»«»

Wednesday morning Hawke slept in. The braying and neighing of his animals woke him. He fed everyone, cleaned the inside paddock, and cleaned the water trough. Then he checked over his saddles and packs, to make sure there weren't any repairs that needed to be made.

His days off were filled with mindless work that helped him to recharge for the coming shift. He threw out all the old moldy food in his refrigerator. "Come on, Dog. We're going to get some groceries."

He purchased his groceries in Alder, the county seat. The town was seven miles from the Trembly's. The drive to Alder was uneventful, other than a buck and two does crossing the highway in front of him.

At the grocery store, he wandered the aisles, trying to decide what he wanted to purchase.
Milk and cereal seemed like a good choice. He bought new bread, butter, and cheese. He could make grilled cheese sandwiches for dinner. Tossing a bag of chips into the cart, he spotted Justine and a woman a few years younger than her.

They wandered up the aisle whispering to one another. Justine didn't look happy, but the other woman was being insistent.

When their cart was in front of his, Justine smiled. "Hawke, this is my kid sister, Leanne."

"Leanne, nice to meet you," Hawke said, nodding his head.

The younger woman glanced in his shopping cart and frowned. "That doesn't look like substantial food for a man your size."

He stared at the woman. Was she flirting with him? While his ego liked the idea, he also knew she was here because of an argument with her husband. "I don't buy a lot because I'm not home much." He smiled at Justine. "See ya around."

The second before he gave his cart a push, he saw the younger sister elbow the older one.

"Hawke?" Justine asked, her voiced raised a bit.

He stopped and glanced over his shoulder, "Yeah?"

"Would you like to come over for dinner tonight? You could bring Dog. He can play in the backyard with Shilo and Sun." Justine's eyes were guarded, her smile not genuine.

Something was up. He didn't know what but figured the best way to find out was to join them for dinner. Facing them, he put a smile on his face. "Only if I can bring dessert."

Justine nodded. "That's fine. Come by about six-thirty?"

He glanced at Leanne. She was grinning.

"See you later." Hawke pushed his cart to the front of the store and glanced at his watch. He'd have to get checked out quickly to get to the bakery before they closed at three. If he was bringing dessert, he planned to bring the Donut Hole's signature dessert—huckleberry cheesecake.

Chapter Eight

Hawke stared at his reflection in the mirror over the small sink in his bathroom. He'd showered and put on deodorant but really wasn't sure if he should dress up or wear everyday clothes. It had been a long time since a woman who wasn't married to a co-worker or family asked him to dinner.

Remembering the whispered discussion between the sisters, he opted to wear a t-shirt he'd bought two years ago at the Tamkaliks Pow-Wow held in Eagle every July. That, along with jeans and his boots, would have to do. If he was invited because the married sister was interested, he wanted none of that.

He combed his wet hair back off his wide forehead and studied his aging face. There were more lines around his eyes and corners of his mouth, but his cheek bones were still prominent. He didn't have any fat to give him a baby face or cause him to become jowly. His job helped keep him looking younger than his fifty-two years. Horseback riding, hiking, and dehydrated meals kept him in shape. He didn't carry snacks and fattening food with him in the wilderness and when he wasn't on the mountain for work, he made sure to run and eat properly. He wasn't going to become a fat, drunken Indian like his stepfather.

A glance at his watch had him moving. He grabbed the bag from the Donut Hole out of the refrigerator, picked up his truck keys, and headed down the stairs.

"Look at you." Darlene said, standing by the arena watching a teen-aged girl ride a buckskin around.

"Giving a lesson?" he asked to take the attention from him.

"I am. But I'm more interested in you being dressed nice," she sniffed, "smelling good, and carrying what I would suspect is a Donut Hole cheesecake."

He grinned at the woman who had become as close a friend as he'd ever had in life. She and her husband had invited him to dinner many times over the years. They knew a good bit of everything about each other.

"I was invited to dinner, but it is all platonic. Just friends." The Trembley's knew about his ex-wife and the scars she'd left on his heart and his belief in marriage.

"So, it is a woman…" Darlene glanced at her student. "Avril, post. And make that horse do what you want not the other way around." She returned her attention to Hawke. "There is nothing wrong with platonic relationships. But if it wants to go further, don't fight it." She put a hand on his shoulder and walked through the arena gate.

Hawke shook his head. He and Justine were friends. He'd met one woman in the last year, who'd made his heart speed up and pulse race. But he didn't have to worry about running into her enough to think his bachelor life would be compromised.

He whistled for Dog. As was normal, he came bounding out of the horse's paddock.

Dog jumped into the truck bed. He loved hanging his head over the side and having the wind flap his ears.

Hawke placed the bag with the dessert in the passenger seat and headed down the drive. His curiosity about Leanne was the only reason he'd agreed to the dinner. He would never give a woman the false hope he would be interested in them. Especially, one he called a friend and wanted to keep it that way.

The drive was calming. He enjoyed the end of summer heat. While it had turned the grass on the hills a tawny yellow, the green leaves of the cottonwood trees and the trickle of water in the creeks gave the valley the feeling of a place where your cares could be forgotten. One of the selling points the Chamber of Commerce used to bring tourists in to help perk up the dwindling economy. Once the lumber mills were put out of business, the county lost their biggest means of employment. Since then they'd worked at bringing in art and tourists any way they could.

He passed through Winslow, glad he wouldn't be eating in a restaurant tonight. The thought of a homecooked meal had his mouth salivating as he turned into Justine's driveway. The chorus of barking started the second the truck tires hit her drive. By the time he parked, it had grown in volume.

Justine came to the door. The barking, except for a woof now and then, stopped once the dogs saw her.

Hawke grabbed the cheesecake. "Dog, come."

They walked up to the door.

"I hope you have a big appetite tonight. If you don't, I'll be eating Leanne's pasta dish for weeks." Justine took the bag with the cheesecake and headed through the small living room.

Hawke wasn't sure if he was to follow or remain in this room. It was the only one he'd seen while they'd worked out his adoption of Dog. Who, now, followed the woman without preamble into the other room.

If his dog had run of the house, he might as well.

Hawke stepped into the kitchen as Justine opened a back door, letting Dog outside.

Leanne glanced up from the steaming pot she held in her hands. "Glad you could make it. Justine, get our guest something to drink."

From the way the two women were dressed, they weren't trying to impress him, which washed away some of his hesitation about the evening. They both had on the pants that stopped mid-calf and T-shirts. Nothing that said either one had a notion to try and seduce him. Just clothing fit for the warm weather.

"Beer, soda, iced tea, water, milk?" Justine had her hand on the refrigerator door.

"I'll take iced tea now and maybe a beer later, when I have some food in me." He sniffed, inhaling a tomato, Italian spice, and garlic aroma along with what his mouth hoped was sausage.

"It's my go to dish for company," Leanne said, stuffing big round macaroni with what looked like a meat and white cheese mixture.

"I'm sure it's a hit." He took the iced tea Justine handed him.

"Want to sit out on the back patio while Leanne

finishes up? It's cooler out there," Justine said.

Knowing Dog was in the backyard as well, Hawke nodded and followed the older sister out to a covered, paving stone patio. A medium-sized barbecue sat at one end. A round table set for three had three chairs. A patio swing for two sat on the end opposite the barbecue. Justine sat in the swing.

Hawke pulled up a wicker foot stool and sat. "You have a nice place. I've not seen the back side of the property before." The Wallowa River rushed by fifty feet from the backyard fence. In between sat the barn and corral with two horses wandering within the metal panels.

"Thanks. I work hard to keep it up." She sipped her soda.

He didn't know her whole story, only bits and pieces of rumors. She grew up here, moved away after high school, and returned ten years after that a different person, according to those who'd known her before.

"Everything is in the oven." Leanne walked out with a beer in her hand. She scowled when her gaze landed on Hawke sitting on the foot stool. "You're the guest. You should be sitting in the swing not on that old rickety thing." Leanne gave him a little shove on the back.

"I'm fine. I prefer looking straight on when I talk with people." It appeared the younger sister was trying to fix up her older sister. By the way Justine squirmed, this hadn't been her idea.

Leanne sat on the swing with her sister. "What do you do around here?"

Justine glared at her. "I told you he was a game warden."

"I'm making what's called small talk, Justine." Leanne rolled her eyes. "You really need to mingle more."

Hawke understood how Justine felt. He couldn't mingle in this county without word getting out he was dating someone he wasn't, or he was two-timing. "I could ask you the same, Leanne. What do you do when you aren't here causing your sister embarrassment?"

Justine's gaze sent him a thank you.

"I work for a restaurant supply company. I go around my district helping the restaurants decide what to stock, given their past sales and the community's needs." She puffed up and pride rang in her voice.

"Sounds like a fulfilling job. Kind of like your sister training and placing dogs with the right owners." He wasn't going to let the younger sister put down the one who took her in when she needed a place to go.

"Touché, Hawke." Leanne jumped up. "I better go check on things. Justine, you can start bringing the other dishes out to the table."

Hawke found himself sitting alone on the patio. He watched Dog and Justine's two bird dogs wrestling in the back half of the fenced-in yard. The chain link fence would keep dogs in and coyotes and other wild animals out.

The door opened.

He stood to take one of the bowls from Justine.

"Thank you. I'm sorry Leanne is so pushy. When she found out I knew you today, she insisted we had to have you over for dinner. She's worried I'll end up an old maid." Justine placed a fruit salad on the table and took the bowl of green salad from him.

"There's more to life than being tied to another

person," Hawke said.

Justine peered into his eyes. "Exactly. Why don't others understand that?"

He shrugged. "I guess because others are happy with a mate, they don't understand those of us who prefer to be alone."

The first genuine smile spread across Justine's face. "We have more in common than Dog. This night might not be so bad after all." She spun back into the house.

Hawke smiled. He'd allayed her worries about him wanting any romance with her. She wasn't bad looking and did have a genial personality, but he wasn't looking for someone to live with. He liked not having to worry about anyone wondering when he'd be home.

The two women returned with the rest of the food.

They all sat. Justine became the bubbly hostess he knew from the restaurant. Leanne studied both of them.

He and Justine talked about the dogs and the regulars at the Rusty Nail. Leanne asked a question now and then.

"Did they try to get information out of you the morning you came and checked on me?" Justine asked.

"Yeah. But I learned more from them." He winked.

Justine laughed.

"What did they want to find out from you?" Leanne asked.

"He found a body on the mountain. Everyone has their own theories of what happened." Justine ripped a piece of bread in half.

Hawke dipped his bread in the spicy tomato sauce that covered the sausage filled macaroni. He hadn't said anything at the restaurant and didn't intend to say anything over dinner.

"A body? As in someone dead?" Leanne asked, picking up her beer bottle and staring at him.

He nodded.

"It was an accident? Some hiker had a heart attack?" she asked and took a drink.

"No. It was a local restaurant owner. Murdered," Justine said.

Leanne choked on her drink.

Justine patted her back. "I thought that would intrigue you, not make you choke."

The younger sister caught her breath. "Who?"

"Who what?" Hawke asked, becoming interested in the woman's reaction.

"W-who was murdered?"

"Ernest Cusack." He picked up his glass of iced tea to hide his scrutiny of the woman.

"Ernie? Oh my!" Leanne stood. She glanced around and sat back down.

"You knew Ernest?" Justine asked.

Leanne picked up her beer and downed the rest before answering, "Our company sold him the linens for his restaurant." She stared down into her plate. "Murder?" Her gaze latched onto Hawke. "Do they know who did it?"

"Not yet." He wasn't going to tell her they were waiting for forensics.

"H-how did it happen?" Her question didn't sound as frightened as all the others.

"I'm not at liberty to say." They had kept the collar out of all media and had hopes that would be how they caught the killer.

Leanne narrowed her eyes. "Not at liberty or don't

want to?"

He forked another bite into his mouth.

"Leanne, I've known Hawke since I moved back here, and he doesn't tell anyone anything about his job." Justine put a hand on her sister's arm. "I'm sorry you knew the man. But most around here are glad he's gone."

Hawke studied Justine. Had she also been one of the women Cusack chased away from his restaurant?

"Are you glad?" he asked.

Justine shook her head. "He was handsy and I know there were a lot of husbands and boyfriends who were happy to hear what happened, but no one deserves to die before their time."

The sorrow in her eyes, made him wonder if someone she loved had died a violent death. Perhaps now that they had established a friend relationship, he'd learn a bit about her past.

"What do you mean he was handsy?" Leanne asked.

"There were many women who started working at his restaurant then left because he wouldn't keep his hands off their butts." Justine picked up her drink and sipped.

Leanne looked angry. "How many women?"

"I'd say over the years nearly every woman who worked at the restaurant who were between the age of sixteen and forty." The older sister nodded her head. "I'm surprised his wife hadn't chopped his hands off."

"She knew about his roving hands?" Hawke asked. She was the most likely suspect. Given the tracks he'd found, she could have paid someone. He stood up. "I'll be right back. I just remembered I was supposed to tell

Darlene something from Herb." He pulled out his phone and walked to the far end of the yard where the dogs were still playing.

He dialed Sergeant Spruel.

"Spruel," his superior answered.

"Sergeant, this is Hawke. I was wondering if anyone thought to pull Mrs. Cusack's financials and phone records? She could have paid the second person I found evidence of to kill her husband."

"We already put in for a subpoena for the records. Just waiting for Judge Vickers to sign off. The D.A. is dragging his feet about the autopsy, but I think Dr. Vance convinced him it was necessary." Spruel cleared his throat. "I thought you were taking a couple days off."

"I am. I was just having dinner with friends. They started talking about the murder and the thought popped into my mind."

"I'm glad you're enjoying dinner with friends. Don't give anything away."

"I'm not. They are doing all the talking." He watched the two sisters. It was clear Leanne had been upset by the information.

"As is most of the county. Thanks for checking in." The sergeant ended the conversation.

Hawke shoved his phone back in his pocket and returned to the patio.

"I can't believe you are this upset over a man you barely knew." Justine picked up the plates and headed to the kitchen.

Hawke sat down. "You must have known the deceased more than just to sell him linens."

Leanne glared at him. "Why would you say that?"

"Because of how upset you are." He waved a hand up and down in front of her face. "No one goes through this many emotions over someone they met once or twice."

"I'm an emotional person. My husband tells me that all the time, like it's a flaw." She used a napkin to dry her eyes and then picked up dishes, leaving him sitting by himself.

Within minutes, Justine returned. "Sorry Leanne is so rude. She's been that way since she was small. Demanding, insistent. Mad one minute and laughing the next. It was like living with more than one sister."

"Is she bi-polar?" He'd dealt with people with this disorder before.

"No. I think it's more an attention getter. She's done it so long it's second nature to her now." Justine had a full beer bottle in her hand. "Would you like that beer now?"

If he drank the beer he'd have to stay longer than he wanted to make sure he wasn't too impaired to drive. "I think I'll stick to iced tea. Beer doesn't go very well with huckleberry cheesecake."

She nodded. "That's true. The mood Leanne is in, I'll bring our dessert out here."

Chapter Nine

Dusk had descended into the valley as Hawke drove home. Over the cheesecake, he'd managed to learn Leanne's last name and that she lived in La Grande. He planned to pull out his laptop when he returned home and look up her information. She'd been too upset about the victim to have been a casual acquaintance.

As he passed through Winslow, he slammed on his breaks as a man staggered into the street.

Hawke parked his truck and hurried over to help the man. The sour stench of alcohol oozing out of the man's pores brought back memories of his stepfather and the times he'd had to help him from his car into the house before the cops arrived and cited him for drunk driving.

"Archie, you can't stagger around the streets. I'm taking you to the Sheriff's Office. They'll keep you safe until you sober up." Hawke put his arm around the man's waist, helping to keep him on his feet as they slowly walked over to the pickup.

Dog hung over the side of the truck bed, sniffing as Hawke lowered the drunk onto the seat and buckled him in.

Hawke sighed as he drove by the road to his place and continued on to Alder where the County Sheriff and jail resided.

At the station, he parked in front and hauled the incoherent drunk into the building.

"Looks like you found Archie tonight," Craig, the dispatcher, said, opening the door to the inner offices of the building.

"Where should I put him?" Hawke turned the drunk's open mouth away from his face.

"In the first cell. It's reserved for him. I'll call back and let Ralph know you're coming." Craig sat back at his desk.

Hawke hauled Archie, who was no longer helping, down to the heavy metal door at the back of the hallway.

Ralph's round face peered out at him from the security window. He opened the door and grabbed the other side of Archie.

"Haven't seen Archie in a week. Wonder what set him off this time." Ralph had the cell door open. They eased the man down onto the cot.

"I don't know. I found him wandering down the middle of the street in Winslow." Hawke stepped back as the jailer, a young man in his early twenties and fifty pounds overweight, pulled the cell door closed but didn't lock it.

A couple of men were in cells at the far end. They

didn't stir. Hawke turned to the door to leave.

"Wait. You have to sign, date, and put down the time you brought him in." Ralph handed him a clipboard.

He signed, dated, and added the time.

"Thanks. Most officers give me a hard time about having to do this. They tell me to do it, but it has to have their signature."

Hawke nodded and walked out the door. With no one in the office, he decided rather than go home and crank up his laptop, he'd just use one of the computers here. They were hooked up to more information sites.

At the front of the hallway, he knocked on dispatch's door frame.

Craig jumped and faced him. "I'm not used to someone coming up behind me."

"Sorry. Since I'm here, I'm going to use a computer. Which one do you suggest?" He didn't want to sit down to anyone's desk without someone's approval.

"First office on the right is for visiting law enforcement."

"Thanks." Hawke backtracked to the first office and turned on the lights. He sat behind the desk, wiggled the mouse, and opened it to a site where he could type Leanne Welch into Department of Motor Vehicles.

Up popped information on two vehicles owned by Leanne and Roger Welch. He had their address and a business name that was registered to one of the vehicles. Welch Applications.

He put that in the business directory. Welch Applications was an agricultural aviation business that applied sprays to crops. He clicked on the web page. A small hangar with a prop plane beside it were both emblazoned with the logo for Welch Applications.

Hawke clicked on the photos to make them larger. A man stood beside the propeller of the plane. He had on a ball cap and aviation sunglasses making it hard to see his features.

Back at the DMV site he typed in Roger Welch. Not only did his business name and driver's license photo come up, but also a government identification number.

He scribbled the number down and clicked into the government data base. In the search box, he typed in the number.

The screen flashed, and a copy of a contract with Welch Applications to fly wildlife biologists glared.

Was Leanne's husband Roger the same Roger Marlene referred to? He'd ask her tomorrow. For now, he was going home to bed. Too many long hours and near sleepless nights this week had him dragging.

«»«»«»

The next morning, he cared for his horses and mule, cleaning the paddock and making sure their water was fresh. He peered up at the mountains he spent so much time traversing, and even though it was his day off, he was thinking about going on a hike.

"How was your date last night?" Darlene asked, walking alongside the outdoor runs.

"It wasn't a date." Hawke turned off the water and gave his attention to his landlord.

"If it wasn't a date then you wouldn't mind telling me her name." The sixty-year-old woman took off her gloves and peered at him from under her straw cowboy hat.

"The problem with telling you the name is even if you just say to someone, 'Hawke had dinner with so-n-so', the next time that person runs in to so-n-so they will make a comment about a date and are we getting married." He shook his head. "I know how the gossip around here works. No, thank you."

She laughed. "That is very true. Even if I say I won't mention it to anyone?"

He grinned. "No. Because I know somehow it will get brought up in a conversation and you won't be able to help yourself."

"It must have went well. You came home after ten." The insinuation in her tone made him laugh.

"I was in Alder at nine after nearly running over Archie when he stumbled onto the highway as I drove through Winslow. I took him to the Sheriff's Office and used one of their computers to look things up."

"Thanks a lot. Herb and I were betting that you and your friend were having too good a time for you to leave."

"You lost. I'm going to the lake. Come on, Dog!" he called.

Dog came bounding around the end of the barn.

"Enjoy the beautiful day!" Darlene called after him.

He raised a hand in acknowledgement, loaded Dog in the back of the truck, and climbed in the front. The Trembley's were great people to have as landlords, but they did tend to have too much fun at his expense.

A few miles down the road, he swerved into a turnout and pulled out his phone. He found the La Grande Fish and Wildlife number and dialed.

"How may I direct your call?" a woman's voice asked.

"I'm State Trooper Hawke. I'm trying to contact Marlene Zetter."

"She's out in the field today. You can try her cell phone, but she may not be in service."

"I'll take that chance."

She recited a number.

"Thank you." He ended the call and punched in the numbers he'd been given.

"You've reached the mailbox for Dr. Marlene Zetter, biologist with the Oregon Fish and Wildlife, please leave a message."

"Marlene, this is Hawke. I have a couple questions for you. Please, give me a call." He left his phone number and tucked the phone in his pocket.

He pulled back out onto the road and took the backroads to Prairie Creek, the small town at the entrance to Wallowa Lake, one of the most beautiful attractions in Oregon. Every time he saw the lake and drove around to the south end, he understood his ancestors' love of the area.

The majestic mountains grew berries and animals for their consumption and lodgepole that had made excellent tipi poles. The lush valleys to the north had fed their cattle and horses. He grieved as much over the loss of the land as if it had been his, but he didn't dwell on it as so many others did who lived on the reservation and drank away their grief and anger. Or the younger generations who took drugs and committed suicide because they couldn't see a way to a better life.

At the south end of the lake, he drove past the shops, go-kart tracks, gondola, and horse rides to the end of the road where the hiking trails began. He'd only brought water and a snack with him, he didn't plan to go very far, just enough to shake off the energy buzzing in him and help him sleep better tonight.

Dog leapt out of the back of the truck and started up the trail.

"Don't run over anyone!" Hawke called to the animal and started up the path. He'd only gone fifty yards and his phone buzzed.

"Hawke."

"This is Marlene Zetter. You wanted me to call you."

"Yes. Thank you for calling back." He looked around and found a stump to sit on. "Give me a minute to get something to write on."

"Sure. Are you out on the mountain like I am?"

"Sort of." He dug into a side pocket of his pack and pulled out a notepad and pencil. "I'm off today, but Dog and I are out for a hike."

She laughed. "You go to the woods even on your days off just like me."

"I ran into Roger Welch's wife yesterday."

"Leanne? She's a great gal," Marlene said with emphasis on great.

"Do you see much of them outside of work?"

"Why are you asking this?" Her tone told him she was leery.

"She was at her sister's because she'd had an argument with her husband."

"All marriages have their arguments. But that explains why Roger was trying to get out of flying for me today. He probably wanted to come there and patch things up with Leanne."

Hawke didn't buy the patch things up. Leanne hadn't acted like a woman who'd been in an argument with her husband. She'd been a free-spirited woman until Cusack's death came up.

"Do you know who Leanne works for?"

"Why didn't you ask her yourself?" Marlene huffed.

"Because when I wanted to know, she wasn't talking to anyone." He'd rather approach a rattlesnake than a woman in a foul mood.

"Roger has talked about how moody she is. Said he was glad they didn't have kids because he didn't need more than one teenager in the house." Marlene laughed.

Hawke didn't understand the marriage. It sounded as if they were both unhappy. What it had to do with the body he found, he wasn't sure, but he was going to find out.

"Where she works?" he asked again.

"Dunberry Restaurant Supply. They're based out of Spokane, but she is the district rep for Eastern Oregon. Is that all you needed?"

Scribbling the information on the paper, he said, "Yeah. Thanks. I'll buy you a beer the next time you're in the county."

"I'll hold you to that."

The connection went dead. He stared at the notes he'd scratched on the page. He wondered how often Cusack placed orders. Or how often the Eastern representative visited the Firelight. He'd have to see if the restaurant was still open with the owner dead. He might have to stop in there for a drink on the way home and see if he couldn't learn if the representative from Dunberry showed up more than once as she'd insinuated.

Chapter Ten

After the hike, Hawke felt too sweaty and dusty to stop in at the restaurant on his way home. He did a drive-by to see if it was open and made reservations for seven that night.

Now, cleaned up, and Dog back at the Trembly's keeping the horses company, he parked his truck in the restaurant parking. There were at least two dozen cars in the parking lot. A big crowd for a Thursday night. He was beginning to wish he hadn't made the reservation.

He stepped into the building and found people sitting and standing in the entry. They stared at him. It appeared the owner of the restaurant getting killed had made the place popular.

"I'm sorry. But as you can see you will have to wait for a table," Mrs. Cusack said to a woman standing in front of the cash register. The victim's wife was working at the restaurant and taking charge. Her gaze traveled over the woman's head to him. "Trooper

Hawke your table is ready."

The woman in front of him spun around and his heart started racing. What was she doing here?

"Hawke, are you meeting anyone?" Dani Singer asked.

"No." He was stunned to see the spunky pilot in the Firelight.

"Then how about sharing your table with me?" She hooked her arm through his.

He nodded, unsure what to say. He'd considered asking the woman to dinner a time or two, then realized it wasn't a good idea. She was the one woman who could get him hooked.

"This way," Mrs. Cusack said.

Hawke kept his gaze on the victim's wife. She wore a black dress and sweater, but her face was animated.

"Here you go. Enjoy."

Dani released his arm and slid onto the booth seat.

He dropped onto the one across from her, still trying to figure out how he'd ended up with her as his dinner partner.

"That worked out well, us running into one another," she said, picking up the menu. "Don't worry. It will be separate checks. This isn't a date."

He picked up the menu but studied the woman. Her short-cropped curly hair accented her high cheekbones and large eyes. The first time he'd seen her, she'd taken the air out of his lungs. He knew many would find her plain, but he found her looks, ambition, and tenacity appealing.

"What are you doing in Alder?" he asked, finally opening the menu.

"Waiting for a family of four to arrive so I can fly them up to the ranch." She put the menu down.

"It will be late by the time you eat, surely you aren't going to try and land in the dark." His gut twisted, remembering the short airstrip with trees and a mountain side that needed to be averted to land.

"I'm meeting them at oh-six-hundred. I flew in an hour ago. Thought I'd grab something to eat and walk back to the motel. I didn't dream this restaurant would be so full. It's my favorite place to eat when I'm in town."

He narrowed his eyes and studied her. "Why is it your favorite?" Could she have had a fling with the victim?

"They have the best triple chocolate cake." She studied him. "Why? You look like my ex-boyfriend when he was jealous."

"Nothing." Hawke picked the menu back up and willed his emotions to settle.

"Do you think there are so many people here because the owner was killed?"

He glanced over the menu but didn't say anything.

"What do you think all these people would do if they knew you found the body and I lifted it out of the wilderness?"

He glared at her. "I hope you don't go around publicizing that."

"I don't. But it got you to say something. This is going to be a boring dinner if all you do is stare at the menu." She tilted her head and peered at him.

Hawke set the menu down and was saved by the waitress. She was a woman in her fifties, a little overweight, a don't mess with me attitude, and name tag that said, Estella.

"What would you like to drink?" she asked.

"Dark beer for me," Dani said. "And these will be on separate checks."

The waitress raised an eyebrow and glanced his direction.

"She butted into my reservation," he said. "I'll have a beer. The local ale."

"Are you ready to order?" Estella asked.

"I am. I'll have the ribeye with baked potato and honey mustard dressing on the side of my salad." Dani handed the menu to the waitress.

Hawke had barely looked at the menu and had only been in here once before. It was the kind of place a person didn't come alone. He nodded toward Dani. "I'll have the same as her, but ranch dressing, please."

"And the steaks?"

"Rare to medium rare," Dani said.

"Done. No blood oozing anywhere." He had a thing about eating anything that had a bit of blood showing. His ancestors would have laughed at him.

"I'll get the beers and salads right out." The woman hurried across the restaurant toward the kitchen.

"No blood? Is that because of your work?" Dani played with the silverware in front of her.

"No. Childhood. My stepfather thought thawing meat and browning it on the outside was good enough. He made me and my sister eat barely cooked venison and beef when my mom was working." He shook his head. Even if he were starving, he didn't think he could stomach eating raw meat.

She nodded. "Childhood events hold a strong role in what we do as adults."

He studied her. What in her childhood had made her go into the Air Force Academy?

Estella returned with their beers.

Mrs. Cusack walked by, talking over her shoulder to the Trembley's.

How on earth had they ended up here the same night as him?

"Hawke! What a surprise!" Darlene stopped and smiled at Dani. "I don't believe we've met. Did you just move here?"

"Darlene," he said in a tone that he hoped would have her backing down.

"I live at my Uncle Charlie's lodge on Bald Mountain." Dani picked up her glass and sipped.

Darlene's gaze landed on him. "Was this your date the other night?"

Dani stared at him over her glass.

"No. That wasn't a date, and neither is this."

Estella arrived with their salads.

"You might want to catch up to your husband," Hawke said as Herb stood by a table four over from his.

"We'll talk tomorrow." Darlene hurried over to her husband.

Hawke groaned.

"Who was that? I realize there isn't much to do in an isolated area like this, but that woman knew a lot about you." Dani picked up her fork and jabbed it into her salad.

"Those two are my landlords. I rent an apartment and paddock from them. And they do know way too much about my life." He ran a hand over his face and picked up his fork. Eating was the best way to avoid talking.

"Sooo, you were on a date the other night," she said it innocently.

He glanced across the table. She watched him intently. "It wasn't a date. I hope Darlene isn't going around telling everyone that it was." He groaned. This definitely looked like a date. She'd tell all her friends about how Hawke was finally dating. "I hope you don't mind being linked to my name."

Dani stabbed her fork into her salad. "I didn't tell her my name."

"But you told her where you live. She'll figure it out. Darlene is like a bloodhound when she wants to know something." His stomach wasn't feeling up to salad even though he didn't get fresh lettuce like this very often. He shoved the plate to the end of the table.

"It's not that bad." Dani shoved the plate back in front of him. "Eat. I've seen the nasty stuff you eat when you're on the mountain."

He studied her. She cared what he ate. That little statement eased the tension tightening his shoulders and neck.

Estella stopped by the table. "How is everything?"

"Good," Dani said.

"Fine. Has it been this busy since Mr. Cusack died?" He needed to ask the question though he would have rather done so without Dani as an audience.

"Ilene left the restaurant closed one day, then boom, soon as she opened there's been a flood of people. Some have been back every day." She shook her head. "One thing good from the boss's death is the fact the restaurant is doing great." She wandered off.

"Did you come here to investigate?" Dani asked, sliding her finished salad plate to the edge of the table.

He didn't say a word, just kept forking the greens into his mouth and chewing.

A younger woman stopped at the table, offered to fill their water glasses, and reached for the empty plates.

"How is everyone holding up with Mr. Cusack gone?" he asked the woman, Stephanie, her name tag said.

She glanced at him then away. "Some are happy." She shook her head. "Most employees are happy. He was a bit of a bear to work for."

Hawke nodded. "And Mrs. Cusack, how is she to work for?"

Stephanie's face lit up. "She's great. She gave everyone a raise and isn't as strict."

"She plans to keep the restaurant open then?" Dani asked.

"That's what she told all of us when we were wondering." The young woman scooped up the salad plates and used forks and wound her way through the tables into the kitchen.

"You *are* investigating. And I pushed my way into it." Dani grinned and saluted him with her half full glass of beer.

He shook his head and sipped his beer, watching Mrs. Cusack move from table to table. Moments before Estella arrived with their meal, Ilene walked over.

"Are you two enjoying yourselves?" she asked, her intense gaze on Hawke.

"Yes. I didn't expect this place to be so busy tonight," he said, scanning the establishment.

"I can't believe that losing Ernest could have been such a boon for the place." Mrs. Cusack's cheeks darkened. "I didn't mean that... I meant that...Oh hell! I'm glad his dying didn't kill the restaurant." She stomped off to the kitchen.

Estella peered after her boss, holding their plates.

"Our plates?" Dani said, catching the woman's attention.

"Oh, sure." She placed their orders in front of them. "She's been so much happier since returning..." Estella stopped.

"Since returning from where?" Hawke pressed.

"The trip where Ernest died." The waitress wrung her hands and started to turn away.

"Just a minute. I have a question for you. How often does a representative from Dunberry Restaurant Supply come by here?" He wasn't leaving here without the information he was after.

"Once a month. Nice woman. She and Ernest acted pretty chummy." She sniffed. "At least she didn't find his hand on her butt offensive." Estella marched back to the kitchen.

"Was that a fishing trip?" Dani asked.

"No, evidence gathering." He cut into his steak and was pleased to not see any red. A glance over at Dani's plate, and he made sure not to look there the rest of the meal.

His pushy dinner guest had another beer while he had a cup of coffee.

"Want to share a piece of triple chocolate cake?" she asked as Estella returned with another beer and refilled his coffee.

He nodded, planning to only have one or two bites of the cake.

"I'll have the chocolate cake and bring an extra

fork in case my friend here wants a bite." Dani handed the waitress the two empty beer glasses.

"It goes on your check?" the waitress asked.

"Yes." Dani looked at him. "It's my treat."

The waitress scurried away.

Hawke watched the woman across from him pour the beer from the bottle into a glass. He'd known from the first time they'd met, she was used to giving orders and expecting them to be taken. But he hadn't had a woman boss him around since leaving home for college.

"What makes you think I want a treat?" he sipped his coffee.

"Because I saw the way you were intent on your job. And I know that job isn't a nine to five one. I bet you take very little time to yourself. When was the last vacation you took?" She watched him. "I mean more than a weekend somewhere. Have you ever gone somewhere for a week?"

He put his cup down, folded his hands together, and placed them on the table in front of him. "I could ask you the same thing. You told me you came straight from the Air Force to your uncle's lodge. Have you left it for a week or more since?"

She ran a finger around the rim of the beer glass. "You caught me there. But I've been trying to pull the lodge out of the red. When I do, then I can think about a vacation. You should have weeks, even months, of paid vacation waiting for you."

"I have some. I did hike the Nez Perce Trail to Bear Paw five years ago." That had been the most spiritual thing he'd ever experienced.

"You did? What did you learn?"

"That it is a trip every Nez Perce, treaty or non-treaty, should make. You can't understand the desperation of the non-treaty until you walk the trail and see the places where so many lost their lives." The trip had hammered home what his mother's family had gone through.

"I'll think about it. I have some interest in my father's heritage, but I've never been, oh, I have to know this or that." She sipped her beer and put it down. "Does that make me a bad person to not want to investigate that side of my DNA?"

He shook his head. "Look around you. I would bet only two percent of the people sitting in this restaurant care about their heritage. I am one of the two percent." He picked up his coffee as Estella returned with a large, three-layer piece of chocolate cake.

"Enjoy," she said, placing the cake in the middle of the table and placing a fork in front of each of them.

Dani's eyes lit up as she sunk the tines of her fork into the cake.

Hawke sat back, watching her slide the bite into her mouth, close her eyes, and lick her lips. Sheer rapture softened her features. He wondered what they put in the cake to make her look as if she were Aphrodite, the Goddess of Love.

He shook his head and told his dick to stand down. He'd put this woman off limits in his mind the minute he'd met her. Just because his body had other ideas was no reason to let his guard down.

She opened her eyes and sunk the fork into the cake for another bite. "Come on try it. You'll be glad you did."

It took mental strength to remember she was

talking about the cake. He picked up the fork with a shaking hand and cut off a small bite.

"Why is your hand shaking? Are you scared of chocolate cake?" She giggled at her joke.

He wondered if she normally had three beers in a row. And how safe she'd be walking back to the motel. The minute the chocolate hit his tongue, he understood her attraction to the cake. The combination of sweet, bitter, and chocolate made his taste buds dance with delight. It was rare he found food that woke up his senses.

"This is good." He stuck his fork in his side of the dessert.

"I told you. I would walk down off the mountain to get this cake once a month." She slid another bite between her lips.

Twenty minutes later, the cake and drinks were finished. Hawke walked out into the summer night with Dani.

"Want me to walk you to your motel?" Alder wasn't known for rowdies or random attacks, but it seemed the gentlemanly thing to ask.

"If you want to keep me company for three blocks, I won't stop you." She grinned and started down the sidewalk.

Hawke shook his head and caught up to her. "How many men did you boss around while in the Air Force?"

She stopped. Her good mood dissolved in a heartbeat. "Are you one of those men who can't take orders from an inferior woman?"

"No. I ate the cake when you told me to." He'd hoped for a smile, but she just marched down the street.

He caught up to her again. "I didn't mean anything

by it. Just wondered what you did beside fly a copter around."

"Then why didn't you ask it that way?" Her hands clenched into fists. "I'm so sick of men thinking I'm a ball buster just because I was an officer and I did order other airmen around. But there were women I ordered around as well."

"Okay. Lesson to me. Don't bring up bossing people around."

She'd slowed her pace.

"How often do you come to town?" he asked, changing the subject.

"When I have guests to pick up. I try to order supplies to be ready when I make a flight down. Saves on fuel and time." She relaxed.

"How long before you stop taking in families and start taking in hunters?" He had a hunch he knew, but it was the best he could come up with to ask at the moment.

"I have three more weeks of families coming in to stay and hike the trails. I already have hunters. Bow hunters. I'm glad Uncle Charlie's friend Clive is willing to stay up there through the hunting season. At first, he talked like he wanted out of the mountains before then. I would have had to hire someone new at the beginning of a crucial season."

"Is Clive leaving you for good after hunting season?" He wondered what she'd do with no one to help her with the horses and guiding.

"That's what he said. I plan to have him bring all the horses out when he comes out the end of November. I'll fly out and spend December through March looking for employees." She stopped at the corner of second and Alder by the Wagon Wheel Motel. “This is me.”

“Where are you going to stay for the four months you’re down here?” He didn’t have a clue anymore what was for rent. Once he landed with the Trembley’s, he’d stopped scanning the ads.

“I’ll see if someone will rent me a room or mother-in-law apartment.” She smiled and winked. “You offering me a bed at your place?”

He sputtered as his heart raced and blood rushed to his lower body. “I only have two rooms.”

She laughed. “We don’t know each other well enough for me to move in with you so don’t worry.” Dani sauntered into the motel without a backward glance.

Hawke let out the breath he’d been holding. If she had taken him up on it, he would have cleaned out his closet to make room for her clothes. Damn! He didn’t need that kind of a distraction in his life.

Chapter Eleven

Hawke walked into the ODFW and State Police building with a mission. He'd decided after gathering the information he had so far, he wanted a chance to continue with the investigation.

He knocked on Sergeant Spruel's door and walked in.

"Hawke, what are your plans for today?" the sergeant asked, his gaze taking in the uniform he wore. Unusual for Hawke to wear the blues this time of year when he spent most of his days on the mountains checking bow hunters.

"I'd like to be one of the investigating officers on the Cusack case," he said and went on to tell his commanding officer what he'd discovered about the victim and Leanne Welch.

"We have the phone records from the restaurant and the victim's home and their bank account statements," Spruel said. "You can take a look at them."

Hawke nodded. While he didn't usually volunteer for this type of work, he had a connection to the case by finding the body and the possibility Justine's sister could be involved. Which made him want to solve the homicide, much like following a track and wanting to discover where the creature was going and why.

Spruel handed him a folder.

He took it to his desk and turned on his computer before wandering down the hall to the break room. He poured a cup of coffee and plucked three cookies from a platter on the table.

Back at his desk, he glanced through the Cusack's house phone records. When he checked the number called most often, it was for the restaurant.

The victim's cell phone record had two numbers he called often. He typed the first number into the computer and up popped Leanne Welch's name. That answered that question. They were having an affair. Ernest didn't need to call his restaurant supply rep three times a week.

He typed in the other number that the victim called the days he didn't call Leanne. It was a Mrs. Abigail Kahn of Lewiston, Idaho. Age forty-five, married to a man who owned a construction business. He didn't think the victim had been calling her about construction. He would have called the husband. Mrs. Kahn could be the rental car seen at the Cusack's when Mrs. Cusack was out of town.

There was one more number that the victim had called several times the last two weeks of his life. Hawke looked it up. It belonged to a law firm in Hermiston, Oregon. Could he have been consulting with a lawyer out of the county because he wanted a divorce? If he was planning to leave his wife, which woman was he choosing? And did his wife know?

He picked up the phone and buzzed Spruel's office.

"Spruel."

"This is Hawke. You might want to send a trooper to Krank and Foster Law Offices in Hermiston. The last couple of weeks the victim was calling there a lot."

"I'll send the request. Anything else?"

"I suspect he was having an affair with two married women. At least he called the two numbers every other day and they belong to married women. One was his restaurant supply rep." Hawke found it hard to believe that Justine's sister was being unfaithful to her husband, but then he and his sister had different thoughts on many things.

"Give me the names. I'll see that the appropriate agency questions them." Paper rustled in the background.

Hawke gave Spruel the names, phone numbers, and addresses. "Any chance I could be there when the women are contacted?"

"I'll see what I can do. No guarantees."

Hawke replaced the phone and pulled Mrs. Cusack's cell phone record up. She called her home office in Portland every week day, a number that turned out to be her mother, and the last month calls had become more frequent with another number in Portland. He looked that number up. It belonged to a Private Investigation Agency. That answered his question if Mrs. Cusack knew her husband had been cheating on her. Someone else to be questioned.

He pulled out the bank records. Mrs. Cusack had an account in her maiden name. She'd managed to accumulate ten thousand dollars over the course of her marriage. And after her first phone call to the PI, five grand was taken out.

She definitely knew her husband was cheating on her. But did she know he'd been talking to a lawyer? She could have been gathering information on him to use in a divorce herself. Had she decided she wanted it all and not just half of it?

The bank records for the restaurant took longer to go through. Interestingly, there were two checks written out to Dunberry Restaurant Supply a month. One in which the numbers looked like supplies and one with a nice round number. Checking the records, the checks were deposited in different accounts. A scan of the records found a check a month written out to Kahn Construction for the same amount.

Not only did he have two lovers, he gave them money monthly. Something he didn't do for his wife. She was sure to see this if she took over the restaurant and took the time to go back over the books.

He jotted all this information down, circled the instances on the paperwork and walked the folder back to Spruel's office.

Hawke placed the folder on the sergeant's desk. "There's interesting information in the bank records and on the wife's phone records."

"Something you want to check out?" Spruel asked.

"Yeah, I think so. At least I'll go have a chat with Mrs. Cusack. You might want to get someone in the Portland area to talk with a PI, name of Wes Chesterfield. The victim's wife paid him to do some work for her."

On the drive to Alder and the Firelight Restaurant, the man who'd hid from him at Boundary Campground when he'd gone back up to the murder site started tapping at his brain. The camp space had been empty when he'd returned from the mountain. Could that have been the PI? But why would he be following Cusack when he was with his wife?

He pulled into the parking lot noticing there were still a good number of vehicles for a Friday at two in the afternoon.

He entered the restaurant and found a young woman manning the front. Her name tag said Pixie. She appeared to be the type Mr. Cusack favored. Had she been one of the man's harassment victims?

"Will you be sitting by yourself?" Pixie asked, picking up one menu.

"I'd like a booth, but I'd also like you to let your boss, Mrs. Cusack, know I'm here and would like to talk to her."

The woman's eyes widened. "Is this about her husband's death?" she whispered.

"I can't say." He smiled and motioned for her to take him to a seat. He might as well grab a late lunch while he was here.

"Right this way," Pixie said, striding through the empty tables to the opposite side of the room from where the other patrons sat.

He applauded the young woman's keen sense that her boss wouldn't want this conversation overheard.

"I'll get Mrs. Cusack, and your waitress will be right over." Pixie disappeared through the kitchen doors.

A plump older woman walked up to his table carrying a glass of water and a coffee pot. "I'm Gladys. I'll be serving you today. Coffee?"

He turned his coffee cup over. "Yes, please. I'll have a BLT with fries."

"I'll place the order." She poured coffee and retreated as Mrs. Cusack peeked out the kitchen door before stepping through it.

Hawke studied the woman as she approached. Her round face sagged and wrinkled with worry. It was much less animated than it had been the night before.

When she stood by the table, Hawke indicated the seat across from him. She dropped onto it as if her legs had gone out from under her. The floor under his feet vibrated.

"What are you doing here?" she asked as Pixie hurried over to the table with another glass of water before retreating to her place by the front door.

"We're trying to discover the person who murdered your husband. While going through records, I discovered you have been calling a private investigator and you paid him five thousand dollars. That's a lot of money. What did you pay him to do?" Hawke sipped his coffee and watched the woman.

She bit her bottom lip. It was easy to see her mind was running a million miles a minute behind her lowered eyelids.

"We'll find out from him soon enough, but I thought I'd give you the benefit of telling us before it looked like you had something to do with your husband's murder."

"I didn't!" Her voice rose, then dropped. "I didn't have anything to do with his murder."

"But you knew he was dead."

She shook her head.

"I followed your tracks from his body to where I found you on the mountain. You knew he was dead." He stared at her.

She blinked, and tears formed in her eyes. "Yes. He did leave me alone, saying he was going to check an area for a camp. When he didn't return, I went looking for him and found…" she sucked in air. "Him lying on the ground, that thing around his neck, and his pants…" Her face turned red and her eyes sparked with hatred. "His pants were undone as if he'd…" She gripped the water glass with both hands. "I couldn't believe he'd brought me up on the mountain and had the gall to have an assignation with one of his whores." She took a swallow of the water. "Yes. I'd paid an investigator to find out who my husband was screwing and to get evidence I could use. I wanted it all. I'm sure with as small as this county is, he had to be screwing someone he wouldn't want others to know about. If I had her name, it could get me more than half of the restaurant. I wanted it all and he'd let me have it to keep me quiet."

"Why did you really go up on the mountain with your husband?" Hawke asked as Gladys arrived with his lunch.

The older woman snorted and placed his food in front of him before hoofing it away from the table.

"Because he said he was willing to give me a divorce if I came with him. He said we could talk things out without interruptions on the mountain away from the restaurant and my job. We could figure out an agreeable settlement." She narrowed her eyes. "After the hours I spent with him on the mountain, I think he took me up there to get rid of me. He would have never parted with half of his money or even a slice of bread without an incentive."

"What makes you think he was trying to get rid of you?" This brought up an interesting twist to the investigation. Had there been someone set up to kill her?

"He kept stopping and trying to get me to get off my horse and walk around. After the third time, I began to wonder what he was up to. The last time, I thought he was going to tell me to get off and walk around, but instead he said he was going to look for a camping spot. When he didn't return after a couple hours, I began to wonder if he had decided to walk off the mountain and leave me and the horses. It didn't make sense." She sighed. "I finally dismounted, tied the horses, and walked the same direction he had. That's when I found him."

"And you zipped up his pants and tightened his belt?" This accounted for the belt being one notch too loose.

"Yes." Her gaze snapped to his. "Do you think the whore who killed him was watching me?"

"Someone was watching. Either the killer or someone else. I found tracks of another person in the same area." He studied the woman. She gave a slight nod as if she agreed. Mrs. Cusack wasn't telling him everything she knew.

"Why do you say a woman killed him?"

"Why else would his pants have been undone?" She glared.

"He could have been taking a leak and someone came up behind him."

"Out in the open? He thought himself God's gift to women, but he wouldn't have stood in the middle of a clearing and peed." She leaned back in the booth and crossed her arms.

She'd made up her mind one of the other women in his life had killed him.

"You can go. But I'll be back when I have more questions."

Mrs. Cusack flounced out of the booth and marched to the kitchen.

Hawke finished his lunch and left the restaurant, wondering if the victim's wife even cared who'd killed her husband.

His phone buzzed as he started to open his vehicle door.

"Hawke."

"This is Shoberg. Sergeant Spruel said you were interested in going with me to question Mrs. Welch."

"I am." Hawke climbed into his vehicle.

"As soon as you can get out to La Grande we'll go have a chat with Mrs. Welch."

Chapter Twelve

The usual time driving the speed limit to get to La Grande from Alder was forty-five minutes. Hawke made it in thirty.

It was three-thirty when Hawke pulled his vehicle in behind State Trooper Shoberg's at the address of Leanne and Roger Welch.

"You made good time," Steve said, when they both met on the sidewalk in front of the one-story house in a residential neighborhood on the west side.

"I used the lights when I needed to." While he wasn't one to get to places in a hurry, he'd wanted to make sure he was here when Leanne was questioned.

They walked up to the front door and Steve knocked.

"Just a minute!" Leanne called out.

He'd thought about calling Justine to see if her sister was in La Grande or still staying with her.

The door opened and Leanne appeared. Her face glistened with perspiration and the clinging workout clothing revealed dampness between her breasts.

"Oh!" She wiped at her face with a towel and didn't open the door any farther.

"Mrs. Welch, I'm Trooper Shoberg and this is—"

"Game Warden Hawke," she interrupted. Her eyes narrowed on Hawke.

"You two have met before?" Steve's gaze landed on him.

Hawke wasn't going to let either one of them keep him from being part of the questioning. "Mrs. Welch is the sister of a friend of mine. We met earlier in the week." He pulled out his notebook. "While I had dinner with Mrs. Welch and her sister the matter of the deceased Ernest Cusack came up. Mrs. Welch excused herself and I didn't see her again until now. I have, however, discovered evidence that proves she and the deceased knew each other better than she let on during the conversation on Wednesday."

"You've been digging into my life?" She didn't allow the door to open a fraction of an inch.

There was the uppity attitude he'd witnessed the night of their dinner.

"Mrs. Welch, you can either let us in or we can take this discussion down to our offices," Steve said, nodding to the door.

Her gaze lingered on Hawke before she backed up, allowing them entrance.

The house was modestly furnished. The amount of money she'd been receiving from the victim should have given her money to decorate with abandon.

She stopped in the living room, dropping onto a recliner. "What did you find out about me and Ernie?"

Steve and Hawke sat on the couch, facing her. The

other trooper nodded for him to start.

"I know that you visited the victim twice a month and talked to him several times a week." He'd start with the information least likely to get her upset.

"We were lovers. Is that what you want to hear?" She leaned back in the chair. Tears glistened in her eyes.

"Did his wife know about you?" Hawke was sure the PI hired by Mrs. Cusack had given her names and addresses by now.

"That old sow didn't care her husband was finding pleasure elsewhere. All she wanted was his money." Leanne's lip curled in an unbecoming sneer. "She didn't understand how virile he was."

"Is that what groping all his female employees was about? Him being virile?" Hawke saw her jealousy rising just as it had at Justine's at the mention of the man's hands wandering. "They thought it was harassment and creepy."

"He didn't grope all of them. They just wished he did." She spat back, defending the lecherous dead man.

"Why was he paying you five thousand dollars a month?" He slipped that in to see what she'd do.

She sucked in her breath. "What are you talking about?"

"His bank statements show him making two payments a month to Dunberry Restaurant Supply. The lesser amount was deposited in the Dunberry account but the one for five thousand dollars was deposited in an account in another bank under your name."

She dropped her face into her hands as her shoulders shook.

Hawke glanced over at Steve. He raised an

eyebrow.

"Mrs. Welch, why did Mr. Cusack pay you that much money every month?" Steve asked in a quiet voice.

Leanne raised a tear streaked face and peered at them. "He was saving it for when we were married. He said this way his wife wouldn't get everything when he divorced her."

Hawke studied her. Did he dare tell her she wasn't the only woman socking away money for him? Having seen her jealous nature, it might be the tipping point for getting the most information out of her.

"You weren't the only woman holding money for when the victim divorced his wife."

Her eyes narrowed, and she leaned forward. "What are you saying?"

"He had another woman he called the days he didn't call you and who also was receiving five thousand dollars a month in an account in her name."

Leanne shot to her feet. "Why that no-good, two-timing bastard! I wondered why he'd get mad when I called or showed up when it wasn't the days he'd told me. He was afraid I'd hear him or run into the other woman." She picked up an ornate box that sat on the end table and flung it at the wall across the room. "Bastard. He told me we would be married as soon as he had enough money put away that Ilene couldn't get her hands on." She turned on Hawke. "Is that what he told the other woman?"

He shrugged. "I haven't talked with her yet." Changing the subject seemed to work. "Are you the one who drove rental cars to the Cusack house on the days his wife was out of town?"

Her face grew stormy again. “No. I could come and go with my company car. No one questioned that I showed up twice a month to get orders and show him new catalog items.” She slammed the heel of her foot against the foot rest on the recliner. “He took the other woman into his bed while I had to settle for doing it in his office on the desk!” She began pacing. “That conniving bastard. I believed all his words and thought he loved me.” Leanne’s arm whipped out, knocking the lamp to the floor with a crash. “I’d kill him right now if he weren’t dead!”

“Mrs. Welch, did your husband know about your affair?” Steve asked.

Her head swung around, and she stared at Steve. “My husband? He wouldn’t care as long as I keep the books up to date. Roger only cares for his airplane and helicopter. I come in third.”

Hawke studied her. Regret softened the anger in her eyes. Had she pushed her husband away thinking she would soon be the wife of a restaurant owner?

“Where is your husband now?” Hawke asked.

She glanced at the clock on the DVD player. “He’ll be tucking his precious flying machines into the hangar for the night.”

“Thank you. We may have more questions for you, please don’t leave the area.” Steve stood.

Hawke followed his lead. “Do you want me to call Justine?”

Leanne shook her head. “I told her too many lies while I was there. She won’t want to see me.”

“You are family,” he said.

“Family doesn’t lie to one another. That’s her cardinal rule.” Leanne sank down on the chair.

Hawke walked out of the house and found Steve waiting for him by his vehicle.

"How is it you know Mrs. Welch? You stayed behind as if you were consoling her." Steve studied him.

"She's the sister of a friend of mine. Like I said we just met this week. I asked her if she wanted me to call her sister." He shook his head. "I have a feeling Leanne's adultery would put a wedge between the two sisters." He'd discovered something about Justine's past that she'd been keeping from everyone.

"Let's go see what the husband has to say." Steve headed to his vehicle.

Hawke slid in behind the wheel of his truck. Did the victim like the woman in Idaho more than Leanne because he allowed her into his home, or had Leanne been so needy for contact that she'd accepted the office and it was handy for the victim? He shook his head. The more he learned about the victim the less respect he had for the man, even if he was dead.

Steve parked in the indicated parking area of the Welch Agricultural Aviation building. Hawke pulled up alongside the patrol car.

The large hangar door was open. They used that as entrance to the building.

A man of about fifty stood beside a helicopter talking with a man in his sixties.

"This bird has to be ready to go in the morning. This fish and wildlife contract is all that is paying our wages," the younger of the two men said.

"Mr. Welch?" Steve asked when they were within ten feet of the other two.

"Yes?" The younger man turned toward them. His

eyes widened. “Did something happen to Leanne?” His worry appeared genuine.

“No, she’s fine. We have some questions for you about the man Trooper Hawke found on Goat Mountain Sunday.” Steve held out his hand. “I’m Trooper Shoberg.”

Mr. Welch shook hands.

“Fish and Wildlife Trooper Hawke.” He held out his hand and the man shook, but his gaze remained on Hawke.

“What about the body?” he asked.

“Biologist Marlene Zetter said you gave her the quadrants that had her stumble across the body. Had the signal you found been steady or did your instruments catch it all of a sudden?” He’d wondered at the man in the helicopter picking up a signal that would take the biologist to the dead man. He would have had to have flown over or not far from the clearing to catch it or he knew the body was there and wanted it found, so gave her the coordinates to get her to walk over it. Yet the collar had been a new. The frequency hadn’t been set up on the ODFW monitoring equipment.

Roger took his time thinking about his answer.

The older man held a wrench inside an opening in the helicopter but wasn’t moving. He was listening.

Hawke held his hand out to the older man. “Trooper Hawke,” he said.

“Ned Bartley.” The older man shook his hand. “I’m the mechanic. Don’t know nothin’ about the doin’s on the mountain.” He stuck his hands back inside the helicopter body.

“Mr. Welch, I’d think that was an easy question to answer,” Steve said, evidently not as patient with men as he was with women.

"I'm trying to remember. I listen to lots of beeps from the computer I carry around to tell the biologist where to find the collared animals. I can't remember exactly how I picked up the signal or if it was the signal of the collar on the… you know." Roger pulled a handkerchief from his back pocket and a packet of gum dropped to the ground.

Hawke retrieved the gum, hoping it would match the wrapper he found. This gum happened to be the small rectangular pieces not the long thin kind.

"Do you remember seeing anything in any of the clearings as you flew around?" Hawke asked, handing the gum back to the pilot.

"There were some horses to the southwest of the clearing and a hunting camp a good three to four miles to the southeast. A few people wandering the trails." Roger wiped at the perspiration beading his brow under a cap with an airplane and the WAA logo for the business.

"You can remember all of that on Sunday, but you can't remember anything about the beeping that sent the biologist to the body?" Steve spoke in a tone that said he didn't believe the man.

"I told you. The beeping all blends into white noise after a while. Especially, if there are a lot of wolves on the same frequency in the same area."

"Were there a lot of wolves in the area where you sent Marlene?" Hawke asked.

Roger wiped his face again. "I don't—"

"I don't want to hear you don't remember. Sunday was a day different from any other you'd had. I'd think once you heard about a body, you would have thought back over the day to see if you had anything that would help the investigation." Steve stepped closer to Roger.

"I put what happened on the mountain out of my mind when I got home and found my wife had left me." Roger ground the comment out between his teeth.

Anger. At last the man was showing some kind of emotion.

"Your wife left you? Why?" Hawke subtly shook his head at Steve, hoping the trooper picked up they weren't going to mention the wife.

"Yes. She left a note saying she wasn't willing to come after my work and toys. She'd told me about a party we were to attend, and I got the call from Marlene to fly for her on Sunday. I want Leanne to have everything and that means working weekends. Only she doesn't see it that way."

"Where did your wife go?" Hawke asked.

"To her sister's in Wallowa County. That's where she always goes when she's mad at me." Roger shoved the handkerchief and gum back in his pocket.

"She get mad at you often?"

The man stared at him. "What's this have to do with if I heard beeping from the collar?"

"Just getting an idea of where your mind was at while flying." Hawke wondered if the man had any idea his wife had been fooling around.

"Oh, like I was thinking about Leanne and not paying close attention to the beeping." Roger grinned and relaxed. "I was thinking about how mad she'd be about me missing the party and that I'd have to put up with one of her tantrums."

"Tantrums?" Steve asked. His gaze flicked to Hawke and back to the pilot.

Hawke surmised from that brief glance Steve was remembering the way Leanne had broken items in the house without a care. He could see the woman killing a man in a fit of rage. But the collar around the victim's neck was done in a calculating way. That Mrs. Cusack said the victim's pants were open, he had to believe a woman had seduced him to the clearing under the pretense of sex and placed the collar on the man using the same ploy. No, he didn't see Leanne being that cold and calculating.

"Leanne is like a teenager. She doesn't get her way, she throws a fit—a tantrum of sorts. I've learned to let her vent and then she's willing to listen." Roger shook his head. "I really expected her to be home when I got there."

"Is she home now?" Hawke asked, wondering if the man knew his wife had come home.

"She came home yesterday. Said she was sorry for leaving and hoped I'd forgive her. I don't know what her sister said to her, but I'm grateful." Roger nodded.

This time Hawke sent a glance toward Steve. The man standing in front of them had no clue his wife had been screwing another man and had come home to him when that man was murdered.

"Thank you for your help. If by chance you remember anything about why you sent Marlene to the quadrant you did, give me a call." Hawke handed the man his card.

"I will." Roger tucked the card in his breast pocket.

Hawke and Steve walked out of the hangar and stopped at the vehicles.

"You think he doesn't know his wife was screwing someone else?" Steve asked.

"If he did figure it out, he's a damn good actor." Hawke stared at the hangar. "The more I think about the way the victim was killed, it had to be someone cold and calculating. That isn't Mr. or Mrs. Welch."

"I agree."

"I'm going to Lewiston tomorrow to talk to the other woman the victim was paying and playing with." Hawke opened his truck door. "When you get the information from the lawyer in Hermiston and the PI in Portland, send it my way."

"Copy." Steve disappeared into his car.

Hawke pointed the nose of his truck toward the county. He was relieved to not have Leanne at the top of his suspect list. He wasn't completely ruling either her or her husband out, but he had a hard time believing either one capable of the murder. That left Mrs. Kahn in Lewiston and Mrs. Cusack. While she'd acted lost and was the first to admit her husband's death benefited her, he wasn't ruling her out of cold bloodedly killing her husband.

Chapter Thirteen

Hawke woke Saturday morning feeling as if this could be the day he caught a break in the case. While he had to see this through and follow the trails, he was more than ready to get back up on the mountain and chat up hunters and sleep under the stars. He loved the comforts of his apartment, but too many days back here and his feet started to itch to be back out in the woods. Winter was coming which meant less time on the mountain and more patrolling in the truck.

His phone buzzed as he buckled his duty belt.

"Hawke."

"Trooper Hawke this is Nez Perce County Detective Orson Watts, I was asked by the State Police to conduct an interview with you today in Lewiston."

"Yes. I'm just now leaving Wallowa County. I can be there in ninety minutes." Hawke knew that was a short time considering Rattlesnake Grade. But he could use the lights on the straight stretches of the road.

"There's no hurry. I have to take my daughter to soccer practice and pick her up before I can do the interview."

"Then do you want me to meet you at the Sheriff's Department at noon?" Not having to hurry would give him time to get something to eat before heading over.

"That works. See you at noon."

Hawke poured himself another cup of coffee and leaned back against the counter debating whether to go to the office and type up his contacts for this week or wait until he returned. He decided to do it when he returned.

He finished his coffee, grabbed his hat, and headed down to his vehicle. Dog sat by the horse trailer, his tail wagging. He was ready to get back up on the mountain as well.

"Not today. You keep Horse, Jack, and Boy company. I have to make a road trip." Hawke scratched the animal behind his ears and walked over to the state police rig.

Herb stood by the hay barn. He whistled and waved his arm, indicating he wanted a conversation.

Hawke sighed and changed direction. The only thing he'd venture the man wanted to know was how the case was going and possibly information on the woman sitting with Hawke at the restaurant.

"You working the weekend?" Herb asked.

"I always do this time of year. Why?" Hawke studied his landlord. The man had a way of sneaking up on you with questions.

"Darlene hasn't stopped talking about you and your date the other night—"

"That wasn't a date. She happened to need a table.

I was eating alone. Or thought I was eating alone."

"Uh-huh. You two left together. Seen you walking down the street side-by-side." Herb cocked one bushy eyebrow.

"I was a gentleman and walked her to her motel. That was it." And why am I acting like a teenager who was caught making out? "I have to meet someone in Lewiston." Hawke spun on his heel and strode to his truck.

"Maybe you should reconsider that dating thing!" Herb called out.

Why everyone felt a need to be in his personal business he'd never understand. It would make sense if he was one of the old-time families or a long time local, but he was a relative newcomer and shouldn't have so many people wondering about his love life. He didn't have a long line of county heritage to keep alive.

He drove to Alder and was thankful to see only three vehicles in the parking lot of the Tree Top Café. It was close to the courthouse and sheriff's office, making the café the go to place for take-out and quick meals for the local LEOs.

The bell over the door jingled when he walked in. A new waitress stood behind the counter and three men sat at a table drinking coffee.

He walked up to the counter and settled onto a stool.

The waitress was in her forties, bleached hair pulled into a ponytail, and enough makeup to hide any wrinkles or flaws.

"Morning stranger," she said in a raspy smoker voice.

"Morning. I'll have two eggs over easy, hash

browns, and ham." He flipped the coffee cup over on the counter, and she filled it.

"I'll get Mort on it." She spun around and hollered his order through the window into the kitchen.

Hawke raised the cup to his lips to drink.

She spun back around. "I haven't seen you here before."

"I haven't seen you either." He sipped and tried to ignore her.

The waitress had other ideas. "I'm Janelle."

He pointed to his name tag.

"Hawke? That's your last name. What's your first name?"

He tapped the name tag again.

"You're Hawke Hawke?" She laughed. "Why would a parent name their child like that?" She put her hands over her mouth, her eyes wide. Slowly, she lowered them. "Not that I was bad-mouthing your mother. I'm sure in your culture that is normal."

His entire life, he'd come across this type of person who thought because he was Indian there was a significance to his name. His family name was Hawke, shortened from Black Hawke two generations ago and his first name, Gabriel, was from the Bible. That was his mother's doing. His father had wanted him to be named Tuff. Wanted him to be a rodeo cowboy, like him. But his mother won with his name, and ultimately, getting away from his father. Hawke didn't care for the name Gabriel and had always used his last name as his first name as well.

He shrugged. He didn't tell strangers his life. That was kept to himself.

"Order up!" the cook called.

Janelle whipped around, picked up his plate, and set it in front of him. “Do you need any hot sauce, ketchup, or whatever?”

“Nope.” He picked up his fork and went to work on his meal.

The bell jingled.

Footsteps grew near and someone sat on the stool next to him. He glanced over.

“Looks like you’re filling up before going on duty,” Ralph, the young jailer, said. “Or are you coming off?”

“Did Archie sober up?” Hawke asked.

“Yeah, he was released the next day. You saved his life bringing him in. Kept him from getting run over.” Ralph turned his coffee cup over.

“The usual?” Janelle asked.

“Yes, please.” Ralph smiled at the woman as if she were twenty instead of old enough to be his mother.

Hawke finished his food and wiped his mouth. He downed the rest of his coffee and tucked a ten and a five under his plate. “See you around.”

Ralph nodded.

Janelle smiled. “Come back again.”

At his truck, Hawke called in that he was on duty and headed to Lewiston to question a woman about the Cusack homicide.

He headed out the North Highway and eased up on the accelerator to enjoy the drive.

«»«»«»

At Lewiston, he used Highway 128 to cross the Snake River and end up at the Nez Perce County Sheriff’s Office. He parked the truck in front of a large red brick and white building. The half-arch over the entry was eye-catching. He was thirty minutes early but couldn't think of anything to do to kill time. Lapwai, where his father's side of the family resided, was too far away to be back by noon. And he shouldn't use the state truck to make a visit to his family.

He pushed through the two sets of glass doors and entered the lobby. Straight ahead was the detention center. To his left, he spotted several women behind a counter.

"May I help you?" one of the women asked.

"I'm waiting for Detective Watts," Hawke said to the woman.

"Have a seat. I'm sure he'll show up soon."

He sat in the chair along a wall of windows and pulled out his phone to see if he had any messages. Two emails caught his attention. The autopsy on Cusack and forensics on the hairs he'd found at the scene.

The door opened. A man, ten years younger than him, walked through. He was dressed in civilian clothes. The bulge of a gun at his waist under his jacket revealed he was a detective.

"Trooper Hawke?" the man asked, holding out his hand.

"Yes." He shook. "You must be Detective Watts."

"I am. I understand the woman you wish to speak to may have something to do with a homicide in your area?"

"Yes. We don't know if she is directly implicated, but she has been receiving money from the victim. We'd like to know why." Hawke slipped his phone back on his belt.

"You could have called to ask her that." Watts crossed his arms.

"If that was all we wanted to know. And I prefer to see the reactions of the person I'm questioning." Hawke placed his hands on his duty belt.

"I see. I do want to warn you, the woman you plan to question is a prominent member of the community." Watts didn't look like the type to cater to the rich and powerful, but he could have been cautioned by his superiors.

"Murderers can come from all walks of life."

"Just warning you." Watts walked to the door. "We'll take my car."

Hawke followed the man out to a tan sedan. He folded himself into the front passenger seat, trying to remember the last time he'd ridden in a car.

"Are you going to fill me in at all?" Watts asked as he drove away from the station headed east.

"Mrs. Kahn had been receiving five-thousand dollars every month from the victim. There has been a rental car at the victim's house when his wife has been gone on overnight trips. I've established the other woman who also received money wasn't the person in the rental cars." He glanced at Watts. "If the husband is home, I'd like you to keep him busy in another room while I ask Mrs. Kahn about her relationship with the victim."

Watts let out a slow whistle. "You have a shit load of questions for Mrs. Kahn."

"Have you met the woman before?" Hawke wondered about a woman who had a well-to-do husband, taking money from the victim. Even if she was holding it for them to marry and start over.

"Once. She was at a school board function. Seemed like a nice woman." Watts shook his head. "But our line of work, you begin to question everyone and everything they do."

Hawke nodded. "Makes life interesting being cynical all the time."

"You have kids?"

"Not that I know of." He wasn't being flippant, he'd had a couple of one-night stands in college where alcohol had dimmed the events. He didn't know if the women had been on birth control. He knew he hadn't used a condom because he hadn't kept any at the ready.

Watts studied him a minute before shifting his attention back to the road. "It's hard to let your kids play with others knowing what their parents are messed up in."

He could see where that would make things difficult. You couldn't really blame the child for the parents' scruples, but you wouldn't want your children subjected to them.

They drove away from the city and out a tree-lined road that followed a stream. Houses and farm land dotted the area. At a cluster of houses, Watts maneuvered the sedan down the street and parked in front of the largest residence.

"Kahn has a construction company. He built this little community and gave himself the biggest house. As if he's saying, I am your landlord, this is my castle." Sarcasm and contempt rang in the detective's voice.

Hawke opened the car door and pulled himself out. This ride had been a reminder of why he didn't like cars. He followed Watts up the cement sidewalk flanked by colorful flowers on both sides.

The massive wood door could have been the entry to a castle. Watts grabbed the heavy iron knocker and rapped three times.

"Coming!" a female voice called out.

The door opened.

A woman in her forties with long brunette hair, hanging in waves around her face and shoulders, smiled at them. "I believe I gave to the police fund not that long ago."

"Mrs. Abigail Kahn?" Hawke asked.

"Yes." Her gaze traveled from his face to his cap, then his name tag and badge. "Oregon State Police? Why are you looking for me?"

"I have questions I'd like to ask you about an acquaintance you have in Wallowa County." He had a feeling this woman was someone who got down to business.

She glanced over her shoulder before whispering, "Does this have anything to do with Ernest Cusack?"

"Yes, Ma'am."

Flustered wasn't a word most would probably use with this woman, but her hands shook as she opened the door wider. "Do come in. I'll have to make sure my husband heads to his golf session before I can talk with you."

He nodded as he entered the home. Watts followed behind.

"Please. Have a seat in here. I don't want my husband to know about any of this. It was foolish and there is no need to upset him." She closed the door on them and left.

"She was having an affair with your victim," Watts said, making himself comfortable on the small couch.

Hawke peered out the window. The side lawn was well-manicured. An affair didn't make sense. At least not from his point of view. The woman had everything she could want. Why chance it to be with a man that had been depicted as anything but flattering?

A car started up. He continued to watch out the window. A sporty convertible drove by with golf clubs in the passenger seat and a large man driving. He eased out the breath he'd been holding. They'd have been fools if the person driving off had been the woman he wanted to question.

Several minutes later the door opened. Mrs. Kahn walked in carrying a tray with a pitcher of lemonade and three glasses.

"We might as well quench our thirsts from this hot day," she said, pouring the beverage into the glasses and handing them out.

Hawke placed his glass on a coaster on the table beside him and pulled out his log book. When she'd placed the pitcher back on the tray, he asked, "How did you know Ernest Cusack?"

She gripped the glass with both hands. "We met at a fundraiser dinner at Wallowa Lake Lodge three years ago. My husband didn't want to attend the event. His wife was out of town at a conference for her work." The woman sipped the lemonade. "We spent two nights together. It was thrilling. My husband works so hard, he doesn't have the energy to hug me most days. He comes home, eats, and falls asleep. Ernie was quite charming. Making me laugh, telling me how beautiful I looked, and buying me champagne. He made me feel young and loved again."

"And you started driving to Wallowa County a couple times a month to be with him when his wife was gone?" Hawke glanced up from the book he'd been writing in and studied her.

Mrs. Kahn grimaced. "Yes. It was easy to rent a car and tell Howard I was visiting a friend or relative. He didn't care as long as he could work. At first, I felt bad for Ernie's wife. But from things he said and evidence of her things and the way the house was kept, she didn't want to be there anymore than I wanted to be here." Her eyes widened, and her hand went to her mouth in a surprised or stunned expression. "Don't get me wrong. I love my husband. Ernie was a distraction. He knew I didn't love him. That what we did was for the thrill."

"Why did he send you five-thousand dollars every month?" Hawke asked.

"It wasn't blackmail if that's what you're thinking." Her tone became angry and self-righteous.

"The other woman he was having an affair with and paying said it was for a nest egg when they were both free to marry." Hawke studied the woman closely.

Her eyebrow raised. Her lips curved into a smile. "I'm not jealous. I know he had another woman. Younger, more gullible, to think he would allow even half of his holdings to go to his wife in a divorce."

"You mean he didn't plan on divorcing his wife?" Hawke had a similar thought. But the man would have kept everything if Ilene were dead.

"No. He sent me money and the other woman to hide it from the IRS. He may have told the other woman it was for them to run away, but I saw the real man. He was as tight-fisted and greedy as they came with everything except seducing a woman." She sipped her drink.

"How do you keep the IRS from knowing about the money?" Watts asked.

"I hid it in one of the non-profits I chair." She shrugged. "He's dead. I'll give it back to the wife and she can deal with taxes."

"Where were you last Sunday?" Hawke asked.

"At the country club, watching my husband in a charity golf tournament."

"What's the name of the country club?"

She'd been straight forward about everything. Her affair, the money, and he didn't see her lying about where she was on Sunday. It would, however, be remiss of him to not check out her alibi.

"There's only one in Lewiston," Watts said, standing. "Thank you for your time and the lemonade, Mrs. Kahn."

Hawke closed his log book, tossed back the rest of his drink, and placed the glass on the tray. "Yes. Thank you for your time and candid comments." He stood and held out his hand.

She shook and said, "I hope you find who killed Ernest. He had his flaws, but he didn't deserve to have his life end this way."

Mrs. Kahn walked them to the front door.

"If all the people I questioned were as honest as you, my job would be easier." Hawke put his ball cap on as he stepped out onto the porch.

"The country club?" Watts asked.

"If you don't mind." Hawke folded back into the front seat of the sedan.

"Not a problem. I'm curious about this after hearing her side of things." Watts started the vehicle. "She was telling the truth."

"Yeah. I didn't pick up on any secrets other than her husband not knowing about her affair." He flipped open his log book. "You'll have to go back and make enquiries about the money."

"Yeah." Watts drove back to the city, through the downtown area, south along the Snake River before turning east and into the golf course entrance.

Chapter Fourteen

On the drive home from Lewiston, Hawke had his mind on all the other suspects. As he'd expected; the staff at the country club remembered seeing Mrs. Kahn all day long. She was checking on food, the entertainment, and keeping track of the golf teams paying for the opportunity to play in the tournament.

His prime suspects were Leanne, her husband Roger, and Mrs. Cusack. He couldn't see an outraged husband of a woman who was fired for not liking the victim's advances going to such an elaborate means of killing the man.

He was about twenty minutes out of Alder when he picked up a call about a stranded driver on the North Highway. He did a U-turn and found an elderly gentleman and his wife trying to change a tire. Fifteen minutes later, he had them headed to their daughter's in Troy and he was traveling south again.

"Heading to the office to write up reports," he told

dispatch as a vehicle sped by him. "Vehicle headed to Alder at an accelerated speed. Giving chase." Hawke turned on the lights and sirens as he read the license plate to dispatch. He chased the jacked-up silver Ford to the edge of town. There, two city cars were waiting for the vehicle. The driver's only choice was to stop, crash into the police cars, or a building. The city cops had picked a good spot to block the road between two large cement buildings on both sides of the road.

The pickup screeched to a stop. The driver's door flew open and a young man sprang out of the vehicle, sprinting across the parking lot.

Hawke followed. He hated runners. Chasing a runner reminded him of the years he'd tried to be a track star and was always five feet behind the rest in the sprinters. Now, if the guy planned to run for a mile or better, Hawke would catch him. He couldn't sprint worth a damn, but he could outlast most people.

The suspect fled between two houses. A volley of barking, snarling, and growling filled the air.

Slowing his pace, Hawke walked between the houses and found his suspect curled in the fetal position with three big dogs growling down at him.

"Hey boys, good job," Hawke said in a calm but commanding voice.

The dogs all turned their attention on him.

"Good dogs. You caught the runner." He continued talking to the animals, as he walked calmly and with confidence up to the suspect on the ground. "Do you mind if I take him out of your yard?" he asked, reaching down to pull the teenager to his feet.

"Hey! What are you doing back here!" a male voice hollered from behind him.

The dogs started growling and showing their teeth.

"Trooper Hawke. I was chasing this suspect. He ran into your yard. Your dogs did a good job of stopping him." He didn't turn to the man. The way the dogs were acting, he didn't want to turn his back on them.

"They did?" He heard a screen door slam shut. "Shorty, Killer, Fang, come!"

The three dogs stopped snarling and trotted toward the house.

Hawke pulled the kid to his feet and cuffed him before turning toward the man, who stood on the steps. The dogs were nowhere to be seen. "Give your dogs an extra bone tonight. They did good work."

The kid hung his head as they walked by the man on the porch.

"Jerry Robbins? That you?" the man asked, starting down the steps.

"Sir, I need to get him back to his vehicle."

"Hawke, looks like you caught him." City Policeman Don Profitt trotted up between the houses.

"Yeah, had some help from this man's dogs." He nodded toward the man now standing several feet from them.

"It's about time your dogs helped rather than caused a nuisance, hey Pete?" the officer said.

"What did Jerry do?" the man, Pete, asked.

"He was driving over the speed limit, reckless behavior—" Hawke started.

"And has open containers and meth in his vehicle," Officer Profitt added.

The boy groaned.

Hawke handed him over to Profitt. "You can have

the honors. The higher charge was found inside city limits." He walked back to his truck, backed up to a side street, and headed through town. His stomach started grumbling as he caught sight of the Tree Top Café. Not feeling like entering the establishment again today, he decided to grab a burger at the Shake-It-Up drive-thru.

He drove up to the order window and waited. A high school girl arrived, shoving her cell phone in her apron pocket.

"What would you like?" she asked, the fingers of her left hand poised over the cash register.

"Chocolate shake, cheeseburger, and fries."

"That's seven-seventy-five." She held out a hand.

Hawke placed a ten in her palm.

She gave him his change. "Your order will be at the next window."

He thanked her and pulled forward. His radio crackled. There was a domestic dispute in Eagle. County would take twenty-five minutes to get there and the other fish and game trooper was at the lake. He was the closest. Only Alder had city police. The rest of the county had to depend on the Sheriff's Department and State Police. And due to the small population, the fish and game staters had to do the jobs of a state trooper as well as their game job.

The young man held his bag of food out to him. Hawke grabbed it as he spoke into the radio he could be there in fifteen.

Once he was out of town, he turned on the lights and siren and drove eighty, even through Winslow, on his way to Eagle. He hated domestic disputes. He'd been a spectator to many while growing up. Either in his family or neighbors. It usually started with alcohol or drugs.

He pulled into Eagle, turned right onto First Street and left onto Sparrow. A crowd had gathered at a small home that sat back from the road. It appeared to be a guest house of the main house by the street.

Shutting the siren down, he checked his vest to make sure it was all snapped up and he had everything on his duty belt. These situations could get ugly in a hurry.

A woman of about sixty hurried over to his truck. "They're going to kill each other!" she shouted.

"Who Ma'am?" he asked, allowing her to pull him to the house at the back of the property.

"My son and that damn woman he dragged home."

"What are their names?" he asked, picking out a man and a woman standing several feet apart each wielding a weapon. The man had a baseball bat, the woman a large knife.

"Percy is my son. Marigold is what she calls herself."

"Stay back." He walked to within twenty feet of the two. "Percy? Marigold? What's going on here?"

Neither one took their eyes off the other.

"She tried to kill me while I was sleeping in my chair," Percy said.

Marigold lunged at him. He held the bat up, knocking away her arm holding the knife.

"Marigold. Why are you trying to hurt Percy?" Hawke had decided the woman was the more dangerous of the two and worked his way closer to her with his hand on the pepper spray on his belt.

"He's evil." Her hands shook as she held the knife.

He'd bet a month's salary she was high. The drugs that were cooked up locally had become the local law enforcement's worst nightmare.

"No, I'm not! I'm not the one trying to slash someone with a knife!" Percy shouted and swung the bat.

Marigold made a lunge. Hawke grabbed her around the waist and yanked the knife from her as the siren of his back up shrilled through the air.

"Let me go! Let me go!" the woman shouted and clawed at his arms.

He yanked one arm behind her and latched one side of the cuffs. She threw her body forward. It took all his strength to keep hold of her.

"Don't let her loose!" shouted the older woman. "She'll kill my Percy!"

Hawke wrestled the woman to the ground, where he could hold her down by straddling her body as he worked to get both her arms behind her back.

"Don't hurt her!" Percy yelled, coming at him with the bat.

He raised an arm to ward off the blow.

The bat and the man's arm jerked away.

Hawke glanced past the man and spotted Deputy Dave Alden, holding the man's arms behind his back.

"Thanks." He hauled Marigold to her feet.

And he'd thought he'd call it a day two hours ago. Now he had to haul the woman to the county jail, book her, and write up a report before he could head home. And his dinner would be cold by the time he had a chance to eat it.

«»«»«»

Hawke parked his work vehicle next to his truck

around midnight. Between adding his notes to the arrest of Jerry Robbins who was transporting narcotics and writing up the domestic dispute, he'd added about five hours of over-time to his day.

Dog ran up to him, wiggling and talking.

"It's good to see you, boy." He climbed the stairs carrying the cold burger and fries and warm milk shake that he'd tried to drink on the way home but gave up. Even though he was hungry, he couldn't stomach the warm slimy texture. He tossed the cup in the trash and tossed the bag with the burger and fries in the microwave. Undressing as he walked to the shower, he came out clean and feeling better. A punch of numbers on the microwave and his dinner heated up.

He glanced at his phone. Justine had tried to call him twice today. Why would she try to contact him?

Opening his laptop, he sat at the small table he used as a counter and listened to Justine's voicemails.

"Hawke, it's me, Justine. Sorry to bother you, but I wondered if you could come see me. It's about Leanne." The message finished. He tapped the next one. "Hi Hawke. Sorry to be a nuisance, but I really need to talk with you. Call me or come by." A pause. "It's Justine."

Whatever she wanted to tell him must be pretty important that she called twice. He glanced at the clock. Midnight wasn't a good time to call. He'd give her a call first thing in the morning.

He opened his emails and focused on the autopsy.

Asphyxiation was the cause of death. No sign of a struggle. They also noted the belt not buckled in the usual hole. *Bromus marginatus Nees ex Steud* grass seed was found inside his pants. The man's pants had been open when he landed on the ground.

Mrs. Cusack had admitted to him she'd zipped up his pants and buckled his belt. Had she also been the one to humiliate him? There were times in their conversations he could see a mean streak in the woman, while other times she didn't appear to have the intelligence to have thought up such an elaborate scheme.

He moved on to the forensics report on the items he'd found around the body and behind the bush where someone had either watched the whole thing or waited for the victim to arrive.

A click opened the report.

Two hairs were female, one was male. The one found on the bushes was male. The hair he'd found first, on the body, was female. The hair he'd found under the body was female but not from the same person as the one on the body. The one under the victim had forty-eight percent Native American blood.

His mind zipped to Dani. She knew how to fly a helicopter and had spoken up about knowing the victim. His heart raced. Had she been playing with him at the restaurant asking questions and pretending to help him get answers from the staff when all along she was the one who'd killed the victim?

He'd found evidence a helicopter picked up the person behind the bushes. She could have landed there, met with the victim, killed him, and flown away. It was just a short hop to the hunting lodge via helicopter. He remembered seeing her wear a bracelet strung with small glass beads the first time they met at her uncle's hunting lodge.

He didn't want to believe it could be her, given his

body's reaction to her, but she was efficient, cold, and calculating. He'd witnessed those qualities about her.

Shaking loose of where his mind wanted to take him, he concentrated on the other information. There were no fingerprints on the gum wrapper but there was DNA and it matched the Native American DNA. That had to be the person who watched, killed him, and left by helicopter.

His hand shook as he ran his finger across the touch pad to scroll down the rest of the information. The epithelial DNA on the victim's genitals matched gum wrapper and hair. When he found the person who matched the DNA, he was sure they would have the killer. His gut twisted. He'd hate to see Charlie's Lodge go under because he left it to a murderer.

Chapter Fifteen

Hawke woke Sunday morning with a plan to visit Dani at Charlie's Lodge and collect a DNA sample. He didn't know anyone else connected to the case who had Native American roots other than himself, and he didn't kill the man. He hadn't even crossed paths with him until he was dead.

Halfway through saddling Horse and Jack his phone buzzed.

Justine.

He'd forgotten about her calls the day before in his quest to get proof whether or not Dani could be the murderer.

"Hi Justine," he said, leaning against the tack room wall in the stables.

"I decided to call this morning in case you didn't get my messages yesterday." The reproach in her voice made him sorry he hadn't checked his phone earlier the day before.

"Sorry. I was following leads in Idaho and didn't get your messages until close to midnight. I thought it would be too late to call."

"I'm sorry for sounding so abrupt. I'm just…It's something…" She released a long breath. "I think there's something going on with Leanne."

"What do you mean?" He had to remember the woman was still a suspect even if the facts were pointing in another direction.

"She called me yesterday and said she was leaving Roger. That being at my house she'd realized what she was missing in her life."

Her tone sounded as if she were fishing for him to say she had nothing to do with her sister's decision. But he couldn't say that. He had a feeling the younger sister realized she was in a loveless marriage and affair and wanted more.

"Maybe she wants to be single again—like you."

Justine moaned. "Don't say that. Pop will blame Leanne's behavior on me."

He couldn't stop the chuckle. "There isn't anything you can do about this. I need to get to work. I have a feeling Leanne will land on her feet."

"But she also went out and bought a new car. An expensive one. Where do you think she got the money for that?"

The worry in Justine's voice made it hard for him to not tell her that her sister had an affair and had been hiding money for her lover. However, that was all part of his investigation. He couldn't say a word. But he found it interesting that Leanne was spending the money.

"Ask her. I have to go." Hawke ended the

conversation and finished getting ready for a four-day trip into the mountains and a visit to Charlie's Hunting Lodge on Bald Mountain.

«»«»«»

Monday around noon, Hawke rode past the largest log building with the sign Charlie's Hunting Lodge on the front porch roof. He'd started out at the Minam River Trail on Sunday. After several stops to check bow hunters and rest his horses, he'd spent the night near a small creek that barely trickled with the last of the summer snow melt.

He approached the barn and stables. Clive, Charlie's wrangler, who was retirement age, walked out of the barn.

"Hawke, figured you'd be showing up here when bow season started." Clive roughed up Dog's ears and tied Jack to the hitching post in front of the barn.

Hawke tied Horse and began unbuckling his pack and saddle.

"Yeah, already wrote a few citations on the way up. I wish they realized there is a reason the ODFW puts out hunting regulation pamphlets and has a website for them to access."

Hawke glanced toward the new addition to the hunting lodge buildings—two canvas portable structures. One housed Charlie's prop plane and the other had Dani's helicopter.

Charlie had always left the plane sit out. He'd tie it down to keep a high wind from tossing it off the mountain but had never put it under cover. He'd rarely spent the worst of the winter months up here. From what Dani said after their dinner the other night, she didn't plan to either.

"There have been a few changes since I was here last." He nodded toward the canvas covered hangars.

"The new boss said they'll last longer if they're kept out of the elements." The older man rolled his eyes and slid the saddle off Jack. "Charlie never tucked that plane away like it was going to melt from a rain storm. In fact, he always said rain was nature's car wash, or in his case, plane wash."

Something had happened since his last visit. Clive had always been easy to get along with and kept the place running when Charlie had bouts of the bottle. He'd never heard the man say a derogatory word about anyone. Yet, his tone said he was ready to leave and it wasn't because he was getting too old to do his job.

"I heard this is your last season here. Planning anything fun when you retire?" Hawke placed the pack on the ground and carried the packsaddle into the barn behind Clive.

The older man set the horse's saddle down and stared at him. "I don't mind taking orders from a woman, honest I don't, but she's turning this place into a tourist attraction. We don't just have fisherman and hunters anymore. She's drawin' in families. With kids that don't listen and parents who think they know more about the horses and the mountains than I do."

Hawke unbuckled his rifle scabbard from his riding saddle and wandered back out to the front of the barn. "She's trying to make a living, not just exist." And the thought of where the money had come from to put up the two hangars had him wondering if he'd missed a payment from the deceased into an account for Dani Singer.

"Me, Doolie, and Charlie lived fine all those years

scouting and leading hunters and fishermen. She gets a good retirement from the Air Force, she don't need to be bringing in all these other yahoos."

Hawke could sympathize with the man. He understood the solidarity and respect most hunters and fishermen had for the wilderness and the sanctity of silence. He could imagine Clive hiding from the screaming and hollering children as they romped and played around the buildings and most likely while riding the horses.

With the scabbard over his shoulder, he picked up his canvas packs.

"Bunkhouse has room for you," Clive said, leading the way to the building where the wrangler lived and any other male employees.

"Are you the only one employed right now?" Hawke asked.

"No. She brought in a cousin last month to help with the horses. He's living in the bunkhouse with me. And she hired a woman to do the cooking and laundry. She stays in the little room off the kitchen." Clive opened the bunkhouse door. "You can use the bed in the corner if you want. It's that or here by the door. Me and the boy keep our distance. He's good with the tourists but don't know a thing about hunting and fishing."

Hawke dropped his belongings on the bed in the corner. "I saw Dani last week in Alder. She said she was going to spend the winter looking for help. Guess that means she's not keeping the boy and woman?"

"Yeah, they're temporary." Clive kicked at the box at the end of his bed. "I honestly thought I'd die here, on this mountain, helping Charlie. He wasn't supposed to go before me."

"He drank too much for you to honestly believe he'd outlast you." Hawke shoved his scabbard under his bed and placed the pack bags at the end of the bed, so anyone walking into the building wouldn't see the rifle. That was the only problem up here. There wasn't any place to lock it up, and he didn't like packing it everywhere he went. "Do the kids stay out of here?" he asked, noticing the shotgun still hung over the door.

"Yeah. They know better than to come in here. Though Dani's been talking about putting locks on the buildings. Another thing I don't want—a passel of keys hanging from my belt."

"Where's she at?" Hawke asked, ready to approach her with his discoveries and see what she had to say.

"This time of day, she's in the office going over the books." He frowned. "That was my job. She took it away the first day she showed up."

Hawke understood why Clive's feathers were so ruffled and he was ready to leave. Dani had taken away all his jobs that showed he was more than a wrangler. Charlie had always treated Clive and Doolie like partners in the Lodge. Doolie had been killed in June, shortly after Dani took over the hunting lodge. His greed and grief had done him in. Hawke still wondered why Charlie hadn't left half the lodge and the land to his two longtime friends. And then to be demoted from feeling like a partner to just a hired hand, Hawke understood Clive's irritation.

He walked into the lodge. It had been spruced up. No longer a rough and dirty place for smelly outdoorsmen to rest while waiting for a meal. It had colorful pillows on the clean log furniture. Magazines on the coffee table along with a fake flower arrangement. The fireplace mantle had shiny glass frames of Charlie, Clive, Doolie, and some famous guests. In the middle was a photo of Dani in her flight suit standing next to a sleek, black fighter helicopter.

"May I help you?" asked a soft voice.

He turned and peered into the eyes of a small woman possibly ten years older than him. "I'll be spending the night in the bunkhouse." He held out his hand. "I'm Fish and Game Trooper Hawke. I stay here when I'm up on the mountain."

She nodded. "I'll make sure there is another plate at the dinner table." She disappeared as quietly as she'd arrived.

"I see you met Juanita. She's helping me out until we close up for the winter." Dani walked into the great room from the back of the building.

"I did. I understand you also have a young wrangler working here." Hawke leaned his back against the mantle and gave the woman his full attention. He wanted to make sure he didn't miss any changes in her demeanor as they spoke.

"Yes, my cousin, Tyson. He wanted some time away from his friends. They were pushing him to become more like them, and he'd rather take a different path." She smiled. "I just about have him talked into joining the military."

Hawke raised an eyebrow. "Is that what he wants?"

"He doesn't know what he wants other than not getting caught up in the problems young people face on the reservation." She crossed her arms. "There is nothing wrong with the military."

"I agree. But it needs to be his own decision."

Hawke motioned to the chairs and sat.

Dani uncrossed her arms and sat. She didn't lean back and relax. She leaned forward, pushing her point. "I agree he needs to make his own decision, but doing something is better than nothing or getting into trouble. If he joins up for a couple years he will get food, clothing, training and an education while he decides what to do with his adult life."

Hawke waited for her to get a breath and nodded. "There's nothing wrong with the military to make a man out of a boy. It worked for me. But there are some that aren't cut out for that kind of life."

She nodded. "You up here checking on bow hunters?"

"That and following up on the homicide."

Her eyebrows shot up. "I don't know anything. You saw me fly in after the man was dead."

"True. But there is evidence that you could have been there when he was murdered."

Her face grew dark and she shot to her feet. "There is no way you have evidence against me. I wasn't there before you saw me. What is this? Some kind of 'I can't find the real killer so I'll pin it on the next best thing'?"

He held up his hands. Her actions were pure fury, nothing put on. "There was a hair with female Native American DNA."

"Do you know how many people that could be? If it weren't female it could damn well be you. Don't use my heritage to railroad me into a murder I didn't do." She seethed. Her eyes blazed with anger and her body heaved.

"And I followed tracks from the scene to a clearing where a helicopter had landed." He held up his hands.

"There are fewer people with Native American blood who fly helicopters."

"That is what makes you believe I killed the man!" She shot out of the chair and stalked back and forth. "What time was the man killed?"

"Around two pm, a week ago yesterday."

"Follow me." She stalked out the door she'd arrived through.

He followed her down the narrow hall to the room at the very back. It had a computer, printer, new file cabinets, and photos of the mountains. Along with a bed and military trunk.

Dani flipped open the date book on her desk and pointed. "That Sunday at two pm I had the plane full of the Ryan family headed back to Alder after their week with us."

Written in her box letter print on the Sunday in question it said: Fly Ryan Family to Alder at 2 pm.

Hawke was glad that she had an alibi. His gut had been battling with his brain all the way up here. He didn't believe Dani was capable of the type of murder that had been committed, but a woman scorned had caused more than one man to die before his time.

"That is a pretty clear alibi."

She glared at him. "I can't believe you thought it was me. I barely knew the man and didn't care for him, but not enough to kill him."

"I followed the facts and the person who fit the facts." He smiled, trying to charm her back to being friendly. "I managed to write several citations on the way up and save deer from unfair hunters."

"It's going to take more than a smile and a stupid comment to make me feel anything but anger with you right now." She pointed to the door. "Go. I don't want to see your face until chow time."

His mother didn't raise a fool. He retreated from the office and wandered out to the barn to make sure Clive had taken care of Jack and Horse.

A tall, thin young man led a family of five out of the trees and up to the hitching rails.

"Everyone dismount, I'll take care of the horses. See you all at dinner," the young wrangler said.

"Can I help with the horses, Tyson?" a girl of about fourteen asked.

Hawke wondered if she was interested in the horses or the young man.

"I don't think he needs your help," the father said, grabbing his daughter by the arm and leading her toward a cabin.

Hawke walked over and started helping uncinch the horses.

"Hey, you don't have to do that. It's my job," Tyson said, when he came around the rear of the horse with a saddle in his arms.

"It's okay, I need something to do. Dani threw me out of the house until dinner."

Tyson grinned. "You must have done something that made her mad."

"I did. And I'm sorry for it now."

The young man hauled the saddle into the barn and returned, holding his hand out. "Tyson Singer."

"Hawke. I'm a Fish and Wildlife Trooper. I've used the lodge as a base of sorts for a lot of years." He pulled the saddle off the horse.

"Fish and Wildlife." Tyson's eyes lit up. "Mind telling me about your job?"

"I don't mind at all." As they finished unsaddling and putting the animals up, Hawke told him how he became a state trooper and then applied for the Fish and Wildlife job. "Working in Wallowa County I still work both trooper and game angles of the job. It keeps things interesting."

As they walked to the shower house and a tub where the employees washed up, Tyson said, "Dani is pushing the military on me, but I don't think I want to do that. Being a trooper and maybe getting back up here to help the animals, that sounds more like what I'd like to do."

Hawke pulled out a business card. "Here. Give me a call if you decide to go this route. I'll put in a good word."

Tyson's eyes lit up as he shook hands. "It's a deal."

They entered through the back door at the end of the hall where Dani's room and the office were located and walked on into the dining area. There were new photos on the walls and a clean tablecloth on the rough-hewn, long, slender table for a dozen. The benches were still half a log, but they'd been scrubbed and a shiny lacquer applied.

Clive was at his end of the table. Hawke and Tyson took seats on either side of him. Hawke picked up the glass of iced tea and guzzled. He hadn't realized how thirsty he was until he sat down and saw the condensation trickling down the side of the glass.

Excited voices carried in from the great room. Within minutes the family Tyson had brought back, Dani, and several men who appeared to have been hunting, walked into the room filling up the spots at the table.

Dani took the spot at the head of the table and made introductions. He thought it interesting she only said he was Hawke, visiting for one night. Did she think having a Fish and Wildlife officer here would get around and fewer hunters would stay?

The family talked about their adventure on horses that day. The hunters ate, grunted, and left. Hawke made eye contact with Dani, wondering if they always left that early or if his presence might have sent them scurrying.

She seemed oblivious to him. Had pretty much ignored him all meal after introducing him. Which was fine by him. He needed to head to the bunkhouse and not remain around the woman. He'd have hoped she was a suspect that way he could use that as a way to keep distance between them. He wasn't a young buck, but when he was around her, he had thoughts and urges he didn't want. The only thing he wanted to be loyal to and last his lifetime was his job.

The family began rising and he did, too. "See you in the bunkhouse," he said to Clive and Tyson before slipping out the back door.

The night was warm and the lingering sun hanging on the top of the mountains to the east made him antsy. He wandered to the bunkhouse, picked up his straw cowboy hat, dug his rod and reel out of his pack, and headed toward the stream up above the lodge. Fishing was as therapeutic as it was lazy fun.

While fishing and reflecting on the case, he realized there were at least two other women who had more of a reason to get rid of the victim and whose backgrounds he hadn't checked.

Chapter Sixteen

Noon Wednesday, Hawke rolled into the Trembley's. He led Jack and Horse out of the trailer and put them in their paddock. He cleaned out the trailer and unhooked it from his work truck. Today was usually his day off. Now he had half a day off.

He headed to his apartment and took a long hot shower while Dog slept in his dog bed surrounded by his toys.

It was four o'clock by the time Hawke was dressed, hungry, and ready to head to Alder. He planned to have another chat with Mrs. Cusack. This time he'd try not to get on her bad side. An early dinner at the Firelight sounded like a good idea. He planned to eat alone and get more information.

On the drive from the trailhead, he'd placed a call to his sergeant requesting more background information on Mrs. Cusack and Leanne Welch.

Hawke walked out to get in his truck and found

Darlene giving a lesson in the indoor arena.

"Hawke, do you have another date? I don't think I've seen you clean up this nice more than three times a year and now it's been three times in less than two weeks." The twinkle in Darlene's eyes wasn't missed on him.

"I do not have another date. I am not dating anyone. I cleaned up because I've been in the woods for four days." He spun around to walk away.

"You didn't happen to go by Charlie's Hunting Lodge, did you?" The insinuation and merriment in her voice told him she'd learned more about the woman she'd seen him with at the Firelight.

He just waved his hand and kept on walking. She wasn't going to rile an answer out of him. His landlords' need to discover what he did on his off hours was both endearing and aggravating. Dog jumped into the back of the truck. Hawke closed the tailgate and climbed in the truck cab.

In Alder, he drove straight to the Firelight. There weren't as many vehicles parked in the lot. That meant he'd have more of a chance to visit with Mrs. Cusack and less people seeing him there.

Mrs. Cusack was at the hostess stand when he walked into the building. Her smile drooped as he walked up to her.

"You never ate here before and yet, here you are again in less than a week." She didn't move to take him to a seat.

"How do you know I've not eaten here before? You didn't work here until your husband's death," he said, knowing this wasn't the honey he needed to spread to get the answers he wanted.

"I guess you would know that if you had been here before," she said, conceding and picking up a menu.

"I'm hungry, but I wouldn't mind if you'd sit with me for a bit and answer some questions that have been bothering me."

She narrowed her eyes and led him to a booth in the back of the restaurant with only empty tables in the vicinity. "What can I get you to drink?"

"I'll have an iced tea, please."

Her wide backside swathed in a flowy black skirt swung away from him.

He studied the menu and decided on a steak. The last one he'd had here was good.

Mrs. Cusack returned with his iced tea and a glass of water with lemon which she held onto as she sat in the seat across from him. "We're not too busy now. Let's get your questions answered, and I can get back to work."

"Thank you." He tipped the glass to her and took a long swallow before placing the drink on the table and starting. "Did you quit your other job?"

Her eyelashes fluttered up and down as her face relaxed into a surprised expression. "What does that have to do with my husband's death?"

"Maybe nothing. I was just curious because you have been here running the restaurant when I was informed you weren't allowed to set foot in it before."

Her eyes narrowed and anger snapped in the brown depths. "My husband didn't want me to see him touching his female employees. That's why I wasn't allowed in here. Not because I was incompetent to run things. I had a restaurant when I met Ernest. He sweet talked me into selling and moving here."

"That sounds like bitterness in your voice," he said, picking the glass back up.

"Damn right! He's the reason I've had to spend the last ten years feeling inferior and begging for money to buy new clothes and items for the house. Had I known how tight he was with money before I'd married him, I would have kept my restaurant and remained single." She sipped her water. "He had a way about him when he wanted something. He could sweet talk a nun out of her virginity if he'd a mind to or she had something he wanted."

"How about needed."

That caught her attention. "What do you mean?"

"Have you had anyone go over the books for the restaurant?" He hoped he wasn't opening a can of worms and putting a death sentence on Mrs. Kahn and Leanne. "I came across payments he made every month to two women—"

"The sluts he was screwing? I knew there were two women who weren't from around here. If they lived here, I would have heard about it." She slid a finger up and down the water glass. "How much was he giving them?"

The innocent way she asked, he could tell she was fishing for the amount.

"A substantial amount. One said it was given to her to put in an account for him to hide from the IRS."

Mrs. Cusack let out a bark of a laugh. "That sounds about right. He made the woman think he cared about her and used her to evade the tax collector. Poor thing." There wasn't a bit of sympathy in her voice.

He was curious that she hadn't asked the woman's name. And didn't seem to mind there was money that should be hers hidden away.

"Could you tell me about your parents, your heritage?"

Her gaze shot to his face. "My parents? Heritage? Why do you need to know that?"

"I'm Nez Perce and Cayuse. I'm always curious when I meet people to understand where they come from. You look Germanic, but your maiden name Bradford suggests you are more English." He continued to sip his drink and watch her.

"Everyone in the county knows you are Native American and your roots started here. You make sure we all know about it." Her animosity surprised him. "I am German, Irish, and English."

That left him with Leanne. He'd swing by Justine's before going home. They both had the duskier complexion unlike Mrs. Cusack's peaches and cream skin tone.

"I'd like the ribeye steak, well done, baked potato, and salad with ranch, please." He handed her the menu.

Mrs. Cusack blinked several times, took the menu, and heaved herself out of the booth across from him. "I'll get your order up." While she appeared relieved he had dismissed her, her eyebrows were knit together in thought.

He pulled out his phone to see if Sergeant Buckman, his OSP sergeant had come up with the information he'd requested. Nothing yet.

A young male waiter brought him a salad.

Hawke put the phone away and enjoyed his meal.

«»«»«»

Driving through Winslow, Hawke swung by the headquarters. He had a lot of information and contacts to add to his reports and log. If he did the recording now, he could head back up on the mountain on Saturday and take Thursday and Friday off. The other Fish and Wildlife Troopers preferred working locally because they had families. With him being single, he had free reign over the mountains and he preferred being up there.

He parked and let himself and Dog into the locked building. After hours, the building was quiet. It was easier to get reports written and contacts logged in when there wasn't someone stopping by his desk and visiting. He flipped his computer on and wandered down the hall to the break room. Snagging a bottle of water out of the refrigerator, he returned to his desk and began recording the contacts he'd made since he'd last logged into his account.

An hour later, he stretched and opened up the file on the Cusack case. The first thing to pop up was a stater's account of questioning the private investigator in Portland that Mrs. Cusack had hired. The PI said he'd been hired to get evidence that his client's husband was having an affair. He'd discovered the man was playing around with three women.

"Three women?" His mind leaped back to Dani even though she had a foolproof alibi. "The only reason you're thinking of her is because she's the only Indian you know of who knew the victim."

Dog walked over and licked his arm.

"Yeah, I'm talking to myself." He scratched the animal's ears. "And you." Putting both hands back on the keyboard, he pulled up the restaurant's bank statements and went back through them, searching for another large sum of money being paid monthly. He couldn't find one. He skipped back to the PI's report. The private investigator had named the women. Mrs. Abigail Kahn, Mrs. Leanne Welch, and Ms. Geraldine Foster, attorney.

"Krank and Foster!" He clicked back to the information he'd discovered about the victim contacting the law firm of Krank and Foster. "Looks like I'll be taking a road trip tomorrow instead of a day off." He scanned back through the bank statements and didn't notice any extra money going to the law firm or anyone with the last name Foster. "Could all those meetings with her have been about his divorce?" He glanced down at Dog, sleeping by his chair.

Mrs. Cusack seemed to think her husband used women to get what he wanted. Perhaps, this Ms. Foster was a hang-toothed spinster that he'd sweet-talked into helping him.

A glance at the time on the computer screen, and he realized it was too late to stop by Justine's to ask her questions about her family. He ran a hand over his face. And he was too tired to think clearly to ask the questions.

"Let's go home," he said, shutting the computer off and rolling his chair back. He scribbled a note about heading to Hermiston tomorrow and taped it to Sergeant Spruel's closed door. He'd call dispatch in the morning and let them know he'd be out of the county but on duty.

«»«»«»

Hawke was on the road headed to Hermiston by eight. He'd left Dog at home hanging out with the horses. Darlene had been impressed he'd been up and out feeding his animals before her.

Driving toward Eagle, he'd called dispatch and let them know where he was headed and that he'd be unavailable for anything in the county today. He had a two-and-a-half hour drive to Hermiston.

On his way over Cabbage Hill out of Pendleton, his phone rang. Sergeant Buckman, his superior in the State Police.

"Hawke," he answered.

"Buckman. Heard through the grapevine you're headed to Hermiston. Fill me in."

He explained how the third woman named in the PI's report was there and he wanted to visit with her.

"You could have had a trooper closer question her."

"True, but a write up in a report doesn't tell me how she reacted to the questions." He put a lot of stock in his ability to read not only tracks but people.

"Do you think she's the murderer?" Buckman tapped something on his side of the conversation.

"My gut says no, but she might have some information that will direct me to the right person."

"Keep me posted. And stop spending taxpayer's money on over-time." Silence followed.

Hawke grinned and slid his phone back on his belt. He didn't think about overtime. Not when he was on the trail of a murderer. He'd take the next three days off.

Cruising along Interstate 84, he noted the vehicles he drove alongside. One had a driver who appeared nervous and shot glances at the state truck every other minute. Hawke rode behind the vehicle, watching. He put the car's information into his computer and came up with a stolen report on the vehicle.

Hawke called it in to dispatch and turned on his lights and siren. The car took off, dodging through the traffic at a speed of ninety-five.

Knowing there was a patrol car ahead, Hawke didn't pursue the vehicle. He'd let the stater on duty take care of it. Five miles before the Hermiston turn-off, the vehicle was pulled over. The driver was cuffed and leaning over the hood of the car. Hawke waved to the stater and continued.

He hadn't wanted to spend time transporting the driver and writing up a report. Calling for someone in the jurisdiction to handle it was fine by him. He wasn't a headhunter like some law enforcement officers. There was no sense in trying to be the cop with the most arrests or the most tickets handed out. He just wanted to keep people and wildlife safe.

In Hermiston, he followed the GPS to a two-story older brick house with a porch the length of the front of the building. Large cottonwood trees shaded the structure. The freshly painted sign on a brick wall rising four feet from the ground and six feet wide proclaimed: Krank & Foster, Attorneys.

Hawke parked his vehicle and strode up the cobblestone walkway to the screen door. The inside door was open. He walked in and felt a cool breeze floating through the building.

"May I help you officer?" the thirty-something woman at the reception desk asked.

"I'm Fish and Wildlife Trooper Hawke. I'd like to speak with Ms. Foster if she's available." He held his ball cap in one hand and hung the thumb of his other hand on his duty belt.

"I'm not sure. Let me go ask her." She stood, took

two steps, and stopped.

"What is this regarding?"

"A death in Wallowa County." He didn't feel more than that needed to be said.

Her eyes widened, and she scurried down the hallway, knocking on the second door on the right. The woman slipped just her head through the open doorway.

Within seconds, she hurried back down the hallway. "This way, please."

He followed the woman to the door.

She stopped. "Trooper Hawke," she said, and motioned for him to enter.

An attractive woman in her fifties sat behind a large shiny wood desk. She stood and extended a hand. "I'm Geraldine Foster."

He grasped her hand. "Fish and Wildlife State Trooper Hawke."

She sat back down and motioned for him to take the chair in front of her desk.

Hawke sat and studied the woman. She seemed too poised and well put together to have fallen for the victim's lies.

"Why did you want to talk to me?" she asked. Her light green eyes held interest and a bit of apprehension.

"I'm working a homicide. Restaurant owner Ernest Cusack—"

"No!" she said, shaking her head.

"Ma'am, I need to know about your relationship with him." Hawke flipped out his log book and jotted down the time as the woman pulled herself together.

"Of course. That explains why he didn't return my calls." She dug through a stack of file folders on her desk and pulled one out.

"Why were you trying to contact him?"

"I'd received the investigator's report on his wife and thought he'd like to know she had a private investigator following him." She sniffed as if her investigator was more important in status than the one the man's wife had hired.

"He was trying to get information on his wife for a divorce?" He knew the truth but wanted to hear it from her.

"Yes. He wanted a divorce but also didn't want to give her everything. The goal with the investigator was to see if she was fooling around when she went to Portland for her work. The only person she met, other than her co-workers, was the private investigator. I was going to tell him, it was going to be next to impossible to get out of giving her half of his assets as she had sold her business to buy his restaurant in Alder." She had turned all business. As if her first emotional outburst had been a random thing. The slight tapping of the pen in her right hand was the only sign of a nervous tick. It could be just that she wanted to get on with what she'd been working on when he arrived.

"I see. Did your investigator know what Mrs. Cusack's PI found out?" He expected her to flinch, but she remained still as a boulder.

"No. To get that information would be illegal." She stared him straight in the eyes.

"I'll enlighten you. He had two mistresses…" he paused to give time for that to sink in.

Her nostrils flared, and her eyes flashed before she lowered her eyelids.

"One he was giving a large sum of money a month to hide from the IRS and the other he told the money was for them to have a nest egg when he divorced his wife."

The pen started tapping harder and faster.

"Then there was you."

Her gaze landed on his face. "What about me?"

"The PI report had photos of you and Mr. Cusack having fancy dinners and standing in front of a house, that I'm pretty sure is yours, kissing." He hadn't brought the photos with him, but he could tell she would cooperate if only because she was ticked the man had duped her.

"He was a smooth talker." She didn't elaborate.

"I would appreciate anything he might have told you in confidence." Hawke studied her. She didn't shield her eyes. In their depths, she was struggling with what she might know and could in good conscience tell him.

"I had a feeling he was shielding money, but I thought it was from his wife, not the IRS. Had I known that, I wouldn't have given him suggestions."

"Such as?"

"I said he could give so many dollars a month to a relative, who could put it in an account for him."

"Did he ask you to hold money for him?"

"No. And I would have turned him down. It's unethical for me to do that for a client." She scowled.

"But he was more than a client."

She nodded. "He was becoming that way. The last couple of months, he'd stayed longer and we…well we became closer. I knew I wasn't breaking up his marriage because he'd come to me to get a divorce. I didn't see…" She dropped the pen and rubbed her hand across the back of her neck. Tension. "I didn't see a problem if we should remain friends after his divorce was final."

"From what I've learned, he was a giving, caring, sweet talker until he had the woman caught. Then he showed his true colors."

Her dark eyebrows raised. "Then I'm lucky I hadn't fallen all the way."

"Hadn't you?"

She shook her head. "I was intrigued and flattered by his attention. And felt a bit reckless and wild meeting at motels and restaurants in the tri-cities. But falling in love. No."

"Did he talk about anyone who might have it out for him?" He didn't want to say women. He'd given her two people to point an accusing finger toward.

"He was having some trouble with a supplier. He said the representative was getting his orders messed up, and he wasn't going to pay for items he didn't order."

Hawke knew the truth to that. He'd heard it from the truckdriver's mother. But him saying that Leanne had messed up the orders…had he told her boss the same thing?

"Anyone else?"

She folded her hands together and placed them on the top of the papers on her desk. "Can you tell me how he died? You said homicide."

"He was strangled while on a trip in the wilderness with his wife."

Ms. Foster's hands smacked down on the desk. "And you aren't questioning his wife?"

"I have been. After I found the body, I found her wandering around on the mountain. I haven't been able to conclusively prove she killed him."

She studied him. "And you don't think she did."

He gave only a brief nod. While it would be simple and the most logical to say Mrs. Cusack killed her husband, the evidence wasn't pointing toward her.

"Did you come here expecting to find your killer?"

"No. I came here hoping to gain information that would help me connect the dots." He stood. "Thank you for taking time out of your day to answer my questions. If you think of anything that might help the investigation, feel free to call." He handed her one of his business cards.

"I'm not happy to hear the circumstances behind Ernest not returning my calls, but I'm glad to know why he hasn't returned them."

He nodded and left the office. On the way past the receptionist, he said, "Thank you."

Outside, he placed his cap on his head and walked to his vehicle. He'd grab something to eat and head back to the county. On the way, he planned to stop at the La Grande Fish and Wildlife building. While talking with Ms. Foster it dawned on him, he had yet to find out how the murderer got their hands on a tracking collar.

Chapter Seventeen

Hawke maneuvered his truck through the slight downtown traffic in La Grande and headed to the southwest end of the town. He found the small ODFW building tucked in a residential area and parked.

The receptionist, Shirley, greeted him.

"Hawke, long time no see." She smiled and walked over to the nearly chest high counter. "What brings you here?"

"I have some questions. Who has access to the wolf tracking collars?" He leaned on the counter.

"Only personnel who work in this building. Those are expensive and aren't left lying around." Shirley leaned her side against the counter and studied him. "This have anything to do with the body you found?"

"Yes. Can you give me a list of the personnel and anyone else who has access to the building?"

"Sure, but I can't think of anyone in this building who would have had a beef with a restaurant owner in

Wallowa County." She pushed off the counter and settled at a desk. Her head disappeared behind a computer monitor. "You also said people who have access to the building?"

"Yes. Anyone you can think of in the last month who was in the back. Maybe talking with a biologist or doing maintenance." He opened the gate at the end of the counter. "Mind if I take a look around in the back, see if someone could have entered without being seen?"

"Knock yourself out."

Hawke ventured down the small hallway peeking into the offices. He waved at the biologists he knew and continued. There was a back door, but it had a keypad lock. Only the personnel would be able to access it. He checked for any signs of forced entry.

Nothing.

Back in the building, he found the storage room. Boxes of various types of tracking collars were stacked in a corner. There were papers taped to the sides of the boxes. On these it appeared the serial number of the collar taken out was marked down. He took a photo of the paper on the wolf collar box. He'd see if the collar found on the body had been taken out of here by someone for the purpose of using it on a wolf and the collar fell into the wrong hands or if someone had taken the collar without marking it down.

Back at the main office area, he grabbed the page the receptionist held out to him. He glanced at the names. The one that stuck out as if it were bold and another color was Roger Welch.

"Thanks."

Since he was in La Grande, he might as well see if he could catch up to Roger and Leanne.

«»«»«»

Hawke pulled up to the Welch house first. There was a shiny new, expensive car sitting in the driveway. He walked up to the house and rang the doorbell.

Nothing.

It was Thursday, late afternoon. They could both be at work. Did Leanne have an office in town that she worked from? He'd go see Roger at the hangars and see what he could find out.

Driving to the Welch Agricultural Aviation base, it struck him as interesting that Leanne would purchase a new car and not use the money to leave a husband she obviously didn't love.

He parked and walked to the open end of the building. The plane was gone. Only the helicopter sat in the hangar. With the building wide open, someone must be around.

"Hello? Anyone here?" he called into the large open area.

A door on the side swung inward. Mr. Berkley, the older man who had been working on the helicopter the other day, approached.

"What brings you back here, officer?" The man's half lowered eyelids and ten feet he'd left between them proved he wasn't about to give away anything that had to do with his boss.

"I was looking for Mr. Welch. I had a couple more questions for him about the Sunday before last." Hawke smiled, wanting to make the man feel more at ease.

"He's out spraying crops. Won't be back until it gets too dark to fly." The man pivoted to walk away.

"Any idea where I could find Mrs. Welch? Does she have an office in town where she works?"

The man flipped back around. "Office?"

"I know she's a rep for a restaurant company, but she must have some place she calls home base." He continued to smile even though his face muscles were complaining.

"Far as I know she works out of her house. Why you want to talk with her?" The protective tone in his voice caught Hawke's attention.

"Just trying to clear up some things. She's not at home. I guess that means she's out on the road. Does the company supply her with a car? I saw a shiny new one in the Welch driveway."

The man walked closer. "She does have a company car, and if it isn't at her house, then you can bet she's on the road. Leave her alone. She's got it hard enough dealing with her marriage." This time the man pivoted and stalked away.

Interesting statement from Welch's employee.

Hawke returned to his vehicle, drove to a fast food restaurant, and scrolled through the reports he'd received today about Mrs. Cusack and Leanne's lives.

He flipped through Mrs. Cusack's, not coming up with anything new or earth shattering that he didn't already know.

The second he opened Leanne's, his attention was glued to the phone. Before marrying Roger Welch, a man twenty years her senior, she was Leanne Berkley. Ned, Roger's mechanic, was her father. He read on further. Leanne and Justine had different mothers. Leanne's mother was Mary Miller of the Confederated Tribes of the Warm Springs.

That was where the Native American DNA came from. But how to prove Leanne was on the mountain.

He thought about the helicopter traces he found while following the tracks from the person behind the bushes. How had he not seen her tracks from the bushes to the victim? Roger had been out flying that day. Had he picked her up after she killed the man she was having an affair with? Did he help for the money and to get rid of the competition?

He needed to gather more information before he confronted either Leanne or her husband. The more proof he had, the easier to catch them up and get the truth.

Instead of waiting for either one to get home, he drove back to Wallowa County, stopping at the ODFW and State Police Office in Winslow to start a list of questions and set things in motion to get the information he needed.

"Surprised to see you here," Sergeant Spruel said, walking by Hawke's desk. "This is usually your day off and you made a trip to Hermiston." His superior leaned against the desk.

"I had a visit with the victim's lawyer. She wasn't holding money for him, but she fell for his charms." Hawke shook his head. He didn't understand how men who had ulterior motives could charm women the way they did. Shoot, he had pure motives and couldn't charm the pants off any woman. Maybe that was it. The women who fell for the Cusack type were looking for excitement, something to make their life less boring.

"To hear most of the population of the county, they didn't think he had any charms." Spruel nodded to the computer. "Why are you so busy writing subpoenas?"

"I need financial records on Welch Aviation, information on Leanne Welch's travel for work, and all legal information I can find. I believe Leanne Welch is our murderer. I just have to find the trail that gives me information to make her talk." Once he'd started tracking the trails from the victim, he had to follow it to the end.

"Let me know if you run into any barricades. And fill Steve in on what you have so far, he's the detective working the case, too. You might see if he hasn't pulled some of that information already." Spruel straightened. "And take your two days off. I don't want any more complaints from the governor that too much money is spent on overtime."

Hawke nodded and continued making his list of objectives for finding out the truth.

«»«»«»

Friday morning, Hawke slept in. He'd woke early and let Dog out and now the animal was scratching at the door wanting in. Rolling to get a visual on his clock, Hawke groaned and wished he'd taken time to grab something to eat before coming home and falling into bed.

His stomach was gnawing on itself. He walked across the floor, letting Dog in. Pouring dog food in the dish, he remembered he'd picked up a box of cereal while in the store the day Leanne talked Justine into inviting him to dinner.

He pressed the brew button on the coffee maker and leaned his rear against the counter as he replayed that incident and the evening. Why had Leanne insisted on him joining them? Had Justine said he had discovered the body and she wanted to know what he knew? She was a good actor. Her stunned look, then tantrum, made him think she knew the man better than a rep and client, but he hadn't picked up on anything other than sadness.

Could her outburst have been remorse for having killed the man?

As much as he hated to string Justine along after their talk of being friends, he needed to speak with her about her sister's visit. He couldn't ask her questions at the Rusty Nail, but he could eat breakfast there and ask her to dinner.

The more he thought about it, the more he liked the idea. He'd make it a picnic. That way there wouldn't be anyone around to hear the conversation.

He quickly dressed and fed the horses and mule. "Come on," he called to Dog who was over smelling the tires on Herb's tractor. It didn't take him long to cross the barnyard and leap into the back of the truck.

Hawke closed the tailgate and slid into the driver's seat. He drove away before Herb or Darlene flagged him down to see what he planned to do on his days off.

Four vehicles were in the Rusty Nail parking lot. That eased the tension in his shoulders a bit. He didn't like the idea of too many people thinking he and Justine were dating.

He walked into the restaurant and was pleased to see Merrilee wasn't in the front. The cook must have not shown up to work. The older woman was in the kitchen cooking.

"Well, look what the cat dragged in," Justine said, smiling and filling the cup on the counter in front of him with coffee.

"It's been a long week." He picked up the cup and studied the woman. She didn't seem any more excited to see him than any other time. Good. "I'll have my usual. And give me a cinnamon roll right now. I'd like to tame the beast gnawing away inside my belly."

Her eyes narrowed. "Didn't eat last night?"

"Too busy." He sipped the coffee while she picked up a plated cinnamon roll, pulled the clear plastic wrap off, and set it in front of him with a fork.

When he sunk the fork into the sweet roll, Justine turned to the kitchen and told Merrilee to make up Hawke's usual. The older woman peered over the counter at him, frowned, and nodded.

She was probably mad he hadn't been back to give her any juicy information about the homicide.

He continued eating the roll, even after Justine placed his plate of food beside his arm. As he ate, the people in the restaurant grew fewer, which lessened the tension about asking Justine out.

When Merrilee walked out the backdoor, to either smoke or cool off, Hawke raised his coffee cup, catching Justine's attention. She walked over with a fresh pot of coffee.

"Here you go." She reached for his empty plate.

He grasped her wrist and leaned a little closer. "Doing anything tonight? Thought we'd have a picnic."

One eyebrow shot up and she glanced around the room. "Sure," she said as soft as he'd asked.

He released her wrist. "Pick you up at six."

She shook her head. "How about we meet somewhere. Like Williamson campground up the Lostine."

That was even better than the lake. Less chance of being seen together. She was as head shy of gossip as he was. He nodded.

Justine cleared away the plates as Dick Harlin

walked up to the cash register.

"You cops figured out who killed Ernest yet?" The man was a farmer in his sixties who wouldn't have frequented the Firelight.

"We're working on it. Did you know Mr. Cusack?"

Harlin handed his money to Justine and sat on the stool next to Hawke. "About as well as I know the other men who play poker on Sunday nights."

This was a new development. "Is that at someone's house?"

Harlin started to stand.

"Never mind. I don't need to know where you play. Who all is there and who usually wins?" If one of the players owed Cusack money, it would be a good reason to kill him, though he still had his money on Leanne.

"There's six of us that usually get together every other Sunday."

"Why Sunday?" He found the day interesting. Almost as if they were thumbing their noses at the God-fearing population.

"That's the day the Firelight only serves brunch till two. Ernest had Sunday nights free."

Hawke motioned for Justine to give Harlin a cup of coffee.

"No. I need to go," the man said, but he remained sitting on the stool.

Justine filled a cup and walked to the other end of the counter.

"Did Cusack win or lose?" Hawke raised his cup of coffee to his mouth and studied the man over the rim. How come Herb hadn't mentioned the card game. Surely, it wasn't a secret if six men had participated.

"He mostly won. But we wouldn't have all kept

playing if we didn't win big now and then." His chest puffed out and his down-trodden face lit up.

"Anyone a big loser lately?" Hawke twisted his stool sideways and studied the room, acting as if the man's question didn't matter all that much.

"Butch and Roger have been leaving with pockets so empty they had holes in them, the last couple of months." Harlin picked up his cup and sipped.

"Losing on a whole or to one person in particular?" Hawke put his cup down and slid it away from him. He was full of the stuff.

The man studied him. "Ernest was the recipient of most of it. They gave him I.O.U.s." He set the coffee cup down. "But you didn't hear that from me."

"Can you give me Butch and Roger's last names?"

"You going to harass them?" Harlin stood, his hands dove into his pants pockets.

"Just curious. I wonder if Mrs. Cusack knew anything about the poker games?"

Harlin started laughing. "That's why we had the games in the back of the restaurant because Ernest told his old lady to keep out of the building."

"And she didn't know what was happening?" He didn't think Ilene Cusack was that dumb. One reason she wasn't completely off his list of suspects.

"No, she didn't care. She was usually headed to Portland for her job on the Sundays we played." Harlin pulled out a set of car keys.

"Where can I find Butch and Roger?" he asked.

The man walked to the door, laughing. "Elgin and La Grande."

Chapter Eighteen

Hawke contemplated having Dick Harlin brought in to the county station and questioned to find out more about the two men from the card game. He'd gone to the station after breakfast and entered the first names into the database along with the towns. Too many Rogers and Butches popped up.

"What are you doing here? It's your day off," Sergeant Spruel said, when he spotted Hawke at his desk.

"Learned the victim had been hosting a poker game in his restaurant every other Sunday and two men had lost a lot of money to him."

"You're thinking someone might have killed him to keep from paying their debt?" The skepticism in his superior's voice had him wondering if he had latched onto this because it was easier than trying to discover more about Leanne and Roger Welch.

"It's something to do while I wait for the

subpoenas to come through." Roger? Could Roger Welch have possibly been the person who had lost money? What if Cusack, being the jerk everyone said he was, made a comment about Roger not only losing his money to Cusack but his wife as well? That would give Roger Welch two very good reasons to want the man dead. He also had access to a helicopter and a tracking collar. One of Leanne's hairs could have been on Roger's clothing and fallen on the victim.

"You have the look I've seen on your face when you are following a trail no one else can see." Spruel tapped the computer monitor. "What did you find?"

"Nothing. But I think I might have connected everything. I still need the records from the subpoenas, but I'm going to have a talk with Dick Harlin. I think I've figured out one of the men he mentioned." Hawke turned off his computer and picked up his ball cap.

"This is your day off. No more overtime," Spruel said as Hawke waved his hand and headed out the door.

There were some things that couldn't wait until he was on duty. He knew Dick Harlin had a place between Winslow and Eagle, up toward the mountains.

Hawke drove up the Harlin driveway and spotted Dick out on a tractor. The farmer was wearing the same red plaid shirt and hunter orange ball cap. It was a combination hard not to notice.

He parked the truck, let Dog hop out, and headed across the field to the other end where the man was baling hay. He'd crossed half the field when the farmer spotted him. The ka-chunk, ka-chunk rhythm of the baler ceased, and he throttled back the tractor.

Hawke lengthened his strides before the farmer decided to take off the other direction. To his surprise, the man drove the tractor and baler toward him. Dog loped ahead, greeted the machinery, and ran back to Hawke.

"What ya want with me?" Harlin shouted, shutting down the tractor and climbing off.

"Is the Roger from the poker game, Roger Welch?" Hawke asked without preamble.

The man recoiled then gathered himself. "Could be. Why?"

"I need you to call all the others together tonight, except Roger." He studied the man. Would this man and the others be willing to answer his questions about a friend.

"Why?" Harlin looked as skeptical as Sergeant Spruel.

"I have questions I want to ask."

"About Roger and Ernest?" Harlin was shaking his head. "Doesn't seem right for us to rat on—"

"Even if he could have murdered Cusack?" He hadn't planned to let that information out, but the man was being hard to negotiate with.

"Roger? We all figured it was Ilene that killed him." The farmer's eyes started twinkling. "I could call the others. What time and where do you want to meet?"

Hawke looked at his watch. Two. "Could you have them to the ODFW building in Winslow by five?"

Harlin shook his head. "I have hay to bale and Oliver is busy harvesting, too. Best I could do would be eight or nine."

He remembered his picnic with Justine up the Lostine River. "Let's make it nine."

"I'll have the boys there at nine." The farmer walked back to his tractor and climbed up. He stopped before he sat down. "You really think Roger did it?"

"I won't know for sure until I hear what all of you have to say and the information I've requested comes in. I'd appreciate it if you kept this to yourselves until I know for sure."

The man nodded, but Hawke had a feeling the word would be spread from one end of the county to the next before they had their meeting at nine.

«»«»«»

The drive up the gravel county road that followed the Lostine River reminded him of why this country was so special. The pine, fir, and spruce in their varying shades of green not only soothed the eyes but the pungent tang revived his senses. There wasn't a scent he liked better than the hot summer sun bringing out the pitch and fragrance of the evergreen trees.

He drove with his windows down, until a vehicle approached. Then he pressed the up button and closed them as the vehicle and its cloud of dust passed by. He'd left Winslow with plenty of time to meander along the road and enjoy the late afternoon.

Had Justine brought one of her dogs with her? He had Dog in the back, his tongue hanging out and ears flapping in the breeze of the twenty miles per hour they were moving.

The sound of the river with the last of the snow melt, splashing over the boulders and downed trees, added to the melody of birds, insects, and crunch of the tires on the gravel road. He spotted the campground on the right and pulled down in. It appeared as if all the camp spots were taken. Scanning the area, he found Justine's truck backed up to the river at a low spot between two campsites.

He parked bumper to bumper with her truck and walked toward the river with two grocery bags of food he'd brought for the picnic.

"Nice spot," he said, sitting on the tailgate beside her. He glanced down at the water where her two dogs were playing. "Looks like Shilo and Sun are having a good time."

"They love it up here." She glanced over at Dog, sitting at his feet. "Why isn't Dog joining in."

"He only goes in water if he's after something. I don't think there's any water dog in him." Hawke pulled out two bottles of cold tea. He handed one to Justine.

"That could be. Or he had a bad experience with water as a puppy." She took the offered bottle, twisted off the lid, and drank.

Hawke kept his gaze on the dogs and the river. He didn't want the woman to think this was anything other than a friendly picnic.

"Why did you invite me?"

Her full-on question, whipped his head around, cracking his neck.

"Ouch! That had to hurt." She shifted and reached out as if to massage his neck.

He slapped his hand over the stinging spot and massaged it himself. "That kind of surprised me."

"I noticed. We established the other night that neither one of us were interested in a 'relationship' other than friends. To have you invite me so serendipitously this morning at the café had me thinking you had a reason." She raised the bottle and drank.

Hawke shuffled everything around in his head.

He'd hoped to lead into his questions about Leanne after they had full stomachs. To give him time, he started pulling the wrapped, cooked chicken out of the bag, the plastic container of potato salad, and the bag of chips.

"Is what you wanted to talk about so bad you're avoiding it?" She picked up the other bag and pulled out the packages of napkins, paper plates and forks.

"I have questions I need to ask you, and thought as a friend, I'd ask them in a neutral setting." He took that moment to glance her direction.

"As opposed to…?"

"The police station."

Her intake of breath and setting the package of plates down was the reaction he'd been trying to avoid.

"Why would you need to take me to the police station? I've done nothing wrong."

Her gaze locked with his. The defiance in their depths told him to tread lightly.

"You haven't done anything wrong. But there is someone in your life who—"

"It's Leanne isn't it? Damn!" She hopped off the back of the tailgate and walked down to the water's edge.

He covered the food back up and followed her.

"You're taking this friendship for granted," she said when he stopped abreast of her.

"I know. But to be truthful, I'm leaning toward Roger."

Her head came up and she stared at him. "You think Roger killed Ernest Cusack? Why?"

"I'm pretty sure the why is because Leanne and Cusack were lovers."

"No!" She stared out at the water.

He gave her several minutes to digest the information.

"Ernest Cusack?" she said, the name softly to herself.

"You'd figured out she was having an affair." He could tell she was going to need some nudging to get the information out of her.

"When she showed up that Sunday. I could tell something was wrong. More than just her and Roger having a fight. It was a bigger fight than over furniture or a vacation." Justine shoved her hands in her pants pockets. "I've been the person on the opposite end of an affair. When I found out my husband had been fooling around with the young receptionist at his office, I couldn't get away from him fast enough. I didn't want to look at him, let alone talk to him."

"I'm sorry." He knew the words probably sounded as hollow as they felt, but he didn't know what else to say.

"When Leanne arrived and said she'd had a fight with Roger, she was too animated. She was talking fast and not really saying anything. She couldn't sit still, couldn't seem to focus on anything." Justine faced him. "When my husband confessed to me, he'd been agitated like that. Words spilling from him as if he couldn't shut them off. That's how I knew the fight was over an affair."

"You didn't figure out it was Ernest Cusack after her tantrum when he was brought up at our dinner?" He didn't believe Justine hadn't questioned her sister's behavior that night.

"She said she knew him as a client and she's

always been flighty about death. Both our moms died in accidents. Leanne has had a hard time believing her mother could have died the way she did."

His mind started racing. "How did she die?"

"She fell while on a ladder. They think she hit her head, became unconscious and her head somehow went through a rung. She was found hanging from the ladder, strangled." Justine shuddered.

"And your mother? How did she die?"

"Childbirth. Having me." She peered out at the water. "My dad married Leanne's mom when I was only a few months old, I've been told. Mainly to take care of me, because he didn't know what to do with a baby. He was in the military. An aviation mechanic."

"Does your father know how to fly a plane or helicopter?" He wondered if the father had killed the man who wronged his daughter.

"No. He's scared of heights. That's why Mama Mary was on the ladder. I guess he was, or still is, a good mechanic. That's why Roger has him work on his plane and helicopter. Dad travels around Eastern Oregon working on planes."

"What time Sunday did Leanne arrive at your house?" He needed to get back to the details he wanted to know.

"It was five-thirty or six. I was just thinking about fixing something to eat." Her gaze shot to him. "Do you think she killed Ernest?"

"I'm just getting my facts straight. It makes more sense that Roger killed him. Did you know that Roger came to Alder every other Sunday to play cards with Cusack and some other locals?"

Her head shook. Her brow furrowed. "He came to

the county twice a month to play cards? I don't even think Leanne knew that. She usually headed out for work on Sundays to do her rounds of the restaurants."

He'd need a list of the places she'd visited and ask about her schedule and route.

"Come on, I don't mind cold chicken but I'm not a fan of warm potato salad." He motioned for them to return to the back of the truck.

When they were settled with food on the plates and resting in their laps, he asked, "I'm surprised you or Merrilee hadn't picked up on the card games. I learned about them from Dick Harlin this morning."

"I thought you were done digging," she said, picking up a chicken leg.

"It just occurred to me. Didn't you overhear us talking this morning?" He watched her from the corner of his eye.

"I tend to tune out what other people are saying. It was through eavesdropping I discovered my husband was fooling around. It's made me shy of listening in." She bit the leg and chewed.

Now he knew her past and understood her reluctance to have another man in her heart.

They finished the meal companionably.

"Thank you for meeting me. I know it's hard to speak about family, however getting information from more than one source helps to put things in perspective for me." He tossed the bags into his truck and closed the tailgate on Dog.

"I understand. But you didn't have to invite me to a picnic to ask questions. I would have answered them just the same had you come by the house." She whistled for her dogs. They raced to the back of the truck and jumped in.

"I'll remember that the next time I have to question you." He smiled, hoping she took it as a joke.

She waved him to take off.

Hawke slid behind the steering wheel and backed out, heading down the Lostine River Road toward Winslow. He could get some work done at the office while he waited for the card players to arrive.

Chapter Nineteen

Hawke leaned back in his chair and rubbed his eyes. He'd been staring at the monitor for two hours reading everything he could find about Leanne's mother's death, Ned Berkley, and Roger Welch.

Leanne's mother died twenty years ago, when both of Ned's daughters were grown enough to take care of house duties. Reading the officer's transcripts from the accident, he could see where they would deem it an accident. However, he found it pretty coincidental that the woman's neighbor had suggested the Berkley marriage wasn't a happy one.

And that both Mrs. Berkley and Ernest Cusack were strangled.

Vehicles pulled into the parking lot. He stood and walked to the door as the sound of the engines all quieted. The four men who entered the office were all men he knew. Even Butch from Elgin. He owned the bar where Hawke had delivered a subpoena his first year in the area.

He led them into the small conference room, took a seat, and pulled out his log book. "Sorry I don't have any coffee or cookies for you."

They all laughed nervously.

"I'm assuming Dick told you why I wanted to talk with you?" He glanced around at the men. They ranged in age from forty to seventy. A couple of them didn't have any business gambling at cards. They barely were able to take care of their families. It saddened him to think that if they gambled every other Sunday, they were probably playing the lottery every week, wasting money.

"We know you want to learn something about Ernest and Roger," Butch said, leaning back in his chair. "I can't believe Roger would kill him over a few hundred dollars."

"Yeah, he can make that doing one large air job," said Lance Devore, an electrician with the Hutchin's Electric Supply in Alder.

"That's all Roger owed Cusack?" Hawke peered at each face. "Anyone know the exact amount?"

Oliver Taylor, the oldest member and a deacon at the Presbyterian church, pulled out a small notebook. "Roger owed Ernest exactly one thousand, two hundred and fifty-five dollars."

Lance whistled. "I didn't know he owed him that much. No wonder Ernest was riding him so hard that last hand."

"What last hand?" Hawke asked.

"The week before Ernest died, we had a game. The very last hand, Roger looked as if he were about to burst. You could tell he had a good hand. Ernest just kept upping the bid and grinning," Dick said.

"Like he was sure he would beat whatever good hand Roger had," Oliver added.

"Did you get the feeling that Cusack cheated?" Having learned how much the man liked his money, he couldn't see Cusack parting with money easily in a card game.

"Nothing we could catch him on and not enough that we felt like we were getting fleeced every time we played," Butch said.

"Do you feel Cusack set Roger up to lose that much money?" Why would the man have done that and then antagonized Roger about sleeping with his wife? Maybe to get rid of Leanne? But then what about the money in her name?

"I don't know about that, but Ernest did mention something about the little woman would have to be away from home more to pay for Roger's losing at cards." Butch studied Hawke. "Was Ernest and Roger's old lady doing it?"

For Justine's sake, Hawke kept his expression blank. "I don't know. I'm just trying to find reasons for someone to murder Ernest Cusack."

"Did you talk to his wife?" Dick asked.

"I have talked with her several times. Why?" Had he missed something key to the investigation?

"Those two fought like cats and dogs. He kept money from her. She wanted to be in the restaurant. Ernest was always griping about Ilene." Oliver closed the book on the numbers. Hawke wondered if any of the other men present owed Cusack a large amount. Dick had said Butch and Roger.

"Yeah. It was like he had the poker game just so he

had someone to complain about his wife to," Lance said. "Shit, none of us ragged on our wives like he did."

"I would have thought he would have killed her before she would have offed him," Dick added.

"He hated his wife that much?" Hawke asked.

"Sure seemed like it. He was glad she went to Portland. Said it gave him peace and quiet when she was gone because when she was there she was always nagging at him," Butch said.

This was a different picture than the Trembley's had painted of Ilene. What he'd witnessed of the woman from finding her in the forest and questioning her, she had more backbone than the Trembley's had suggested.

"Maybe he was more glad to get rid of his wife so he could have his mistresses over?" Lance peered around the table, a smug grin on his face.

"You're kidding!" Dick chortled. "What woman would want to have an affair with that tight-ass?"

Lance shook his head. "I'm all over this county and especially Alder doing electrical jobs. I've seen a rental car at his house every other week when Ilene was out of town." He leaned back. "I even saw the woman come out of his house once when I was driving by. The kiss he laid on her before she walked out to her car wasn't no peck on the cheek."

The expressions on the other men couldn't have been faked. They were all surprised, and it look as if they were a little bit envious.

"What did the lady look like?" Butch asked.

"Nice looking. Great body." He made the motion of large breasts, which Hawke knew was an exaggeration, but he wasn't going to add anything to the gossip. Then they would know he already had a line on the mistresses.

"How old?" Oliver asked.

"Looked in her fifties. Dressed nice." Lance was eating up being the center of attention. Hawke had a feeling the man didn't usually get this much conversation time when they gathered for cards.

"Why did you say mistresses?" Dick asked, giving Lance a stink-eye stare.

"Nancy said when she worked at the restaurant there was a woman came in through the back entrance two nights a week every other week right before closing. And those nights, Ernest would chase them all out before they'd finished with the cleanup.

"One night, Nancy snuck in the back door because she'd left her e-reader on the table in the break room. She said she heard two bodies slapping together in the office, a woman's voice pleading for more, and other noises." His face grew red as he recounted what his wife had told him. "She said there was a car parked behind the restaurant."

"That old dog. He was giving it to two women under his wife's nose." As soon as the words came out of his mouth, Oliver stared at Hawke. "That would be plenty of motive for Ilene to kill him if she found out."

"It would, if she hadn't been working toward a divorce." Hawke studied the men. None of them seemed surprised.

"Rumor around had the two of them splitting up," Dick said.

"Did the rumors say which one was doing the splitting?" Hawke knew the husband had taken the first step but wanted to see what the county gossip said.

"Well, my Raelene said Ilene had pretty much told all the ladies at the last décor party that she was leaving him," Dick said, shrugging.

"Nancy said she heard him making an appointment with a lawyer in Hermiston when she was getting supplies out of the back room at the restaurant." Lance crossed his arms as if he dared anyone to discredit his wife.

"Other than Ilene and Roger, can you think of anyone else who might have had enough of a grudge to want Cusack dead?" He still had his mind set on Roger, but didn't want the men to know that and tip their friend off, if they hadn't already.

They all shook their heads.

"Plenty of people have had beefs with him since he moved here but nothing big enough to want to kill the man." Dick glanced around at the other men. They all nodded.

"Thank you all for coming in and talking with me. Please, don't tell anyone about our talk and most of all, Roger. I plan to go talk with him on Sunday."

The men murmured and nodded as they stood. He shook each man's hand as they filed out of the building.

Hawke walked into the conference room, closed his log book, and turned out the lights. If he didn't take tomorrow off, Spruel would make him take Monday off for keeping on the case today when he should have been off duty. That was the trouble with having been on the scene of the murder first. He had to follow the leads and find the killer. He'd never been able to let something go that he'd started. It was why he couldn't get his wife out of his life. He still called her on her birthday and asked about her to the people who knew her. That the life he'd started with her had ended before they'd completed their journey kept him from allowing anyone close.

His work would sustain him and keep him company. That was why he had to keep digging on this murder. To find the end and keep his mind occupied.

Chapter Twenty

Sunday started with sunshine and high temperatures. Hawke fed the horses and mule while contemplating going for a hike. However, back in his apartment, he'd caught sight of the laptop on his counter. He opened it, becoming immersed in all the notes and reports on the case.

All the facts that pertained to the murder pointed to Roger Welch. The records Hawke had subpoenaed would be available tomorrow. Once he had the financial records, the picture should be clear.

He stretched and listened. Thunder rumbled in the distance. The forecast had mentioned a thunderstorm rolling through the area this evening.

Hawke grabbed a jacket and wandered down to check on Boy. He became agitated during storms. The gelding was starting to prance about. Horse and Jack each stood in a corner of the paddock, one hip cocked, ignoring both the storm and the youngster.

Darlene kept horse tranquilizers for the flightier horses she boarded. Hawke wandered through the barnyard, with Dog on his heels, toward the Trembley's house. He wanted to see if he could give Boy something to curb his nerves, so the horse didn't do something that would hurt him.

As a child, Hawke remembered his grandfather mixing something with grain that he gave the frightened horses during storms. He knew it was an herb, but at the time didn't have enough brains to think he might need to know what it was some day. That was the problem with childhood. So many things he remembered but never asked about could do him well as an adult. Even the times his grandparents would tell him a story and ask him what it meant, he didn't really soak it in as much as he should. As an adult he wished he had those moments back.

He knocked on the back door. His face reddened, thinking of the time he'd knocked and walked in only to find his landlords in an intimate embrace. He didn't walk in anymore.

Herb answered the door. "What are you doing wandering around? Lightning could strike you."

"I wondered if Darlene had a tranquilizer I could give Boy? All the booming and light flashing has him worked up into a lather."

"I'm sure she does. Hold on and I'll get her. She's in her sewing room." Herb poured a cup of coffee. "Have a seat, I'll be right back."

Hawke took the offered cup and sat down. Dog plunked on his haunches beside him. He sipped the coffee and admired the modern design of the kitchen. Every time he sat in this room or visited the house, he'd start thinking it might be time he looked for land and planted some roots.

"Herb said you needed something to calm Boy." Darlene bustled into the room, wearing a T-shirt that said Squares can be Cool with a quilt block on it.

"If you have extra. I'm beginning to think Boy may not be a good choice for my profession." He'd been having these doubts for a while now. He needed a horse he could depend on, especially as he became older.

"Give him another year. If he doesn't grow out of all of this, then I'll trade you Babe for him." Darlene shoved her stocking feet into the cowboy boots sitting by the back door. She grabbed a jacket that hung above her boots and opened the door. "Come on. Best get it in him before he gets so agitated it won't work."

Hawke drank the rest of the coffee and placed the cup on the table. "Thanks," he said to Herb and followed the woman on a mission out to the barn. He knew he'd find her in the tack room.

She was dialing the lock on the cabinet where she kept all the medicine she used on the horses. The door swung open, and she reached in. She pulled out a syringe and a vial. "About three ccs of this will take the edge off of him." Darlene replaced the vial and pulled the needle off the syringe.

"We'll squirt this under his tongue and he'll forget all about the storm coming." She closed the cabinet door and headed out to the paddock.

Hawke grabbed a lead rope and entered the area first. He softly said the words he'd been taught to calm a horse and managed to get close enough to click the lead rope to the horse's halter. He led the animal over to Darlene.

"That's a good boy. We'll have you forgetting all about the booming and lights." She pushed her thumb into Boy's mouth at the corner. When he opened his mouth, she squirted the medicine under his tongue.

Boy opened his mouth wide and wagged his tongue as if trying to rid it of the taste.

"Just pet him a bit and it should start taking effect in fifteen minutes. Thirty for sure." She slipped out of the paddock.

"Thanks!" Hawke called after her.

"You'll get my bill," she said and laughed.

He chuckled and stroked Boy's neck, whispering to the animal until his body stopped quivering and his head lowered.

"Do you have plans for dinner?"

Darlene's voice startled Hawke. He glanced over at the gate where the woman stood with her arms folded across the top. He wondered how long she'd been standing there watching him.

"No plans."

"If you don't have a date, then how about joining Herb and me?"

He shrugged. Not giving away his happiness at having a home cooked meal. "Might as well."

"Good. See you at six-thirty." She spun around and disappeared.

He had a couple of hours before taking her up on dinner. Hawke climbed the stairs to his apartment and dove back into the reports, making lists of the information trails he'd followed.

«»«»«»

"Are you any closer to knowing who killed Ernest Cusack?" Darlene asked as they sat at the table getting ready to dig into a three-layer cake with her signature strawberry frosting.

Hawke had expected this question long before dessert. He grinned and glanced at his host and hostess. "You know I can't tell you what has been determined."

Herb picked up his cup of coffee. "But you can nod your head if what we say is correct."

A belly laugh exploded out of Hawke. When he could talk and had cleared away the tears, he glanced at the two people glaring at him across the table. "You know I can't nod or shake my head. If you want to tell me what you think, I can add it to my file." He poked his fork into the piece of cake on his plate and stuck the bite in his mouth.

"I told you he wouldn't tell us anything," Herb said to his wife.

Darlene glared. "I didn't make this cake to have you clam up and not give me something good to tell my quilting club."

"How about you tell me what your quilting club thinks?" He knew some of the women in the club. Two in particular had no conscience about spreading anything they heard whether it was the truth or not.

It appeared that Darlene was happy to tell him everything. She placed her forearms on either side of her dessert plate and leaned toward him. "Dee said that Ernest had been seeing a woman at his house when Ilene was out of town."

"Did anyone tell Ilene this?" As much as in his gut he felt Roger was the murderer, he couldn't rule out the spouse. The statistics were too high on the case of the spouse being the killer.

Darlene nodded her head. "Dee and Selma both

told Ilene about seeing a car at her house when she was in Portland working. Selma even saw the woman one day. She lives on the same block as the Cusacks. Selma said she saw the car pull up to the house, the woman walked up to the door, fussed with her key chain, and unlocked the door. Selma called Ilene and asked if she was expecting company and had given them a key."

Hawke latched onto this information. "When did Selma call Ilene about this?"

Darlene leaned back, cutting into her cake with a fork. "Oh, about two meetings ago is when Selma told us, so a good month, I'd say."

That would have been about the time Ilene hired the detective. She knew a woman had a key to her house and was rendezvousing with her husband when she was gone. That would have been easy money for the P.I. and kindling for her getting what she wanted in a divorce. But murder… He still didn't understand the trip Cusack had taken his wife on. Why, if he was working on a divorce, would he tell his wife they should go on a trip to the mountains? He needed to talk with Ms. Foster and see what the end results would have been had Ilene taken her husband to court for a divorce.

"That's all your group has been gossiping about?" He didn't want to come out and ask if anyone had heard Cusack was having sex at his office in the restaurant.

"Isn't that enough to take a closer look at Ilene?" Herb asked, shoving his empty plate to the center of the table and settling back in his chair.

"I've been checking out Ilene."

"The spouse is always the first suspect," Darlene said, triumphantly.

Hawke shook his head.

"She's not a suspect?" Darlene asked, leaning forward, again.

"I didn't say that." Hawke clattered his fork onto his plate. "And don't you tell anyone I did. I was shaking my head at the fact you knew the statistic."

"Everyone knows that. It's on all the cop shows," Herb added.

"Nancy Devore is part of the quilting group. She said she thought she heard Ernest in his office one night having sex." Darlene nodded her head.

"How did she know that?" Hawke had asked the question partly to see if the story was the same as Nancy's husband told and partly to see how flustered Darlene would get responding.

"She worked at the Firelight for a couple of months last fall after the kids went back to school, but she couldn't stand watching Ernest patting all the women on the butt, including her."

"Do you think she made her comment to make you all dislike him even more?" Hawke asked.

"No! Nancy isn't like that. She's a nice young woman. Lance offered to go down and give Ernest two black eyes when Nancy told him what was going on. But she talked him out of it and quit." Darlene leaned back and sipped her coffee. She put the cup down and continued, "Anyway, one night shortly before she quit, one of the nights when Ernest had shooed them all out of the restaurant without checking to make sure everything was clean and ready for the next day, she realized she'd left her e-reader in the break room. Knowing the front door was locked, she went around to the back door, thinking she'd have to knock to be let in and worrying she'd be alone with Ernest. But she said the door was unlocked and there was a fancy car parked behind the building. She walked in, grabbed her e-reader, and on the way out heard moaning and what she said sounded like two people going at it coming from the office. Nancy said she hurried out of there before she was caught." Darlene picked up her coffee cup. "Do you think it was the same woman who let herself into his house?"

Hawke had to stop his head from shaking. Any movement at all would get Darlene thinking he agreed or disagreed. "That's an interesting story. Is Nancy working anywhere now?"

"Why?" Darlene asked in an accusing manner.

"So I can ask her to corroborate what you just told me." Hawke finished off his cake and slid the plate to the center of the table.

"Oh! She may not want to tell you." Darlene's face reddened as if she just realized she'd put her friend in an embarrassing position.

"I need to know in her words what happened." He was enjoying his hostess's discomfort too much.

"She isn't working anywhere. Lance got a raise not too long ago, and they seem to be making do without Nancy working." Herb offered, eyeing his wife.

"I'll try to stop by and have a chat with her tomorrow." Hawke finished off his coffee and stood. "I'm going to check on Boy and then call it a night. Thanks for dinner. It was delicious."

Herb walked him to the door. "I know you can't tell us anything, but why did you have Lance and some other men down to the ODFW building in Winslow yesterday?"

Hawke shook his head. “Can’t tell you. It’s all part of the investigation.”

The other man nodded and walked back to the dining room where Hawke heard dishes clanging as Darlene cleaned up.

He let himself out of the house and ran through the pouring rain straight for the paddocks. Dog ran out of the horse stall and greeted him.

“Hey. You look dry and safe.” He looked into the paddock. Horse and Jack were sleeping in their respective corners. Boy stood where Hawke had left him, his head hanging a little lower but not quivering or wild-eyed. The medicine was doing its job keeping him calm.

“Let’s go to bed,” he said to Dog. They climbed the stairs to his apartment. He slipped out of his jeans and sat on his bed, with the laptop on his lap.

Scanning the reports, he found everything he could on the private investigator Ilene hired.

Chapter Twenty-one

Hawke fed the horses and headed straight for the office. He had woken up in the middle of the night with the same questions plaguing him. Ones he planned to get answered today.

At the office, he checked in with dispatch, telling them he'd be on his way to La Grande in an hour. It was seven on a Monday morning, but he had to make the calls before he made the trip to La Grande. The answers he received may make his trip out of the county unnecessary.

He called the number for the PI, Wes Chesterfield.

"This better be good," said a male voice Hawke judged to be about thirty.

"This is State Trooper Hawke. I have some questions for you about services you did for an Ilene Cusack." The man was already surly. Trying to get on his good side wasn't going to happen.

"Did you say state trooper? I already talked to one

last week." The phone went silent.

Hawke hit redial and waited.

"It's early. Call me back this afternoon."

"If you don't talk to me now, I'll send a cop over to your house to watch you as you talk to me. And if you refuse, I'll have you hauled to jail for obstructing a murder investigation." It wasn't often in his line of work that he had to play the tough cop act. It wasn't one he liked, but one he found worked especially well over the phone. His deep voice made him sound like he meant business.

"Okay, fine. What do you want to know that I didn't already tell someone?" The man's surly attitude riled but at least he didn't hang up.

"Were you at Boundary Campground the day Mr. Cusack's body was found?"

The sputtering on the other end told Hawke the man was. "Were you the man in the tent who contradicted your actions?" Without waiting he said, "I'm the Fish and Wildlife State Trooper that you didn't want to speak to that day."

"Fuck," the man said under his breath.

Hawke grinned. He'd been right. The man hadn't been truthful then. "What were you doing there?"

"Mrs. Cusack called me. She was worried her husband was going to do something to her on a camping trip. She asked me to follow them up on the mountain and intervene if her husband tried to kill her."

"Why didn't you call the authorities about this?" Hawke hated it when people took this type of action.

"I thought she was over-reacting. The way that man was dipping his stick in women while he was married to her, I didn't think he'd need to kill her to keep doing it." There was a hint of admiration in the man's voice. "And she paid me another two grand to do it."

"Did you follow them on the mountain?" He knew better. He and Dog had been following the Cusacks and no one else had been.

"I started out following, but they were on horses. She didn't tell me that. Do you know how hard it is to follow horses up the mountain?"

"What did you do when you stopped following them?" Hawke jotted down what the man had said so far in his log book.

"I went back to my tent at the trailhead and waited to see if they returned. When I saw you bring her out with no husband and the trooper and deputy were waiting for her, I thought she'd turned the tables on him."

"You were still there the day after. That's when I talked with you."

"I waited to see who picked up her truck and trailer. The friend who showed up only knew that the husband was dead, and Ilene had been so distraught she'd come to pick up the horse for her. I was taking down my camp when you showed up."

"And that's all you can tell me? You didn't see anything else unusual?"

"I heard two different helicopters flying around. Thought that was kind of odd for two to be in the air at the same area. Were they your birds looking for marijuana?" His tone turned interested for the first time in the conversation.

"Did you see either of them?" Hawke knew one had landed in the clearing a mile from the murder site.

And he knew Roger had been flying for Marlene. He thought they had been the same aircraft. It was unusual for there to be more than one aircraft in the same vicinity unless there was a law enforcement mission happening.

"Only one. It was dark blue and had the letters WAA on the side."

That would have been Roger, flying for Marlene. And it still could have been him who put the copter down in the clearing. He could have seen Cusack from the air and spotted him in the clearing and approached. No, that didn't go with the fact he'd found prints that said someone had waited for Cusack to enter that clearing.

"Thank you. Sorry to have bothered you so early." Hawke slid his finger across the screen on his phone and stared at his blinking computer monitor. Had Cusack gone up on the mountain with the intention of killing his wife? Had the person waiting been someone who was going to help him kill her? Or had the person been there waiting for him. To kill him.

Why would someone wanting to kill Ilene have a wolf collar? To throw suspicion off her husband? The more he dug, more questions popped up.

He'd follow up on the other call.

"Hello?" Geraldine Foster asked.

"This is State Trooper Hawke. I was in the office last week. I have a follow up question I'd like to ask."

"Oh, I remember you. Just a moment. Let me get my breakfast off the stove."

Classical music poured from the phone. He held it away from his ear and watched Fish and Wildlife Trooper Ward Dillon walk into the break room with a plate of something.

The music stopped.

He placed the phone next to his ear.

"Ok, I can talk now. What can I do for you?" The attorney's voice held authority.

"I would like to know how much Ernest Cusack would have stood to lose if his wife had filed for a divorce?"

"On principal, he would have had to give her half of everything. She had proof that he'd talked her into selling her previous restaurant and used the money to purchase the Firelight. She could have been given the restaurant and substantial money made from it."

"He would have been better off to stay married to her or have something happen to her."

"What are you suggesting?"

"That I think the tables turned on him. Thank you." Hawke hung up. He was beginning to think the person Cusack had hired to kill his wife had changed his mind and killed him instead. But why?

"Did you do something relaxing on your days off?" Ward asked, walking up to him with several cookies and a cup of coffee.

"I went on a picnic and had dinner with my landlords." Hawke stood. "I'm headed to La Grande. I have some questions for Roger Welch, the helicopter pilot for Marlene Zetter."

Ward shook his head. "I heard he's the husband of one of Cusack's lovers. Who would have thought that overstuffed blowhard would have lovers?"

Hawke nodded. "That's why I'm going to have a talk with him. Though I'm starting to believe something different may have been planned to play out." Hawke told the other trooper where his suspicions were turning toward.

"Everything you've dug up makes sense. Go see what you can find out in La Grande. I'll take a trip up the mountain and check on the bow hunters."

«»«»«»

Hawke drove straight to the Welch residence. It was Monday and he doubted he'd find anyone home but it was worth a try.

A pickup and the fancy car were in the driveway. He didn't see the car that Leanne had driven to Justine's on the fatal Sunday.

The front door opened as Hawke stepped out of his State Police vehicle.

"What are you doing here?" Roger asked, being confrontational at the onset.

"I have questions for you and your wife," Hawke continued up the walkway to the house.

"Leanne isn't here. She left yesterday to talk to some of her clients. Sundays, Mondays, and Tuesdays are slower at restaurants. It's easier for her to get to talk to the owners and managers." Roger didn't offer to allow him into the house.

"Then I'll have to speak with you and catch up to her elsewhere." Hawke motioned with his hands for Roger to enter his home.

The man stared at him for several seconds before relenting and stepping into the house. He walked straight over to the recliner in the living room and sat.

Hawke closed the front door and took a chair not far from the recliner. "I've recently learned that you owed Ernest Cusack over a thousand dollars and he'd made a threat that you might have to pay with your wife."

Fury heated the man's eyes and reddened his face. "He had no right throwing my wife's bad taste in men in my face."

"You already knew she was having an affair with Cusack before he made the threat?" That would have given him plenty of time to have come up with a way to get rid of his competition.

"I knew what she was doing almost from the beginning. Cusack couldn't wait to let me know he was slamming my wife on his office desk every time she showed up." The disgust in his voice made Hawke wonder at the man's pride to allow it to happen.

"Did you tell Leanne you knew?" He didn't understand the state of some people's marriages.

"No. She thought she was getting away with something. You have to understand my wife. She's like a teenager even though she's close to forty. That was what intrigued me at first. But after a while having a teenager in your life constantly is wearing." He ran a hand through his hair. "She rebels when you put your foot down, which is what happened with Cusack. I can almost tell you the day she started hooking up with him. It was right after I'd told her we couldn't afford to go on some cruise she wanted. She threw a tantrum that night, and the next day she headed to Wallowa County for work. When she came back, she was smug and acting like she was God's gift to men. The next Sunday I went to play cards, Ernest was acting the same way. I put two and two together. I knew to tell her to quit her job or drop the restaurant from her route she'd just have another tantrum and find someone else to rebel with. At least I knew she wouldn't leave me for him. He'd never leave his wife and give her half of what he owned." Roger made a noise like a scoff. "The only person Ernest loved was himself and the only thing he loved better than himself was money."

"Then you didn't know he was giving your wife five thousand dollars a month?" Hawke watched the man's face quiver as a string of emotions flashed across.

"He was giving her money? What for?" Roger sat up in the chair, his jittering eyes reflecting how fast his mind was clicking behind them.

"Leanne said for a nest egg when he divorced Ilene and married her." He allowed that to sink in a few minutes. "But the other woman he was having an affair with said he gave her the money to avoid paying taxes on it."

"That sounds more like him." Roger slapped his hands on his thighs. "He was using Leanne, wasn't he? Having her hide money when he didn't plan to leave Ilene."

"Your card buddies think Cusack had plans to get rid of his wife, other than a divorce." Hawke didn't have to wait long for that response.

"We talked about it when Ernest wasn't around. He talked as if he was getting rid of Ilene, but we all knew he'd never give her money. Not after the way he'd fleeced her and got her to move to Alder." Roger nodded his head. "He was a calculating man who would have talked someone else into doing his dirty work."

Changing the subject, Hawke asked, "Do you ever pick up the tracking collars at the ODFW office for the biologists?"

The man sat back in his chair and stared at him.

"What do you mean? I'm not on the ground when they put the collars on."

The man had avoided his question. "I asked if you picked up collars from the ODFW building here in La Grande for the biologists. Do you know where they are kept?"

"Sure. I know they're in boxes in the building. I've stopped in there to map out where Marlene wants to go on flights, and she's disappeared and come back with collars." He studied Hawke and asked, "Why do you want to know that?"

"Just curious. What about Leanne? Does she know where the collars are kept?"

"I don't understand why you're asking this question. No, Leanne wouldn't know where the collars are kept. She's never been in the ODFW building. She only cares about my work because it pays the bills and she can use her money to buy what she wants." He stopped his mouth half open as if a thought came to him. "Damn! Is the money from Cusack what she used to buy that new car?"

"I don't know, but I would guess so if you don't have any idea where it came from." Hawke wondered at the marriage and was surprised it had lasted as long as it had.

"Do you have a log of the route you took the Sunday I found Cusack's body?"

Roger nodded. "Sort of. I record the general area I'll be in. When I'm listening to the beeping of the tracking collars, I don't know where it will take me."

"Did you see another helicopter in the vicinity that day?" Hawke couldn't believe the two aircraft hadn't come within range of one another, considering where the one had landed.

"I was the only helicopter up in that area."

"How do you know?" He studied the man, trying to decide if he knew more than he was telling.

"I would have noticed another helicopter in the area. It's not like a bird flying by." Roger had an 'I'm not stupid' tone in his voice.

"Where were you when Marlene asked you to contact dispatch?" Finding out where he was when the other helicopter would be taking off would tell if he were lying. Hawke was sure the murder had to have happened an hour and no longer than two hours before he arrived, because there hadn't been any signs of rigor. That meant there was a good chance the helicopters would have been in the air at the same time.

"I had landed at Wade Flat and was waiting for Marlene. I'd given her the coordinates and she had the computer to catch up to the wolves." He shook his head. "I didn't expect her to call and say she'd found a body."

Hawke searched his face. His expression was too schooled. He could have landed his helicopter after giving Marlene the quadrants, hiked to the clearing, and waited for Cusack having seen the man hiking that direction while he was in the air.

"You didn't see Cusack or his wife and three horses while you were flying around up there?"

"I saw people on the ground. Hikers, horseback riders, and hunters with bows. But I don't see everything, there are trees that conceal. I only spot wolves because I can pinpoint them by the beeping." He shrugged. "If I was to swoop down and checkout every person I saw, I'd get turned in to the FAA for harassing people."

The comment raised Hawke's eyebrow. Had he been turned in before? "Are you and the FAA not on good terms?"

"What's that got to do with Ernest being dead?" Roger's fingers dug into the arms of the recliner.

"I don't know. You brought it up." Something else to look into. He was surprised a run-in with the FAA hadn't popped up when he did his search in the government sites. "Have the biologists ever left a collar behind in your helicopter when tagging them?"

The change of subject caught the man off guard. "Not that I can remember. They keep a tight watch on those things. They cost a lot of money."

He'd answered the question without thought. Might be the only thing he was completely truthful about during the whole interview.

Hawke stood. "Do you have a schedule of where your wife will be the next couple of days? I'd like to catch up to her."

Roger rose from the chair. "Be right back. She has a schedule in her office."

Waiting in the living room, Hawke scanned the photos and knick knacks. Leanne had a love of expensive things. The photos on the mantle drew his attention. Leanne sat in a small bubble-like helicopter, smiling. Roger stood on the ground beside her, looking proud. Had he taught her how to fly a helicopter?

"Here's a copy of where she's going to be this week." Roger entered the room, holding out a paper.

Hawke pointed to the picture. "Does Leanne know how to fly a helicopter?"

Roger glanced toward the mantel. "No. She sat in

the seat for the picture. She doesn't pay enough attention to be able to fly a helicopter."

The way the man threw that comment out there, Hawke wondered if he were telling the truth.

"Thank you for the list." Hawke took the paper and left the house.

Seated in his vehicle, he scanned the places she would be. A grin spread across his face. She would be at Alder tomorrow at the Firelight. He noted the time and decided that would be a good time to visit Mrs. Cusack with a few more questions. By now the deceased's wife would have received the full account from her private investigator and would have the names of her husband's lovers.

Chapter Twenty-two

Driving up to the Firelight Restaurant at nine Tuesday morning, Hawke spotted Leanne's car in the parking lot along with Mrs. Cusack's. There were no other vehicles, and he noted the restaurant didn't open until eleven. He wondered when the cooks arrived.

He pushed on the door and it opened. Mrs. Cusack must have left it open when she'd let Leanne enter. The tables were already set with napkins and silverware. Winding his way to the back of the building, he heard voices.

"I'm not buying any more supplies from your company," Ilene's raised voice said. "I don't deal with whores who sleep with other women's husbands."

"I didn't sleep with him. We had hot, passionate sex on his office desk!" The sass and satisfaction in Leanne's reply didn't surprise him.

"Why you little—"

"Ow!"

He hurried into the kitchen and found Ilene's hand fisted in Leanne's long hair and Leanne getting ready to stomp her high-heeled shoe on the other woman's foot.

"Stop!" Hawke hurried over, separating the women.

"What are you doing here?" Ilene accused.

"I tried to see Mrs. Welch at her home yesterday, and her husband gave me her itinerary." Hawke noted the flash of anger in Leanne's eyes at the mention of her husband helping him.

"I want her to leave! Now!" Ilene shouted in the other woman's face.

"You should have called and asked them not to send a representative. But you knew who was coming. Did you plan to do to her what you did to your husband?" He was bluffing.

"What I did? Why, I didn't! I couldn't! I was the only woman who truly loved him. All his whores were just using him." Ilene pointed a finger at Leanne. "Look at her. What in the world would she have wanted with an overweight, balding, man in his late fifties? His merchandise orders? His money?"

Leanne flinched.

"That's what I thought. He gave you money and I want it back." Ilene stabbed her finger at Leanne's face.

She opened her mouth and bit down.

"Ladies!" Hawke shoved the two away from one another. Ilene held her bleeding finger and howled.

Leanne had blood dribbling out the corner of her satisfied grin.

He pulled her arms behind her back and cuffed her. "Do you want to charge her with assault?"

"Damn straight, I do. And my husband's murder. If

she's crazy enough to bite my finger she's crazy enough to strangle a man after having sex with him."

Ilene's comment caught him. Had anyone checked to see if he'd had sex before he was killed? And if he had, how did Ilene know?

"I'll take her to the county jail." He headed Leanne out of the kitchen and stopped. "I'll be back to ask you some more questions."

Ilene shrugged and held her bleeding finger under a water faucet.

Leanne walked docilely to his truck. She didn't struggle or even talk.

He helped her into his back seat, buckled her in, and slid behind the steering wheel.

"Do you realize biting that woman was the last thing you should have done?" He felt sorry for her. More because he was Justine's friend than because he understood or even wanted to understand what she was going through.

"Ernie was always complaining about her. He said she made his life a living hell. Only our moments together helped him stay sane."

He glanced at her in the rearview mirror. She didn't talk like someone who had a fling with a man older than her husband to get back at him. She sounded like a smitten, vulnerable young woman. He was finding it hard to figure out what to believe—the husband and sister who had called her a vengeful teenager who never grew up or the woman's own actions.

The drive to the jail was less than three blocks. He pulled down the alley in the back of the courthouse. A deputy, of retirement age, stepped out the back door to the jail.

"What do you have?" he asked, holding the back door open.

"She assaulted Mrs. Cusack as I arrived to question her." Hawke hauled Leanne out of the truck and escorted her into the jail area. "I'd like to process her and then do an interview."

The man, Deputy Gregan, nodded. "I'll bring her out to you when I finish the intake process."

The deputy opened the door for him to enter the office area. Gregan hollered, "Lucy, I'll need you in the jail!"

A woman in her forties charged out of a room, and nearly ran into Hawke. "Excuse me."

His gaze followed the woman. She entered the jail through the door he'd just exited.

Sheriff Lindsey was in his office. "What dragged you in here, Hawke?"

"I brought you a woman to be held on assault charges." He sat in the chair in front of the sheriff's desk.

"Anyone I know?"

"She's also a suspect in the Cusack homicide." He waited for the man's reaction.

He whistled. "Who did she assault?"

"Mrs. Cusack."

The sheriff chuckled. "I'd like to have seen that."

"You know Ilene?" Maybe he'd get an unbiased opinion of the woman.

"She's one of those women you don't want to mess with. She's had my deputies chasing their tails because she swore there was a prowler outside their house a month ago. Before that she'd call in every time she felt a presence when her husband was gone." He sipped from the cup of coffee on his desk. "I was happy when she got a job that kept her out of town half the time. We had less calls to her house."

"Did she ever say her husband abused her, or she was scared of him?" Her paranoia could have been from her fear of her husband. The prowler outside her house a month ago could have been her own private investigator.

"She never had any marks on her, and she never came out and said she was scared of him, but that's what the women in the county say. She'd confided in a few of them over the years."

"Do you think she has it in her to have killed her husband?" Hawke asked the question he'd been asking himself ever since he found her wandering around on the mountain.

"Some days, yes. Most days, no."

"It only takes that one day to make a person snap." Hawke had learned that from a family experience.

"True."

"Trooper Hawke?" The woman Gregan had called Lucy poked her head in the office.

"Yes?"

"Your suspect is waiting for you in the interview room." The woman disappeared before he could say thank you.

"I better go see what I can get out of Mrs. Welch." Hawke stood.

"Is she any relation to the Welch Aviation who works with ODFW?"

"His wife." Hawke walked out of the office and back toward the jail. He stopped at a door being guarded by Lucy.

"Thank you," he said, and opened the door.

Leanne sat at a table, her hair a mess, her bottom lip quivering, and her leg bouncing. He'd never witnessed her so nervous.

"Do I need a lawyer?" she asked.

"Why do you ask?"

"That's what they say on television. You know. The cop shows."

"You wouldn't be in here and wouldn't be in handcuffs if you hadn't bitten Mrs. Cusack's finger. She has the right to press assault charges against you." He sat in the chair across from her. "Why did you bite her?"

Her lips didn't tip into a grin. "I don't know. It just seemed like the thing to do with it right there in my face. She made me mad, thinking I had been bought like a whore. Ernie gave me that money, asked me to save it for when we were together. He wasn't buying my ass." Her lip stopped quivering and her eyes blazed with anger. "The nerve of that woman saying what she did. Did she ever think maybe he wanted something young and firm to hold onto instead of her sloppy, soft body?"

"Hey, I don't want to hear your thoughts on Mrs. Cusack. I want to know your whereabouts on the Sunday Mr. Cusack was killed." Hawke pulled out his log book.

"That was two weeks ago, how am I supposed to know what I did?" She didn't look at him. She stared at her fingers, tangled together like knots in a rope.

"You ended up at your sister's. I don't understand how you didn't arrive there until well after your husband was in the air flying for Biologist Marlene Zetter." He didn't want to help her with any answers. What she said would be crucial to his case.

"I don't understand what you mean?" She sniffed and continued to study her fingers.

"What time did you have the fight with your husband?" He mentally slapped himself for not asking Roger about the fight that had sent his wife running to her sister.

"I don't know. After Marlene called and asked him to take her up on the mountain. It was Sunday. He'd been flying for eight straight days. I wanted him home. He told me if I wanted all the fancy things I liked, he had to fly any time someone asked." She glared at him. "He always made it sound like it was my fault he stayed away and worked all the time."

"What time did he leave?"

"Around noon, I guess. I didn't pay that much attention." Her gaze dropped to her hands.

"What did you do the five or six hours before you arrived at your sister's?"

"What do you mean?" She didn't look at him. Her fingers tightened.

"It doesn't take that long to pack some clothes and drive to Winslow. What did you do after your husband left?"

"I fumed and talked myself into leaving him. I marched around the house, thinking about what I should do, then I packed a bag and decided to drive to Justine's."

"That's all you did in five hours?"

"What do you think I did?" Lifting her gaze, she peered into his eyes.

This was the rebellious teenager her sister and husband had talked about. He wasn't taking the bait and giving away his suspicions. "I don't know. That's why I'm asking you."

Her eyelids fluttered three times, and she returned her gaze to her hands. "I don't know what I did every minute from the time Roger left to when I drove up to Justine's."

"Did you stop anywhere? Talk with anyone?"

"I told Dad I was going to Justine's and thinking about leaving Roger."

"What did he say?"

"Good for me. I didn't need that ball and chain." Her voice held a note of humor. "Dad never did like being tied to anything."

"Even your mother?"

Leanne's head snapped up, her gaze blazed into his. "Don't bring my mother into this."

"Why? Is it because your parents had a bad marriage that you can't keep yours together?"

"Theirs was different. They needed each other." Her gaze softened. "Mom ran from an abusive husband and lived with my dad to help him out and hide from her husband. I know I wasn't a child made from love, but they both loved me."

Hawke understood the woman running from an abusive husband. He'd seen too many women on the reservation used as punching bags by their drunk spouses. Two times he'd stepped between his mother and his stepfather to prevent her being hit. He'd taken the blows for her and didn't regret it. He'd hold Ned Berkley in higher esteem if he didn't know the man had used the woman as a nursemaid for his daughters and could very well have been the person responsible for her death.

"What was your dad's reaction when you came back to Roger? What did you tell him about that?" Hawke studied her slumped posture, her twined fingers, and pursed lips. She was thinking before she spoke. A trait her husband said she didn't possess.

"He understood that the timing was bad."

"Why do you say that?" Her comment intrigued him. When was the timing right to leave a marriage?

Again, she took her time replying. "Ernie dead, you finding out I'd been his lover, the money he gave me. It would look bad for me to leave Roger right now."

"Like you had murdered your lover for his money, so you could leave your husband?"

Her head whipped up again and she glared at him. "Yes!"

"Did you kill Ernest Cusack?"

"No," she whispered. "I loved him."

"But it was a one-sided love. Kind of like your marriage. I think your husband loves you, but you don't love him." Roger Welch had put up with a lot to keep hold of his young wife. Only love would make a man tolerate what he had.

Tears spilled down her cheeks.

Hawke stood. It didn't look like he'd get anything else out of her right now. He'd go take down Ilene's statement for the assault and ask a few more questions about her husband.

He stepped out of the room.

Lucy appeared from the same office as before. "I'll take her back to the jail."

"Thank you." Hawke walked to the front of the

building and out onto the street. He could have walked through the jail area to his truck, but he hadn't wanted to see Leanne behind bars. As much as he regarded her as a suspect, he respected her sister too much to see that sight. And it would bring back the night he'd locked up his brother-in-law and lost his wife.

Standing on the sidewalk, he breathed in the warm summer air and decided to walk to the Firelight. He'd get his truck later. The stroll to the restaurant gave him time to think about what Leanne had and hadn't said. She'd remained vague about her time between when Roger left and she arrived at Justine's. Was five and a half hours enough time for her to get a helicopter to fly her to a spot not far from where Cusack was, wait for him, kill him, and fly out to drive to her sister's? And what about the collar? How would she get her hands on a collar and why even use it?

He arrived at the Firelight still no closer in any of his thoughts. Drawing in a deep breath, he grabbed the door handle and opened the door. It was after eleven and people had arrived for lunch. He waited in line behind a family of tourists.

Ilene led the family away, but not before she caught sight of him and frowned. He hoped she didn't find something else to do and send out a new hostess.

She returned, but her expression wasn't friendly. "Are you here for lunch or to ask me about that woman who assaulted me?" She held up a bandaged finger. "She's lucky it didn't require stitches. But I made the doctor give me a tetanus shot. You never know what she could be carrying, given her loose tendencies."

Hawke shook his head. "I'll have lunch and take your statement about this morning's incident."

Mrs. Cusack spun on a heel and led him to the booth in the back of the restaurant where no one else was seated.

He took the side that faced the rest of the restaurant.

She handed him the menu. "Do you want to ask me questions now or after you eat?"

"Now. Then I can enjoy my lunch." He motioned for her to sit as he pulled his log book out of his duty belt.

"Why didn't you stop Mrs. Welch from coming to the restaurant today?" he asked.

Ilene's eyes and mouth opened wide. "Why you…" She glared at him. "What does that have to do with her biting my finger?"

"Everything. You knew who she was before she came, yet, you made no move to make sure she wasn't the rep for your restaurant supply company. Some could say you brought it on yourself."

She pointed at his log book with her pointer finger on her left hand. "Are you going to take down my words?"

"Yes. Why didn't you stop her from coming?"

"Because I wanted to see what Ernest's plaything looked like. I was curious. I can't believe someone her age and looks would have fallen for him." She seemed genuinely surprised that a woman other than herself would find her husband attractive.

"I heard you calling her names. How long was she in here before you started antagonizing her?" The woman had known exactly what she was doing and probably had hoped to get more than a bitten finger out of it to sue the younger woman to get her husband's money back.

"I was being civil until she made a crack about I didn't look like a grieving wife." Ilene's round face reddened. "The nerve of her saying something like that to me. She deserves jail and more."

"Did you happen to think she may be grieving, too? And she isn't the only woman."

"The other two don't have the sliminess of coming here and accusing me of not grieving. They have the decency to stay away. I want her to get what's coming to her."

"What do you think that is?" Hawke felt the woman's anger wasn't genuine.

"Whatever she can get for assaulting me, a grieving widow."

He hid a grin. "The law won't be any worse because you are grieving."

Estella, the waitress who had waited on he and Dani, walked up to the booth. "What can I get you today, trooper?"

"I'll have iced tea and a turkey sandwich with chips." He handed the menu to the waitress, and she walked away.

"Does this mean we're done?" Ilene asked.

"Yes." He hadn't needed her statement, having witnessed the altercation, but he'd wanted to speak with her and judge her attitude and truthfulness. That was rating pretty low right now. Every time he questioned the woman, he felt like only half of what she said was the truth.

Estella arrived with his iced tea.

"Thank you. I was here at nine this morning and the only person here was Mrs. Cusack. Is that normal?"

The older woman glanced around and shook her head. “Last night she told us to not come in until ten-thirty today. That she’d do all the prep work. But the cooks arrived and had to work their butts off to get things ready to open at eleven.”

“Had she done that before since taking over?”

“No, she usually flounces in here at a quarter till eleven. We all know it’s because that rep, the one Ernest was doing, was coming in this morning.” A grin spread across the woman’s face. “From the look of the bandage on the boss’s finger, I’d say the other woman left her mark in more ways than one.”

She walked away giggling at her own humor.

Hawke shook his head. Ilene had wanted to meet her husband’s lover alone. Had she planned to do something to Leanne? Was that why she sounded guilty when he talked with her?

This whole case was becoming much too complicated. The trails were converging, crossing, and covering others. He preferred following physical tracks to the paths people took in their lives.

Chapter Twenty-three

After lunch, Hawke walked back to his truck and called the state police forensics. Several holds later, he was speaking with the forensic pathologist who autopsied Cusack.

"Did you happen to check to see if there had been any sexual activity?" he asked.

"When we noticed the belt hooked in the wrong place and found the grass seed inside his pants, we did check. There was no sign of secretions either vaginal or oral." He heard the sound of flipping papers. "I can tell you that there were extra holes drilled in the collar to make it go smaller than was needed on a wolf. We tried to get fingerprints off the dome nuts both on the collar and that were found at the scene, but the surfaces were too small to collect any sufficient data."

"Thank you." Hawke started his truck. On a whim, he drove to the small airport between Alder and Prairie Creek. He knew there was a helicopter at the airport and the man who owned it had worked with ODFW before retiring three years ago. He wanted to know how easy it was for two helicopters to be in the same area and not see or know the other was there.

He pulled up to the small office building and walked inside. Hector Ramirez sat with his feet propped up on a desk, a soda in one hand, and a cigar in the other.

"Mr. Hawke, what brings you to my little shack?" He didn't sit up, merely took another puff of his cigar.

"I had a couple of aviation questions." Hawke grabbed the only other chair in the place and pulled out his log book. "What are the chances of two helicopters flying around Goat Mountain and not seeing one another?"

"What are they up there for? Sightseeing or watching wildlife?"

"One was tracking wolves. The other I believe carried a murderer."

The old man sat up and leaned on his desk. "You talking about the murder a couple weeks ago up there?"

Hawke nodded.

The man whistled. "Well, I can tell you if the one didn't want to be seen and was a good pilot, then no one would have seen them." He took a sip of the soda and continued. "In the war, I learned all kinds of ways to avoid the enemy."

"Wouldn't any aircraft have to file flight plans?" Hawke was wondering how to get a list of pilots who flew helicopters.

"The one working for the government, tracking wolves, would have filed with the ODFW. But the one carrying your murderer, because the Wallowa

Mountains are uncontrolled airspace, they could have come and gone without reporting anywhere." Hector took a draw on his cigar and blew the smoke up into the air.

That would make things even harder to prove. "How would I get a list of people who own helicopters or rent them out?" Hawke studied the man.

He ran a hand over his unshaven jaw. "You could try the FAA. I have to register my bird with them."

Hawke nodded and jotted that down. "You didn't happen to rent your helicopter out the Sunday the body was found?"

"Nope, it was right there in the hangar. I'm waiting for a part. Couldn't have rented it out if I'd wanted to." Hector flipped open a large book on the desk. "But Jason Spencer made a note that the Singer lady from Charlie's flew her plane in and dropped off passengers about two. And at that time, someone was picked up by a helicopter."

"What do you mean picked up by a helicopter?" Hawke leaned forward, putting his log book on the desk and peering at the book the man held open.

"He says a copter landed at the far end of the buildings and someone ran out, climbed in, and it took off." Hector tapped the page. "You want me to call Jason in here?"

"Yes. If he's around."

Hector picked up a cell phone and punched numbers. He placed the phone to his ear.

"Jason, get over to the office. Now." He folded the phone and smacked it down on the desk so hard, Hawke wondered if it would work again. "He'll be here in a few minutes. He was up at the wind tower replacing the sock."

"What does Jason do around here?" Hawke asked.

"He's a jack-of-all-trades. He does maintenance to the hangars and field. And he's an aviation mechanic. Learned it in the Army. He's a good boy but needs some help now and then."

"Help, what kind of help?"

"He lost a couple friends while stationed in Iraq. There's times when he needs an eye kept on him. He gets to feeling so low and thinking he shouldn't be here either." Hector's eyes glistened with unshed tears.

The door opened and a man in his thirties limped in. Hawke restrained his gaze from lowering to see what his problem might be.

"Jason, this is Trooper Hawke. He'd like to ask you some questions about that helicopter that landed here a couple weeks ago."

Hawke stood and held out his hand, shaking Jason's greasy hand.

"Sir," Jason said, releasing his hand, shoving both hands into his back overall pockets. "Not much to tell. I wouldn't even have seen the helicopter if I hadn't been out helping Ms. Singer fuel up her plane. She'd run to the restroom while I topped her tank off."

"Do you remember anything about the helicopter?" Hawke asked. "Or notice anything about the person who got in?"

"The bird was a red Bell four-oh-seven. I think the tail number started N two-four-nine. I didn't get the last two numbers. It looked like a fair-sized man flying it."

"What about the person who got in?"

"A regular sized person." Jason glanced over at Hector. "I don't know anything else."

"Any idea where the person who got in the helicopter came from?"

"I noticed a car parked down by the last building after Ms. Singer left. It wasn't there later when I went home." Jason shifted his weight back and forth.

"Have a seat," Hector said, pointing to the seat Hawke had vacated.

The younger man sighed and lowered his body down onto the chair. That's when Hawke realized Jason had two artificial legs.

"Any memory of the car?" Hawke asked.

"Silver, I think." He closed his eyes. "Ford. Sedan. I didn't see it from the front or back to get a license."

"Thank you. That's more than I had to go on before." Hawke circled the color and make. They fit Leanne Welch's car. He closed his log book. "You've both been a big help. Thanks."

Hawke walked out to his car with one thing on his mind. Making sure Leanne Welch stayed in jail until he'd checked on helicopter rentals and discovered who flew her.

He called the sheriff, asking him to make sure Leanne didn't go anywhere.

"You know this is a small charge. It's going to be hard to keep her in jail for biting a finger." Sheriff Lindsey said it with mirth in his voice.

"Think of something. I believe she is a murderer. I'm working on pulling all the pieces together." Hawke hung up and headed for his office. He needed access to the FAA database. He had the make, color, and first three letters to identify who flew Leanne to the mountain so she could commit murder.

«»«»«»

Hawke leaned away from his computer and stretched. There were five possibilities of who the helicopter belonged to. Three were in the Grand Ronde Valley and two were in the Lewiston/Clarkston area. The later made him wonder if Mrs. Kahn had somehow been involved. He flipped back through his notes to see what she'd been doing that Sunday. She had an alibi. Many in fact.

A thought struck him. Hawke skimmed through his notes. Mrs. Kahn met Ernest Cusack three years ago. She'd amassed close to $200,000 in whichever non-profit she put it in. Leanne had over $100,000 in an account in her name. And Ilene Cusack had her freedom and the restaurant.

He only had Mrs. Cusack's word the trip to the mountain was her husband's idea. That she thought he'd planned to do something to her. Why had she gone along on the trip if she was scared? She did have the private investigator following her, but he'd wimped out and went back to camp. He obviously hadn't been worried for her safety.

The victim had few friends. The only people he could think to ask about the trip were his card buddies or the employees at the restaurant. He'd have to talk with them when Ilene wasn't around.

He picked up the phone and called Butch at his bar in Elgin.

"Lumber In," Butch answered the phone.

"Butch, this is State Trooper Hawke. I have a question. Do you know if going to the mountains was Mr. Cusack's idea or his wife's?"

"I'm pretty sure it was Ernest's. Like we said, he'd been talking a while about getting rid of Ilene. At first, we thought he meant divorce but then when he said they were going camping… well, we figured he'd be coming back alone, not her."

"Thank you." Hawke hit the off button and dialed the number he had for Oliver Taylor.

"Hello?" a woman's voice answered.

"Mrs. Taylor?"

"Yes."

"I'm State Trooper Hawke. I wondered if I could speak with Oliver."

"Yes. Of course. One minute. He's out mowing the lawn."

The phone clunked in his ear, footsteps faded, a screen door slammed, and muffled yelling came through the phone. The door slammed again, footsteps grew in volume, and the phone was picked up.

"This is Oliver."

"Mr. Taylor, I have a question I don't remember asking the other night. Do you know if the camping trip was Mr. or Mrs. Cusack's idea?"

"I thought it was Ernest's. He wouldn't have left the restaurant for a weekend in summer if it hadn't been his idea."

"Thank you." Hawke hung up. There was no sense calling any others.

Instead, he called Nez Perce County Detective Watts.

"Watts," answered the detective.

"This is Oregon State Trooper Hawke. You helped me interview Mrs. Kahn the other day. Pertaining to the same case, I need you to check on two helicopters registered to people in the Lewiston area."

"I can do that."

Hawke rattled off the two businesses.

"You didn't look at who owns the companies, did you?" Detective Watts asked.

"No. Is there a significance?" Hawke had the feeling finding the helicopter was going to be easier than he'd thought.

"Brant Charters is the company the Kahns use."

"How do you know this?" Hawke folded his log book and was headed to the door.

"There was a write up about the company in the paper last month and several of the influential people in the area were mentioned as repeat customers." There was the sound of a dog barking. "Are you headed this way?"

Hawke slid into his truck. "I'll be there in two hours."

"I'll meet you at Brant Charters."

To be on the safe side, after Hawke called dispatch to let them know where he was headed, he called Sergeant Spruel and filled him in. "I'd like a search warrant for a Bell four-oh-seven helicopter N number two-four-nine-seven-three. It's at the Brant Charters in Lewiston, Idaho. I'm headed there now and would like the warrant when I get there."

"I'll see what I can do." Spruel hung up.

Hawke turned on his lights and felt like he'd finally found a trail that would lead them to who murdered Ernest Cusack.

Chapter Twenty-four

Detective Watts's vehicle sat alongside the road as Hawke approached the airport on the hill overlooking Lewiston. The car pulled out in front of him, entering the parking area for the terminal, but taking a right into an area with a large white hangar. He stopped in front of a building with the sign Brant Charters.

They both exited their vehicles and met on the concrete in front of the hangar.

"I've got the warrant," Watts said, holding up a piece of paper.

"I'd hoped it would come through before I arrived." Hawke walked toward the building. "Let's go."

He opened the door and walked in, followed by the county detective.

"What can I help you with?" a man with graying hair, wearing a pair of overalls, asked as he walked toward them.

"We have a warrant to check that helicopter over there." Hawke pointed to the red helicopter with the correct N number.

"I don't know. I'm not the owner, I'm just the mechanic." The man pulled out a phone and punched in numbers. "Mr. Kahn, there's an Oregon State trooper and…"

Watts held up his badge.

"A county detective here with a warrant for one of the birds." The man listened and nodded.

"He said go ahead and do what you need to do. We don't have anything to hide." The man slipped the phone in his pocket. "And he's on his way down here."

As they walked to the helicopter, Hawke said, "You didn't tell me Kahn was an owner."

Watts shrugged. "That wasn't in the paper."

Hawke opened the door. He didn't have a clue what they should look for. He turned to the mechanic. "Can you get me the records for the last month of who chartered this?"

"Is that in the warrant, too?" he asked.

"Yes. The aircraft and any records or files pertaining to it." Watts held the paper up to the man and ran his finger under the wording.

"Okay." The man shuffled across the concrete floor as if he'd been sentenced to the electric chair.

Watts opened the door to the back. "What are we looking for? It's been over two weeks since it was used by your suspect."

"I don't know. Strands of long brown hair that can be matched with ones found on the victim. Small glass beads. Domed nuts like are used on tracking collars. Grass or seeds that can be matched with the type found on the victim. In other words, pick up anything that you can find."

Hawke studied the two seats in the cockpit. He put on latex gloves and swiped his hand between the seat and back of the passenger side. He'd picked up several hairs, dust, and what looked like three beads that matched the ones he'd found at the murder scene.

He pulled out a small plastic evidence bag and scooped everything he'd pulled from between the cushions into the bag. As he wrote down the time and where the evidence was found, the mechanic returned with a file.

Hawke placed the evidence bag in his pocket and reached for the file. "Thank you."

As he scanned the pages, the door to the hangar opened. He glanced up.

Mr. Kahn, the man he had watched leave the house before they talked with his wife, strode toward them.

"Why do you need to search my aircraft?" the man asked without preamble.

"It is suspected to have been used to transport a murderer." Hawke said. "I'm Fish and Wildlife State Trooper Hawke from Wallowa County, Oregon." He pointed to Watts. "This is Nez Perce County Detective Watts."

The man mentioned waved a hand and continued his search of the cabin.

"Why do you believe my helicopter was used?"

"We have an eyewitness who saw this aircraft land at the Alder airport and pick someone up on Sunday, August nineteenth." Hawke scanned the papers in the folder the mechanic had handed him. "But I don't seem to find a notation of this helicopter having flown that day."

"Then I would say your eyewitness is wrong about seeing this aircraft."

Hawke pulled the evidence bag out of his pocket. "The glass beads I found between the cushions look a lot like the same ones I found at the murder scene." He put them back and turned to the mechanic. "Who would have been here on Sunday, the nineteenth?"

"If there wasn't a charter that day, no one. No one works on the weekends unless there is a charter scheduled." The mechanic turned his gaze on his boss as if for verification.

"Is this correct, Mr. Kahn?" Hawke asked.

"Yes. Is there a charter scheduled that day?"

Hawke scanned the records in his hands. "No. Who has keys to this hangar?" he asked, hoping the man would say his wife.

"Melvin, myself, and our pilot, Casey Brant."

"That's the person they showed in the paper and who I thought owned this outfit," Watts said, walking around the front of the aircraft. He handed three small evidence bags over to Hawke.

"Why didn't you tell the paper you owned this business?" Watts asked.

It had nothing to do with Hawke's case, but he could indulge the man his curiosity.

"I'm a silent partner in the business with Casey." Kahn looked at his employee rather than the detective when he answered.

"Could your wife have used your keys on Sunday the nineteenth?" Hawke asked.

"My wife? What has Abigail got to do with this?"

Mr. Kahn became flustered for the first time since entering the building.

"She knew the man who was murdered in the Wallowa Mountains two weeks ago." Hawke watched Mr. Kahn.

His eyes flashed briefly before his lids lowered enough to hide anything else. "Who was the man?"

"Someone she met at Wallowa Lake several years ago." Hawke glanced at Watts. He nodded his head to continue. "Someone she had been meeting several times a month at his home when his wife was out of town."

Kahn's fist slammed into the side of the helicopter. "I knew something was up. Running off all the time to see relatives and friends." He faced Hawke. "Who was he?"

"Ernest Cusack, a restaurant owner in Alder." Hawke decided to lay it all out. The man appeared to not have a lot of loyalty toward his adulterous wife. "I believe she provided the transportation, this helicopter, for another of the man's lovers to actually kill him."

Mr. Kahn smirked. "Abigail wouldn't dream of getting her hands dirty. Melvin, check the Hobbs meter with the records. Officers, you'll have my full cooperation. If my wife had anything to do with this, I want to make sure she gets what's coming to her."

"Sir, if you wouldn't say anything to her until I get all the forensics back, it will be easier to catch her in lies." Hawke had a thought. "On the Sunday I mentioned, her alibi was being at the country club, running a charity golf tournament. I believe you were in the tournament?"

"Yes, the one for the hospital. She was there, but I can tell you about one o'clock I couldn't find her anywhere. I wanted her to run home and get me a different pair of shoes, the ones I wore hurt my feet and made me lose my concentration." He shook his finger. "Does that fit into anything?"

"Are you a pilot?" Hawke asked.

"Yes."

"How long do you estimate it would take to fly from here to Alder, Oregon?"

"Half hour to forty-five minutes."

"Her missing from the country club around one would fit with the time frame I'm working with." Hawke had a hunch today would tie everything up.

The mechanic crawled out of the helicopter and tapped the log book he spread out on the floor of the aircraft. "According to my log this hasn't gone anywhere other than what we have logged."

Hawke stared at the page. This was the helicopter the mechanic at Alder had seen. He didn't see a reason for the man to lie about it. "Is there any way for someone to come in here and change your log book?"

Watts looked as dejected as he felt.

The mechanic shook his head.

"Who do you think flew this?" Mr. Kahn asked.

"That's the one piece of the puzzle I haven't figured out. The woman I believe is the murderer, got in the aircraft in Alder." Hawke studied the man. "Does your wife know how to fly a helicopter?"

Mr. Kahn nodded. "She wasn't gone long enough to have flown there, picked someone up, waited, and returned." He shook his head. "I'd say that would take at least three hours."

Hawke nodded. It appeared all the man's wife did was supply the helicopter. But how did they prove, other than the forensics, that this helicopter had been used? "Would this Brant have helped your wife?"

The man frowned. "By God, he better not have!" Kahn walked away punching numbers on his phone.

The mechanic walked up to Hawke. "There is a way to make the Hobbs meter not record a flight."

Hawke turned his attention to the mechanic and not the man bellowing into the phone. "How is that? And who would know?"

"Any mechanic worth a lick of salt would know how to disengage the circuit breaker from the meter. The meter won't run without it." The man in the overalls, pointed to a panel on the nose of the helicopter. "Take that off and you can unhook the circuit breaker attached to the Hobbs meter. It will stop recording air miles."

This was a break. If someone had tampered with the panel and circuit breaker, they might get prints. "Have you or anyone else touched this since Sunday the nineteenth?"

"No, sir. I wouldn't mess with the instruments that say how long a bird is in the air. I need to know that to make sure all the parts are working right."

"Watts can you get a fingerprint kit and dust the panel inside and out, and then the wires he's talking about?"

"Sure can." The detective strode out of the hangar.

Mr. Kahn stormed over to the aircraft. "Casey said he didn't fly this anywhere for Abigail. I threatened him with pulling my backing. He wouldn't lie to me if it meant losing all of this."

"Your mechanic brought up how this helicopter could have been used and no one realizing it." Hawk hoped they pulled a good set of prints. It would bring him one step closer to the killer.

Watts returned with his fingerprinting kit and went right to work lifting prints from the outside of the panel. "Are you sure you didn't clean this since that Sunday?" he asked.

"No. If it wasn't used, which the log book says it wasn't, I don't dust or clean until someone is taking it out." The mechanic leaned closer to look.

The detective looked at Hawke. "I'm not finding any prints on this panel."

"Open it up," Hawke told the mechanic. "But don't touch the back side."

When the panel was unfastened, Hawke held out gloved hands and the mechanic used a screwdriver to pry the panel loose and have it drop into Hawke's hands.

Watts dusted the inside of the panel. "There are several partials where someone held the panel, putting it in place, I'd say." When Watts had those captured on the print tape, the mechanic pointed out the wires to disconnect the circuit breaker.

"That's too small, there's no way to get a good print from that," the detective said. "If we're lucky, there will be enough from the partials to at least find a name that can be connected to the women."

The mechanic replaced the panel as Hawke and the detective walked over to Mr. Kahn.

"It's important you don't say anything about this to your wife." Hawke studied the man. "Can you do that?"

"I don't know if I can. I think I'll take a business trip. Then I won't say or do anything to harm your investigation. That is, if I can." He glanced from Hawke to Watts and back to Hawke.

"As long as you let Detective Watts know where you'll be and give him a way to contact you." He didn't think the man had anything to do with any of it. He'd been too cooperative.

Hawke gave both Mr. Kahn and the mechanic his card. He took a photo of the helicopter from all angles before he and Watts walked out of the hangar.

"Do you want the prints?" Watts asked.

"The aircraft is from here, there's a good chance so is the pilot who flew it. Why don't you run them and if you come up empty, I'll run them on my end."

"Works for me. I'll be in touch." Watts slid into his sedan and drove away.

Hawke stood by his truck, wondering if there could have been anyone who would have noticed the helicopter leaving that Sunday. It couldn't have been pushed out and taken off without someone noticing. Even on a Sunday.

He glanced up at the air traffic control tower. They would have to log in any flights in and out of the airstrip.

Chapter Twenty-five

The control tower loomed up behind the small terminal. Hawke drove his truck past terminal parking and over to the chain link fence around the tower. An intercom system was attached to the fence by the gate. He called up, stating who he was, and what he wanted to know.

The gate swung open and closed behind him. He walked up to the tower and heard the clang of someone coming down metal stairs inside. The door opened slightly and a woman's face with sharp features and big round glasses appeared. "Credentials," she said.

Hawke displayed his badge and ID with a photo.

The woman checked them over thoroughly and then allowed him entrance.

He followed the woman, he thought resembled a grass hopper due to her thin angular stature and big round glasses, up the stairs.

At the top, she sat in a chair and plopped a set of

headphones on, leaving one ear out from under the ear piece. "What did you want to know?" she asked, flipping through pages on a book.

"I'd like to know if a helicopter N two-four-nine-seven-three requested to leave or land on Sunday, the nineteenth." He held his log book open, hoping the woman could conclusively say the aircraft had left the hangar.

"Here it is. The pilot called to leave the airport at thirteen-ten and was given clearance at thirteen-fifteen." She tapped a page with her finger.

"Did it request clearance to land later?" It would help to have the time frame all neat and tidy.

"The same aircraft requested permission to land at fifteen-fifty-two and was allowed to land at sixteen-zero-five."

"Did the pilot give an itinerary? Or did anyone make note of which direction it went?"

She shook her head. "They don't have to. All we have to do is get them in and out safely."

"Thanks." He let himself out of the tower, the fence, and slid back into his truck.

On the drive back to Wallowa County, Hawke ran all the suspects through his mind. Of all of them it seemed Mrs. Kahn and Roger Welch were the only two who knew how to fly a helicopter. But it had been established that Mrs. Kahn had an alibi for all but the time when the helicopter was taken. And for that matter, Roger had an alibi of sorts as well. He was flying around the area where the murder happened, but the timing didn't feel right or how the murder happened. Welch wouldn't have seduced the man and put a collar on his neck. He would have shot, stabbed, or beat him to death.

The murder felt like something a woman would do. And women were the victim's weakness. The killer had used that to their advantage.

He needed a warrant to search the Welch house for a garment that was missing small glass beads and a sample of Leanne's hair. He was sure she was the one who did the actual killing.

He also needed to find out how Leanne and Mrs. Kahn discovered one another and conspired to kill their mutual lover. Had Ilene Cusack discovered them and the money and used that to blackmail the two into doing what she wanted done?

Pulling into Alder his phone buzzed. Hawke pulled to the side of the road not recognizing the number.

"Trooper Hawke," he answered.

"Trooper, this is Bart, the mechanic for Mr. Kahn. After you left, I got to thinking and remembered that even if the Hobbs is turned off, the air miles are stored in the FADEC. I hooked it up to the ECU. And sure enough, there is a difference of a hundred-twenty-three point six miles than in my log book. That would be around an hour to the destination and the return flight. Which would be to the Wallowas and back."

"Thank you, Bart. That is helpful." Hawke added the new information to his log book. It was nearly ten and he hadn't had anything to eat since that morning. If he was lucky, he'd be able to grab a cold sandwich at the High Mountain Brew Pub. He didn't go in there often dressed in his uniform, but he was tired, hungry, and his mind was spinning like a top, trying to make sense of what he'd discovered.

He was glad it was a Tuesday night. Any other

time of the year besides summer and the place would have been closed. Summer months when the county was crawling with tourists, the businesses, like the brew pub, were open every day and later at night than the other seven months of the year.

Desiree Halver greeted him as he walked in. "Trooper Hawke, I bet you aren't here to drink since you're in uniform." She picked up a menu.

"No, I was working late and need something to eat." He liked the young woman and her family. He'd been called to her family's ranch two years ago to help with a trespass dispute. A hunter from outside the valley had killed a deer on their land, cut down the fence to drive to it and then turned his gun on Mr. Halver. Hawke had been only twenty minutes away and had helped settle the situation.

"The grill is still on if you want something hot." She settled him in a quiet booth in a corner. "Iced tea?"

"Please, and I'll have a steak and baked potato if you still have one." He handed the menu back to her without opening it.

"Salad?"

"Please, with ranch dressing."

The woman nodded and headed to the kitchen.

Hawke glanced around the room. There were a handful of men playing pool and sipping beers. One table had two couples who looked to be in their sixties. Another table had a young couple, completely oblivious to anything other than one another.

It appeared ten was the time to enjoy a peaceful meal at the pub.

Desiree returned with his drink and salad. She hovered at the table after setting the food down.

He picked up his tea and peered at her over the rim. "How is your family?"

"Good." She scanned the restaurant then returned her gaze to him. "Do you know any more about what happened on Goat Mountain?"

Hawke studied the young woman. "What do you know about that?"

"Just what I read in the paper." Her voice rose just a fraction.

"What are you worried about?" He put his glass down and motioned for her to take a seat on the bench across from him.

She glanced around again and sat, her legs sticking out the end as if she planned to make a quick getaway.

"My friend Stephanie works at the Firelight."

Hawke thought back to his dinner there with Dani. He remembered the young woman filling water glasses. "I've met her."

"She was excited when Mrs. Cusack took over. She complained a lot about Mr. Cusack's roaming hands. But Stephanie says lately Mrs. Cusack is snapping at everyone and accusing them of spying. Stephanie says it's as if Mrs. Cusack is guilty of something, which makes everyone wonder if she killed her husband."

Inside he smiled. His questions were making the woman jumpy. Someone with nothing to hide wouldn't be that way. "I'm sure my stopping by the restaurant so much is making her worry about business. Could you give me Stephanie's phone number? I'd like to ask her a few questions about Mrs. Cusack's behavior."

Desiree stood. "I'll go get it off my phone. I know she'd be relieved if you could shed some light."

Hawke shoved his fork into his salad. He'd contact

Stephanie tomorrow after he wrote up his report from today.

«»«»«»

Pounding on the stairs up to his apartment, sat Hawke straight up in bed. He glanced at his clock. 6:30.

Dog scurried to the door and started whining moments before there was a knock.

"Hawke, you up?" Herb called.

"Yeah, I am now." He ran a hand over his face as his landlord shoved the door open. The man looked as if he hadn't slept.

"What's wrong?" Hawke swung his legs over the side of the bed and picked up his jeans flung over the one cushioned chair in the place.

"Darlene went out to feed the horses and she—I don't know what she did. Call nine-one-one." The man turned to head out the door.

"Where is she?" Hawke grabbed his phone on the table by the bed.

"I drug her out of that new horse's stall. The one on the end." Herb disappeared.

He punched in the numbers and relayed the information he knew. Shoving his feet into his boots, he headed to his work truck for his first aid kit and found Herb kneeling beside his wife.

Hawke had never seen the woman look so white. Her chest moved up and down slightly. She was breathing.

"Did you check for broken bones before you pulled her out here?" he asked Herb.

The man shook his head. "I didn't like how antsy the horse was. I wanted to get her to safety."

Hawke stood and peered into the stall. The horse

was still dancing a bit and making chewing motions.

Sirens grew. Hawke hurried out to the front of the house to direct the EMTs to the barn. They threw questions to him he couldn't answer. He felt helpless until he was needed to reassure Herb.

They checked her for broken bones as well as took her vital signs. They discovered a bump on the back of her head before they loaded her onto the gurney and slid her into the back of the ambulance.

"Want me to drive you to the hospital?" he asked.

Herb nodded.

"Do you need to turn anything off in the house?" Hawke led the man toward the house.

"I don't know. How did she hit her head?" Herb stared at him with glazed eyes.

"I'll check it out later. Come on." They checked to make sure there was nothing on the stove or in the oven. Herb grabbed his wallet and hat.

"Wait in my truck, I'll go finish dressing." While he was putting on a shirt other than the one he'd slept in, he called Sergeant Spruel and told him he would be off duty until noon today.

"What did you find out yesterday?" the man asked.

"A lot. I have evidence to go to forensics, and I have more questions for my suspects." He hung up and drove Herb to the hospital.

By the time Darlene had come around and was diagnosed with a concussion and Hawke was ready to leave the hospital, several of Herb and Darlene's friends had arrived. He knew the man would be in good hands. Even though he needed to write up his report on what he'd discovered the day before, Hawke pulled out the phone number Desiree gave him the night before and called her friend.

“Hello?” a young woman answered.

“Stephanie, this is Fish and Wildlife State Trooper Hawke. Your friend Desiree gave me your number. She said you were concerned about your boss, Mrs. Cusack.”

“Oh!” She said something to someone else, and he heard footsteps before the young woman said, “She has been acting weird lately. And jumping on everyone if she thinks they are talking about the murder.”

“Is there a chance I could meet you somewhere and we could talk?”

“I don’t have to be to work for another hour. We could meet at Cuppa Joe’s in ten minutes.”

“I’ll be there.” Hawke started his truck and drove the two blocks to the coffee shop on Alder Street. The Firelight was almost directly behind the coffee shop. He wondered that Stephanie didn’t worry someone would see her talking with him.

He walked in, ordered a breakfast sandwich and coffee. When he finished here, he’d have to go home, feed his horses, and see which of Darlene’s hadn’t been fed. They’d be making enough ruckus he’d be able to tell.

A young woman with long blonde hair walked into the shop. She spotted him, smiled, and continued to the counter. When she had her drink, she sat down at the table across from him.

“What did you want to know?” She sipped her drink and watched him over the rim.

“Have you noticed Mrs. Cusack taking any calls or visitors in the office and shutting the door?” He had to find a connection between the women.

"She took a call Sunday evening that seemed to start her bad temper. Then Tuesday after that rep bit her finger…you would have thought each of us had bit her. She was jumpy all day. A deputy came in last evening. I think for the statement from Mrs. Cusack to charge the woman who bit her. I could tell when the deputy left he wasn't happy with whatever she'd said to him." The woman took another drink. "Darryl said he heard the deputy ask her why she wasn't pressing charges and she said because she thought it over and didn't want to."

Hawke had wondered if the woman would go through with the charges. That she hadn't, only confirmed his assumption the two were working together. But why had Leanne bitten the woman who could take away the money Cusack gave her?

"Thank you for meeting with me." Hawke finished off his coffee and stood.

"Is that all you wanted to know?" The young woman looked disappointed.

"That's all. Thanks again. If you see or hear anything else," he held out a card, "Give me a call."

She smiled and tucked the card in her purse. "I will."

He sat in his truck for several minutes debating whether or not to visit Mrs. Cusack. He still had too many unanswered questions. But not enough information to ask her anything that might give him answers.

The summer sun, warm air blowing through his windows, and glimpses of the mountains had him wishing he was up there checking bow hunters instead of down here trying to figure out a murder. He pulled into the yard, and Dog came bounding out to greet him.

As he'd expected, choruses of neighs punctuated by Horse's braying filled the air.

Two hours later everyone had food and fresh water.

A vehicle pulled in as he finished putting the wheelbarrow away.

A woman and teenaged girl stepped out of the vehicle.

"Can I help you?" he asked.

"Nellie is here for her lesson," the woman said.

"I'm sorry but Mrs. Trembley is at the hospital. She had an accident this morning."

"Oh my! Will she be…"

"Mom, we need to go check on her!" the girl said, opening the vehicle door.

"She had a concussion. I'm sure she would appreciate a visit from you." Before he finished talking, they were both in the SUV and headed out the drive.

The mention of the accident reminded him he'd told Herb he'd check on how it could have happened.

He grabbed the halter and rope hanging next to the horse in question's stall. The animal had calmed down since this morning. Hawke caught the horse and tied it up in the alleyway. He returned to the stall and tried to figure out what could have caused Darlene to fall backwards and what she hit her head on.

The mare was a bay. The light-colored hair he found in the crack of wood by the door had to be Darlene's. Why had she fallen backward? He stood in front of the spot and walked away from the wall. About five feet out he felt something under his foot. Kicking the shavings around, he discovered a curry comb. Whoever left that in the stall was sure to get a good lecture on taking care of their equipment.

He hung the curry outside the stall on a nail and put the horse back where it belonged.

His phone buzzed.

Watts.

"Hawke."

"This is Watts. I got a hit on the partial fingerprints from the military database. It's a Ned Hillman Berkley."

Hawke's jaw dropped a bit. "That's one of my suspect's father. I had him on the radar, but someone made a crack he was scared of heights. He's the mechanic for his son-in-law's crop-dusting outfit. It didn't occur to me he could be a pilot. Thanks!"

"I'll send you a copy of the prints and all the documentation." Watts hung up.

A break! Now he had to get the warrants and get the beads and hair off to forensics.

He jogged up to his apartment, put on his uniform, and headed to his work truck. Dog trotted up to the truck.

"Not today. We need you to stay here and guard things until Herb gets back." As if the animal understood, he trotted over to the steps of the house and sat down.

Hawke smiled and drove to Winslow and the office.

Sergeant Spruel approached him as soon as he arrived. "Where are you on the Cusack case?"

Hawke filled him in on all that he'd learned the last day. "I think we'll have this cleared up as soon as I get some warrants." He held up the bags of evidence he and Watts had collected from the helicopter. "Do you mind if I hand deliver this to forensics in Pendleton? I'll spend a day with my family. Hopefully, when I get back, there will be warrants to serve, and I'll know more from the evidence found in the helicopter."

Spruel nodded. "Makes sense to me. Just don't stay there longer than two days."

Hawke laughed. "My family will drive me crazy after one day." He sobered. "While I'm gone, could you pull up everything you can find on Ned Hillman Berkley. I believe he flew the murderer and knew what was going to happen." Hawke stared at the list of questions he'd made in his log book the night before. The pilot had been determined. But the wolf collar still nagged at him.

He wrote up the warrants to search the phone and bank records of the three women involved and to search all property belonging to Leanne and Roger Welch. He needed to find the clothing that placed her with the victim.

After making sure he'd ordered all the legal documents he needed, Hawke picked up the evidence bags and headed to his truck.

As soon as he was headed out of town he called Marlene.

"Marlene," she answered.

"It's Hawke. Did you ever get a chance to figure out how that collar ended up in someone other than a biologist's hands?"

"Just a minute. You're breaking up."

Lucky woman. She was up in the mountains. That's where he wanted to be.

"Did you ask about the collar we found on that man?" she asked.

"Yes. Did you figure out how someone else got

their hands on it?"

"From the serial numbers it appears it was taken out for a tagging and must have fallen out of a bag. Whether it was in the helicopter or on the ground and someone picked it up, I don't know."

"Thanks. That helps." He hung up with a pretty good idea who'd picked up the collar. And not from the ground.

Chapter Twenty-six

Hawke dropped the evidence off at the forensic lab in Pendleton and headed east toward his mother's home on the edge of town. He hadn't called her, but knew she'd be there. Since the death of her husband, she had started watching children for the young mothers in her neighborhood while they worked. The weekends she went shopping. If it was Saturday, he wouldn't find her home until after the bingo game at the center.

It always amazed him that even though he hadn't felt as close to the people on this reservation as he had the ones at Lapwai when he was younger, his throat still tightened as he approached. Perhaps it was knowing he'd see his mother or the thought of immersing himself in the culture he grew up with but rarely practiced while away.

Maybe what he felt wasn't nostalgia but guilt? That thought left a lump in his gut.

Two little boys around four-years-old were

wrestling in the yard when he pulled up. They stopped, looked at his vehicle, and immediately bolted for the front door.

It was rare for a state police rig to be seen on the reservation. The reservation police dealt with issues here.

He stepped out of his truck as his mother came to the door.

She smiled and waved for him to come in.

Hawke's heart beat with a renewed joy seeing his mother. He wouldn't call himself a momma's boy, but the two of them had gone through a lot. First the rejection by his blood father and then the abuse of his stepfather. They had a bond that was different than his younger sister and mother had.

He took off his duty belt and vest and locked the truck before walking across the dried lawn. Stepping through the door, familiar scents sent him back in time. To the days when his stepfather was on the road for his job and Hawk would come home to fresh-baked cookies and soup simmering on the stove.

"My boy. It's good you came to see me. I've been thinking about you a lot," his mother said, walking up and giving him a hug. Her graying head came to his shoulder. Her thin arms wrapped around him in a warm embrace.

"I've missed you, too." He hugged her and stepped back to get a good look at her. "You are growing too thin."

Four children ran around them and out the door, giggling.

"You don't have to watch children. I can send you money." He always offered. She always turned him down.

"You need to keep your money for the day you decide to buy a house and settle down like a proper husband." Her gaze scanned him from head to foot. "You look good."

She wandered into the kitchen and he followed. Pieces of chicken were in different stages of preparation to be fried.

"Would you like me to help?" he asked, remembering the days of the two of them preparing meals.

"No. You sit and talk to me while I work." She plopped a glass of iced tea in front of him and went back to rolling the chicken in flour. "You are in your work truck. Does this mean you won't stay for dinner?"

"I can stay for dinner. If it were up to my sergeant, I'd stay for two days but I'm this close to finding what I need to pin a murder on a suspect." He held his thumb and forefinger an inch apart.

"That isn't close at all." His mother put her fingers together. "If you were this close you would have the truth."

"I know who did it. I'm just trying to get the proof before I arrest her."

His mother put her hands on her hips and glared at him. "You don't arrest people. Your job is to catch hunters who devalue their privilege to hunt. Not catch killers."

He'd told her in the beginning when he joined the state police that his goal was to be a game warden and not be in the middle of situations that could get him killed. He'd known he would be in just as much danger, but it made her feel better. "Mom, I found the body on the mountain. I followed the tracks that showed how the man was killed. I want to be the one to bring the killer in. She's the sister of a friend of mine. I feel I have to be the one."

Her gaze traveled over his face. "This friend, is it a she?"

"Yes, it's the woman who found Dog for me."

Her face lit up. "So, she is special to you?"

He shook his head. "Special as a friend. I don't want her to be devastated when her sister is arrested. That's why I want to be there." His mind flashed back to stepping into his house and finding his wife and all her clothes gone before he could tell her he'd arrested her brother. Someone else had told her first. And she'd left him for doing his job. He wanted to be the one to tell Justine before anyone else did.

"She is only a friend? Have you been seeing anyone else? Someone who could make me grandchildren?"

Hawke shook his head. Mom had been mad at him for a long time after Bernie, his wife of five years, divorced him. She'd thought he should have tried harder to make Bernie come back. He'd tried to talk with Bernie twice. Both times had been torture. He'd loved her, but she couldn't see past what she thought of his being a traitor for arresting her drug trafficking brother. His only solace was that they'd had no children and he wouldn't have to worry about her druggy brother being around his daughter or son. Hawke had signed the divorce papers, and decided then and there, he was finished with marriage. But his mother wanted grandchildren. His sister had yet to find a man worth marrying.

"Mom, you'll have to hope Miriam finds a decent man at the Cultural Center. I won't be marrying any time soon. And any woman I'd marry would be too old to bear children." His mind flashed to Dani.

"You do have your mind on a woman." His mother jumped on his comment like a cat on a mouse.

"There is a woman who interests me, but that's as far as it can go." He didn't think the Air Force Officer was a one-night type of woman. And he couldn't give her anything more, considering she wasn't giving up her inheritance and he wasn't giving up his job until he could no longer perform his duties. "Have you seen Linda around?"

"You are not going to bed her tonight," his mother said, frowning. "That woman makes her living on her back. You don't need to catch any of what she has."

He knew his old classmate and junior year girlfriend had fallen into the trade after her husband was killed. She'd always been a pretty girl and had grown into a nice looking woman. He'd asked her why she didn't remarry, and she'd said, she'd rather not get close to another man. It hurt too much when they died.

"I wasn't going to sleep with her. I just wondered how she was doing. Mike's death was hard on her."

"We all lose men. But we don't all sell our bodies." She slammed a pan on the stove and plopped a spoonful of bacon grease in.

"Mimi," a young woman's voice called from the other room.

"In here, Sherry," his mom called.

A woman in her twenties walked in carrying one of the boys he'd seen when he pulled up.

"Is there some kind of trouble—" Her gaze landed

on him.

"This is my son, Gabriel." His mom waved the spoon in her hand toward him and then toward the woman. "This is Sherry Dale and her son, Trey."

Hawke stood. "Pleased to meet you."

"That's right. You said your son was a game warden in Wallowa County." The woman held out her hand. "Pleased to meet you."

Her cheeks darkened. "Mimi, your first husband must have been one handsome man."

His mom scoffed, and Hawke shoved his hands in his pockets. They didn't speak much about his father. The man had dumped him and his mom on her parents' doorstep and never came back.

"Here's the money for watching Trey. Thanks again. I think I got the job. I'll know tomorrow." She put a ten-dollar bill on the table. "If I did, will you be able to watch Trey?"

Mom picked up the money, shoving it into her apron pocket. "As long as it isn't nights or weekends. I only watch kids from seven in the morning to six at night." She squinted at the woman. "The rest of the time you should be home with your children."

"I know. I am. Thank you. I'll let you know as soon as I hear from the bank." Sherry glanced at him. "Nice meeting you." She spun on a heel and left the room, and from the clap of the screen door, the house.

"Nice girl. She got knocked up in school. Got her GED and took college classes in business and now is out there looking for work. I wish more girls did that." She turned to the sizzling chicken.

"Good for her." His phone buzzed. He glanced at it. Sergeant Spruel.

"Hawke." He walked out the back door and watched the three children still there run into a small playhouse.

"I went over the bank and phone records. I couldn't find any contact between the three you suspect, but I did find that they all purchased burner phones in the same week. It was on their credit cards. When the warrants come through, we can search each of their residences for the phones and connect them."

"Good. I'm having dinner with my mom then I'll head home. If by chance the warrant for the Welch home comes through tonight, let me know. I can meet whoever serves it."

"Will do. Enjoy dinner." Spruel disconnected.

When he stepped back into the kitchen another young woman stood in the room.

"Oh!" she said, seeing him walk through the door. "Did something happen?"

His mom went through the introductions as she manned the frying pan.

This woman took two of the children, leaving one little girl who came in and sat at the table.

"You a big man," the girl said, wiping at her milk mustache with the back of her hand.

"You're a pretty girl," he said, picking up a cookie from the plate his mom had placed in front of the girl along with the glass of milk.

The girl frowned at him. "You shouldn't steal cookies. You're a policeman."

He laughed. "I thought the cookies were for both of us."

"Mimi always gives me three cookies. Now, I only gots two."

"I'm sorry." He picked up the plate, carried it to the cookie jar on the counter and put two more cookies on the plate. Sitting back down, he said, "Now you have your three and I have one more, because they taste so good."

She grinned and nodded, picking up another cookie.

"Mimi?" a male voice called.

"In here, James," his mom called back.

"That's my daddy," the girl said, wiping her hands on her jeans and jumping off the chair. She hit the man, wrapping her arms around his legs as soon as he appeared in the room.

"Hey bug, did you have a good day?" he asked, totally absorbed in his daughter.

"I did. I made a new friend." She pointed to Hawke.

The young man followed her arm and froze. "What are you doing here?" His arms automatically tightened on his daughter.

There was a story here.

"It's okay, James. This is my son, Gabriel. He's not here to take Annie." Mom walked over to the two and patted Annie on the back. "He's visiting. Besides, we won't let Annie's grandparents take her away from you. You are a good father."

Hawke smiled and held his hand out. "Pleased to meet you, James."

The young man relaxed his hold on his daughter and shook hands. "Sorry. I've received so many threats from my wife's parents, I don't know who to trust."

"I understand. Annie is a precious girl." Hawke smiled at the child.

"I have to work overtime tomorrow. Can I drop Annie off early?"

"You can drop her off here any time you need to. She's no problem." Mom squeezed the child's cheek and went back to frying chicken. "You're welcome to stay for dinner, if you want. I made plenty."

James glanced at Hawke. "Not tonight. You have company, and I need to get laundry done."

Hawke didn't invite him to stay. He preferred a quiet dinner with his mom before he headed home.

"It was nice meeting you. See you in the morning, Mimi." He and Annie walked out the door with the child waving and grinning.

"What happened to the wife?" Hawke asked.

"She overdosed. Parents blamed James, but Carla was just unstable. Always had been. He loves that little girl and is bringing her up strong. We won't have to worry about losing her to drugs."

She placed the chicken on the table along with potatoes, gravy, and beans. "Sit. Dinner is ready."

He enjoyed the meal, reminiscing with his mom and asking her about the children she watched.

"You are the best thing that ever happened to these young people who need childcare. I'm proud of you." He gave his mom a hug as he got ready to leave.

"Thank you. I think I did a pretty good job bringing you and your sister up, considering our circumstances. I feel that gives me the guidance some of these children need."

"I agree. I'll come stay a couple days next time."

"You better. A few hours isn't enough." The tears glistening in her eyes, made his heart ache. He didn't come visit often enough.

"I promise." He climbed into his truck and headed over the Blue Mountain pass back to La Grande.

His phone buzzed when he was on the summit. "Hawke."

"Hey, it's Shoberg. Your warrant for search of the Welch home and hangar came through. I can have it at their residence in twenty minutes."

"I'll meet you there." He flicked on the lights and pressed on the accelerator. He wasn't going to miss the search.

Chapter Twenty-seven

Three law enforcement vehicles sat in front of the Welch residence when he pulled up. Shoberg stepped out of his cruiser with papers in his hands. A county deputy and a city detective met them at the door.

Introductions were made, and Hawke pushed the doorbell.

"They know we're here, someone looked out the window five minutes before you arrived," Shoberg said.

Roger answered the door. His gaze took in all four officers. "What do you want?"

Hawke held out the papers. "This is a warrant to search your premises."

"For what?" He took the papers and stared at them.

"For evidence your wife was involved in the murder of Ernest Cusack." Hawke moved into the building. "Is she here?" He knew she'd been released when Ilene dropped the assault charges.

"I haven't seen her since Sunday. She's usually

back home from her rounds by now." Roger stood back while the other lawmen turned to Hawke.

"We're looking for a burner phone, dome nuts, and clothing that is missing small glass beads." He pointed to the others. "You look in the garage, you the kitchen, you stay with Mr. Welch. I'll take the bedroom." He was the only one who knew the size and type of bead they were looking for. If he didn't find any clothing with the beads, he'd check the laundry room.

"Bedroom?" he asked Roger who seemed to be in shock.

The man pointed down the hall.

Hawke opened doors until he found the master bedroom. He looked through the drawers for the phone and beaded clothing. Nothing. The closet was crammed with women's clothing. He didn't see a single piece of men's clothing. He searched each garment, looking for beads. There was a bulging pillow case on the closet floor. He dumped it and wadded up in the middle of the other clothing was a blouse with small glass beads and a section that clearly had lost beads. He took a photo, bagged it, and wrote down the facts. He continued through the closet, checking pockets and the various purses for a phone.

The master bath turned up nothing.

He walked out of the room and entered the other bedroom. He'd thought it was a guest room, but while searching, realized it was Roger's room.

Leaving that room, Shoberg walked out of the office. "I didn't find a thing in there."

"Check the hall bathroom. I'll see if the others found anything." Hawke met up with the city cop in the kitchen.

"I haven't found a phone, but I haven't made it to the pantry yet."

Hawke nodded and opened the door to the small walk-in pantry. There was little food. It appeared the two rarely ate at home. He picked up several cereal boxes and shook them. They sounded like cereal, nothing heavy like a phone.

If she was still contacting Ilene and Mrs. Kahn, there was a good chance she had the phone with her and they were looking for something that wasn't here. Roger said she was usually home by now. He had a pretty good idea where she was. Close to Ilene and where she could keep an eye on what was happening in the investigation.

He dialed Justine.

"Hello, Hawke. What are you doing calling this late?" Justine asked.

"I was curious. Have you talked to Leanne lately?" He wasn't going to tell her they were looking for her.

"She's here. Why?"

"Roger called worrying about her. Did she go to your place after the police let her go?"

"Police? What are you talking about."

The younger sister was using her older sister. He didn't like his friend being used. "She bit Mrs. Cusack's finger, and the woman was going to press charges then changed her mind." He had a thought. "Is she listening to this conversation?"

"Yes."

"I know she's your sister, but you could be in danger if she thinks you are giving me information—"

"I don't understand. What are you talking about?"

"Justine, you have to trust me. Be careful. I'll

swing by your place on my way home. I'll be there in an hour." He hung up and handed the bagged shirt to Shoberg. "Take this to Pendleton for them to match with the beads I brought them earlier today and were sent to them right after the murder." He turned to Roger. "Don't call and tell your wife we've been here."

The man nodded.

All of the officers walked out together.

"Where are you going?" Shoberg asked.

"To make sure my suspect doesn't harm someone else."

«»«»«»

One faint light shone inside Justine's house when Hawke pulled up. The dogs made enough noise that anyone inside would know he'd arrived. He stepped out of his vehicle as Justine opened the front door. It was eleven. Not that late, but he didn't know when Justine went to bed.

"Hawke, I don't know what's going on, but as soon as I hung up from talking to you, Leanne pulled a different phone from her purse, talked on it, and grabbed her things and left." She pulled him in off the porch. "What is going on?"

"I believe your father helped her and two other women kill Ernest Cusack." He didn't know of any other way to say it than the truth.

Justine fell into the closest chair and stared at him. "Dad and Leanne? What are you talking about? How? Why?"

"I know your father used a helicopter from a charter service in Lewiston, owned by one of the other women, to pick up Leanne at the Alder airport and take her to the mountain where Cusack's body was found.

Her hair and beads from one of her shirts were found at the scene. The murder weapon, a wolf tracking collar, had to have come from Roger's helicopter, which your dad services. I believe he found the collar after Roger had taken biologists out to collar wolves and whether he took it to make money or because your sister was already contemplating murder, I don't know."

Justine moaned. "I could see Dad doing this. But Leanne? Why did they do it?"

"I believe she realized Cusack was never going to leave his wife and discovered his other lover and the money he'd been giving her to avoid the IRS. This made Leanne realize Cusack was using her. She had over a hundred thousand dollars in an account with her name. How she and the other two got together and planned it, I'm not sure." Hawke was still puzzling that out.

"If Leanne calls you, or returns, you can't let her know all of this. But you need to let me know where she is if she tells you. I'll have a warrant for her arrest as soon as I get the lab results from the clothing." Hawke put a hand on her shoulder. "Are you going to be okay?"

She nodded her head. "I can't…My dad and sister killed someone?"

"I'll call you when I have them in custody."

She nodded again.

He walked to the door and let himself out. If she'd been anyone else, he wouldn't have said a word, but she was his friend. He didn't want her finding out at the restaurant when she went to work.

He had a pretty good idea that Leanne had fled to Ilene's. He'd know when the Alder City police got back to him about what cars were parked at the residence.

«»«»«»

When he arrived at the office in Winslow on Thursday, he had a warrant for Ned Berkley's arrest, authorization to confiscate the helicopter, and he had a warrant for Leanne's arrest for murder. He sent the warrant for Berkley to the state police in La Grande to pick the man up. Finding Leanne was going to be easy. The Alder City Police had called and told him Leanne's car was parked at the Cusack residence.

It was going to give him pleasure to pick her up. He called Ullman, one of the other game wardens, and Deputy Novak, asking them to meet him at the Cusack residence.

They all arrived at the same time. Leanne's work vehicle was parked on the street. Hawke motioned for Ullman to keep an eye on it and for Novak to go to the back of the house. He walked up to the door with the arrest warrant. It was early enough that Ilene wouldn't be at work yet. And if she had the visitor he expected, he figured they were making plans.

The doorbell had a pompous ring to it. Something he wouldn't have envisioned the tight-fisted Cusack to spend his money on.

Ilene opened the door and started to close it.

Hawke shoved his foot and leg out to keep the door from closing. "I have a warrant for the arrest of Leanne Welch. I know she's here, her car is parked out front."

"Stop, police!" Ullman called out.

Hawke spun around in time to see him put cuffs on Leanne. When she was apprehended, he faced Ilene. She was looking a bit too smug. "Now I have a warrant to search your premises."

Her mouth dropped open, and she stared at him.

"Mrs. Cusack, here is the warrant. Please step outside." Deputy Novak had ran to the front of the house after Leanne.

"Deputy Novak, take Mrs. Welch to the station, and then return to help with the search," Hawke said.

Deputy Novak nodded and drove off with Leanne as Ullman stepped into the house.

Hawke pulled out his phone and called Sheriff Lindsay. "Deputy Novak is bringing a murder suspect into the county jail. I need his assistance at the Cusack residence for a search as soon as he can get back here."

"I'll send him right back."

Mrs. Cusack stood on the steps, her arms crossed over her large breasts, her face wrinkled in a deep frown. He had lots of questions but refrained since there wasn't a recording device present.

She finally spoke. "How long do I have to stand out here?"

"Until we finish searching your house."

"That could take hours," she whined. "I have a restaurant to run."

"You'll have to call and tell them to continue without you today." He had no doubt the restaurant would run fine today, and until someone took over. The staff was well-trained and conscientious.

The county car approached, siren wailing and lights flashing.

"Tell him to turn his lights and sirens off. People will talk," Mrs. Cusack said, pushing her body against the house as if it would hide her.

Deputy Novak jogged up to the step. "I hurried back."

"Watch Mrs. Cusack while Ullman and I start searching her house." He handed the warrant to the deputy and entered. The entry was clean and uncluttered. He spotted a purse hanging on a hall tree. He checked it for a burner phone. Nothing. He checked the living room, finding only Ilene's regular phone.

Ullman walked out of the kitchen as Hawke stepped into what appeared to be an office.

"I'll check the back rooms," Tad said.

Hawke nodded and began sifting through papers, files, and going through drawers. He discovered a file with the payments Ernest had made to Leanne and Mrs. Kahn. Their names, phone numbers, and addresses were written in pen on the inside flap of the folder. He took a photo of it and the contents, then stepped out into the hallway.

"Tad."

"Yeah?" The other trooper stuck his head out of the bedroom.

"Any luck?"

"No."

"Could you grab a couple evidence bags big enough for a file folder?" Hawke ducked back into the room, knowing the man would.

He'd gone through all the drawers in the desk. An oak file cabinet sat between two book cases. A tug on the top drawer opened it. Files that seemed to pertain to Ilene's job. The next drawer had household files. He skimmed through them as Ullman entered with the bags.

"That file on the corner of the desk shows she knew about the other two women." He pulled drawer three out. It had photographs. Expecting the photos to be of Ernest and his lovers, he was surprised to see they were of the three women sitting at a table in a restaurant.

He whistled. What were these doing in this cabinet? Had Ernest known they were getting together? Or had someone else put one and one and one together and blackmailed Ilene?

"What do you have there?" Ullman asked.

"More evidence." He put the photos in an evidence bag and closed the drawer. The bottom drawer had miscellaneous electronic cords.

"Still no phone. The photographs are incriminating enough but if we can link them by the phones, that would seal the conviction."

"I haven't finished in the bedroom. That woman is a slob." Ullman left the room.

Hawke stood back and studied the room as he would an area in a forest if he were looking for tracks. What in the room was out of place? His gaze started to the right and worked around the room. The printer paper on the printer stand stuck out an inch from the open end of the stand. The stand was wide enough to accommodate the paper.

He knelt at the stand and pulled out the paper. Against the back wall of the stand was a burner phone. He took a photo of the hiding spot, used one of the evidence bags to pick it up, tucked it in the bag, and stood. This was what he wanted to find in the search. The other evidence was a bonus.

Ullman was in the master bathroom opening the cabinets and rifling through them.

"I found it," Hawke said, after watching the other man work a few minutes.

"Good. I don't think I could take another minute in this perfume scented bathroom."

Hawke had to admit the room smelled like he imagined brothels would have smelled back during the days when people rarely bathed.

They exited the house.

"Deputy Novak, bring Mrs. Cusack to the sheriff's department."

The woman started to protest. "Why would you take me in?"

"As an accessory to your husband's murder."

Her mouth snapped shut.

Hawke stepped into his truck and his phone buzzed. Watts.

"Hawke."

"Watts here. We issued the warrant and recovered a pay as you go phone. I'm taking it and Mrs. Kahn into custody."

Hawke filled him in on what they had accomplished this morning. The photos, the phones, and the evidence that was coming back from forensics.

"I'll see what I can get out of her. You're sure about the pilot being Ned Berkley?"

"Yes. And I believe he's the one that took the collar out of Roger's helicopter."

"Then I'll question her with what I know. And keep you informed."

"I'll do the same." Hawke shoved his phone on his belt and headed to the Sheriff's Department. He had some questions for Leanne.

Chapter Twenty-eight

As Hawke walked into the County Station the sheriff called him over.

"We just received the results from the forensic tests. You'll want these when you question the Welch woman." Sheriff Lindsay handed him a file with several sheets of paper.

"Thanks." Hawke took them to the back room to read through before he stepped into the interview room with Leanne. There was no way she'd be able to talk her way out of the murder. Her DNA was found on the victim's penis. Her hair was found at the scene and wrapped around one of the bolts on the collar. The beads found under the body and at the spot behind the bushes where she'd waited, matched those on the shirt he'd found in the pillow case. And her DNA was on the gum wrapper he'd picked up by the bush. If she was smart she'd give up her accomplices and take them down with her and not be a martyr.

"What do you want us to do with Mrs. Cusack? She's sitting in the jail wailing that she should be allowed a phone call." One of the deputies walked into the room.

Knowing that Mrs. Kahn and everyone else involved in the scheme were in custody, he shrugged. "Let her make a call. But only one. I'll question her when I finish with Mrs. Welch."

The deputy nodded and headed to the jail.

Hawke walked down the hall and entered the room where Leanne was being held to keep her from knowing Ilene had been brought in as well.

She looked up. Fear rounded her eyes and lightened her complexion. Her hands were cuffed in front of her.

He took a seat and punched the button that recorded interviews. "Please state your name for the record."

She said her name, her gaze locked onto the cuffs binding her hands.

He didn't say anything else, just studied her. The longer he said nothing, she began avoiding eye contact.

"Why'd you do it?" he asked.

"Run? I didn't know what you wanted." Her attempt at attitude didn't quite hit the mark.

"Why did you kill Ernest Cusack?"

Tears trickled down her face. "I didn't kill Ernie. I loved him."

"You loved his money, not the man."

Her head snapped up. She stared at him.

"We know you somehow lured him to that clearing, showed him how much you cared, and then tightened that collar around his neck." He studied her as he went through the scenario they'd figured out.

She shuddered but didn't say a word, studying the hand cuffs.

"Why were you picked as the one to put the collar on him?"

Her gaze rose to his. "What are you talking about?" She didn't ask it as if she had no clue. She was fishing to see what he knew.

"We've pieced together that you, Ilene, and Abigail worked out how to get rid of Ernest and keep all his money. But finding photos of the three of you meeting at a restaurant, clenched it."

Her face grew redder, her fingers twined together tightly.

"You might as well tell me your side of it, because Detective Watts, in Lewiston, is questioning Abigail right now, and when I finish with you, I'll be bringing Ilene in to tell her story. You'd be dumber than I thought, if you didn't think the two of them would throw you under the bus. After all, their hands are clean. They aren't the ones who tightened that collar and left DNA, are they?"

Her jaw clenched and her eyes sparked.

"What you tell me can make the difference in what you are charged with." He motioned to the handcuffs. "How long do you want to stay in jail?"

"That pig Ilene contacted me. Said she knew I'd been helping myself to her husband. She said she didn't care, but I was going to have to give the money back he'd given me. I'd ruined my marriage and had sex on an office desk for that money. I wasn't giving it back to her."

Leanne's face had contorted into such a disgusted

grimace, he wondered how she'd lived with herself.

Her fingers picked at the handcuffs. "She started sending me letters through my work, saying she was going to tell my husband how I'd whored myself and other things until I couldn't stand her accusations anymore. I asked her what I could do to keep the money and keep her mouth shut. She told me to buy a pay-as-you-go phone and only use it to contact her. I called her and that's when she told me all I had to do was meet her up on Goat Mountain. She'd have Ernie there and I had to seduce him." Her hands shook. "Someone else could kill him. She said if I did that, she'd forget about the money and that she knew about my affair with her husband."

Leanne leaned back in her chair. "They told me the man picking me up in the helicopter would be the one who would do the killing." She shook her head. "The surprise was on me when the helicopter Abigail sent for me at Alder was flown by my father.

"I started to get out of the helicopter, but he grabbed my arm and yanked me in. He said we'd both get what we wanted. He'd get money enough to quit working, and I'd get rid of my husband." She glanced down at her hands. "I didn't understand what he meant by get rid of my husband until I saw the wolf collar."

Hawke studied the woman. The fact she'd helped her dad kill someone seemed to upset her more than the act.

"How did you know where to find Ernest?" he asked.

"Ilene had me send a text to Ernest that I was camping on Goat Mountain, and if he wanted to do something kinky, I'd meet him at the coordinates she gave me."

"Then he wasn't surprised to see you. Didn't expect anything unusual?" Hawke wondered at the man being so sure he'd do away with his wife and have a fling with his lover at the same time.

"No. I was waiting behind the bushes when he arrived. I don't know where Dad was. He said he'd stay out of sight." She became agitated. "It was like a bad dream. Ernie arrived. I walked out toward him. He was happy to see me. Said something about we couldn't take too long, his ball and chain might come looking for him. Dad had given me the collar. Ernie asked about it. I said it was the kinky I was talking about. I told him how I'd read that when a man put a collar on, he became more excited. He was always up for something kinky. I put the collar on to where it was snug, without the fasteners. Then we knelt on the ground and starting making out while I gently tightened the collar. He started moaning and Dad appeared. He came up behind Ernie and motioned for me to leave. I ran back to the bushes, picked up my pack, and ran to the helicopter. Dad came back about fifteen minutes later. He climbed in, started the helicopter, and we didn't say a word all the way back to Alder." She heaved a sigh. "I wasn't sure Ernie was really dead until you said something at Justine's."

"I'll have this transcribed, and you'll need to sign. It appears to me, you are an accessory. But your father will be going away for murder."

"I don't think it's the first time he's done it," she said quietly.

Hawke had the same thought. He left the room and motioned to the female deputy waiting in the hallway.

"Stay with her until she signs her statement, then put her in holding."

The woman nodded.

He walked into the sheriff's office and sat down. Telling Sheriff Lindsay what he'd heard, they determined it was best to let the officers interrogating Berkley know they had him.

Hawke called and talked to Detective Donner. Once the detective was up to speed on what he needed to know to continue his questioning of the murderer, Hawke asked that Ilene be brought into the interview room.

She tried to deny everything. Halfway through his interview, he called Watts and relayed what Abigail Kahn had told him.

"You told Abigail Kahn that if she didn't help you kill your husband, you would tell the IRS she was laundering money in her non-profit organizations."

Ilene started to protest.

"Mrs. Kahn is a shrewd woman. She recorded you with her phone."

That bit of news crumpled the woman's wall of objections. She admitted to everything. Even to asking the private investigator to follow them, giving her proof she wasn't with her husband when he died, but the weasel, her words, had bailed on her and she refused to pay him.

When everyone was lodged on charges, Hawke logged into the computer at the Sheriff's Office and read the transcriptions of Mrs. Kahn and Ned Berkley.

Mrs. Kahn told her story without Detective Watts asking very many questions. Her story matched what Hawke already knew. He was interested though in the fact it was Ilene's private investigator who gave her the name of Ned Berkley as a person who could take care of their problem. That would be one more person going down for the death of Ernest Cusack.

Hawke pulled up Ned's transcript. As he'd figured, Detective Donner had to do a lot of talking with very few answers. Until the detective told Ned his daughter and the woman who contacted him had given him up. The curse words and names he called the two women made Hawke wonder how the man had dealt with his demanding daughter. And how the two girls hadn't known their father was a murderer for hire?

The one thing that had puzzled Hawke the most was how he'd missed their trail to and from Cusack. Two people had walked into and out of the clearing and all he'd found was the dome nut. How had they done that?

Ned began telling how they'd waited and he'd tightened the collar on Cusack's neck. He'd broken off a limb on a bush and used that to brush out any tracks. He'd made the path wide and random enough to look like something had been blown by the wind. The man was cunning and covered all his tracks. Hawke believed that was how he'd gotten away with other murders.

Once the man started talking, he was like a fountain of past deeds. He told how he killed his second wife. And when he got away with it, he realized his job as a roving mechanic would take him anywhere, giving him reason to travel and take care of people's problems and add to his bank account.

Hawke wondered how many unsolved murder cases were because of Ned Berkley? He read to the end of the file and turned off his computer. It was time to go home and get a good night's rest.

Now it was up to the District Attorney to decide what the charges would be.

The hardest part would be telling Justine about her family.

«»«»«»

Hawke decided even though he was beat, Justine deserved to hear about her family in person. His body tried to override his mind as he drove past the road to his place. He was dead tired, but he owed his friend a face to face discussion.

He drove into Winslow and turned down the road toward Justine's. He was getting more tired as he drove, but he had to face her tonight. By morning everyone in the county would know who had killed Cusack and all the people involved in the case.

Turning into Justine's lane, the dogs started barking. A light went on, and Justine came to the door with a shotgun.

She must have noticed the state vehicle because she lowered the weapon.

Hawke exited his vehicle and sauntered up to the porch.

"What are you doing here so late?"

The quarter moon didn't illuminate her face well enough for him to see if she'd already heard the news.

"As your friend, I wanted to tell you, your father has been arrested for the murder of Ernest Cusack, and your sister was an accomplice." He figured there was no need to withhold the truth.

She gasped and the weapon started to slip through her hands.

Hawke caught it before it hit the ground and

grasped her arm, leading her to a chair on the front porch.

"Is there any doubt they didn't do it?" she asked, her head bowed.

"We have confessions." Hawke rubbed his face. There just wasn't any way to break something like this to family members.

"We? You were the one who caught them?" Her tone had turned icy.

"Yes. I was part of the team who gathered the evidence." This was feeling too much like when he'd arrested his brother-in-law. He didn't want to make excuses for his job. It was who he was and he wouldn't break any rules for anyone.

"You can go. I'll be fine." She stood, took her shotgun away from him, and walked into the house.

His shoulders drooped and his chest felt heavy. They'd just begun to be friends. Someone he could do things with and know they didn't expect any strings attached. He sighed and climbed into his truck. Sometimes this job played hell on having a life outside of the job.

«»«»«»

After a good night's sleep and checking on Darlene, Hawke headed to Winslow for breakfast at the Rusty Nail and to write up the last of the reports on the case. Then he was taking two days off.

The minute he stepped into the restaurant, he knew word had gotten out about the murderer being found. Everyone was solemn. Dick Harlin sat at a table drinking coffee with other farmers. He made eye contact then went back to the conversation.

Justine stood behind the counter. There wasn't her

usual welcome smile. He hoped she didn't blame him for her family being in jail. It was their own actions. He'd just done his job.

"Coffee?" she asked, holding up the pot.

"Yes, please." He turned the cup in front of him over.

"How's Darlene?" Merrilee asked, shuffling over from the far end of the counter.

"She's fine. I feel sorry for the student who left the curry comb in the stall." He sipped his coffee and caught Justine's gaze over the cup.

"I'll bet she does give whoever did it a piece of her mind. A woman her age shouldn't be messing around with horses anyway," Merrilee said.

Hawke laughed. "Have you said that to Darlene?"

"I wouldn't dare, she'd take a swipe at me." Merrilee grinned and shuffled back to the kitchen.

"Your usual?" Justine asked.

"No. I'd like a sausage omelet today." He peered into her eyes. "Life is too short to fall into a rut."

"Point taken," Justine said, placing his order and picking up the coffee pot to refill cups.

Hawke sipped his coffee, it appeared Justine didn't hold a grudge like his ex-wife.

«»«»«»

Mouse Trail Ends

Book Two in the Gabriel Hawke series

Prologue

Sunday Morning

"Momma, since we have to leave today, can I go look for more wildflowers to put in my scrapbook? Please?" Kitree knew if she was polite her mom was more likely to say yes.

Her mom looked up from rolling clothes to put in her backpack. "Only if you don't wander far. Stay within sight of the camp, and be back in an hour. I know your dad doesn't want to get home late. He has work tomorrow."

"Thank you!" Kitree dropped the clothing she'd been rolling to put in her backpack and grabbed her wildflower book. She patted her jacket pocket, making sure she had her book, *My Side of the Mountain Pocket Guide.* Darting out of the tent before her mom changed her mind, Kitree headed up the slope behind their camp.

Piles of snow in dips on the mountainside glittered in the sunlight. Where the snow had melted and the warm summer sun shone all day long, she was able to find a small scattering of buttercups. She'd found lots of the small flowers with shiny yellow leaves and many Indian Paintbrush on their hike up the mountain and around the lake. She was hoping for a lily or a bluebell.

Her scrapbook of wildflowers wouldn't be complete without those two flowers.

A boom ricocheted around the bowl of earth that

cupped Minam Lake.

Fear froze her feet.

Another boom resounded in the quietness the first had caused.

She'd been on a hunting trip with her dad just this past fall and knew what she'd heard were gunshots. They'd sounded close. The only people at the lake this weekend had been her family. They'd hiked around the edge to make sure. Who would be shooting? Her father hadn't brought a gun on the trip.

Kitree ran down the side of the ravine toward the camp.

Out of breath when she reached the tent, she raised her face to draw in more air and caught sight of motion at the top of the ravine where the trail disappeared over the edge. A man's back and head. Dark longish hair and a plaid shirt.

Lowering her gaze to the area in front of the tent, she spotted Daddy lying on the ground. She ran over to him and dropped to her knees. Her gaze landed on a small red spot on his shirt, where his jacket had flopped open.

"Daddy?"

He didn't look at her. His eyes stared up at the blue summer sky.

A cold shiver of fear rippled through her body. She leaned closer to try and feel breath on her cheek.

Nothing. Her chest squeezed. How could he be dead? He was Daddy. He held her tight when she was scared.

"Daddy?" she barely whispered.

A clank in the tent drew her attention. Momma! She wasn't alone.

Kitree shoved to her feet and ran to the tent. Throwing back the flap, her gaze landed on her mom lying face up in the middle of the tent. Blood and pink bubbles oozed from her mom's chest. Her eyes were closed.

Kitree knelt beside her. "Momma? Who did this?"

"Run… Kitree," her mom wheezed. "Take… all… can… carry." She sucked in air and more pink bubbles formed on her chest. "Find… Ranger Station. Don't talk… anyone."

"I don't understand. Why can't I talk to anyone?" Kitree wanted to scream and shake her mom. She wasn't going anywhere. She'd stay here and help her mom. They would both leave together. All they had were each other with Daddy dead.

Her mom's eyes fluttered open. Slowly her gaze focused on Kitree. "The man…this." She sucked in air and her chest bubbled out more pink. "Kill you…don't let… him… see you… Go! Take food... Go!"

"I can't leave you and daddy." Kitree cupped her mom's cheek. Her heart and mind raced trying to figure out what to do. Her mother needed her, but to get help she had to leave. They had no way to contact anyone. And then she had to stay away from a man. Fear for her and her mom made it hard to make a decision. Thoughts and fears banged into one another in her head. Finally, she knew of no other way than to find help. "I'll get help. I'll come back with –"

"No… Too late... Save… Self… Take map… Stay… off… Trails… Ranger Station…" Her mother sucked in air and coughed. Blood trickled at the corner of her mouth.

"I'm not leaving you," Kitree said, dabbing at the

blood drizzling out of her mom's lips with her bandana and trying to hold back tears. She had to be strong for momma. To get her help.

"No… I'm leaving you," her mom barely whispered the words. Her body shivered and went still.

"No Momma! Don't leave me alone!" Kitree fell on her mother, crying. Grief tore at her heart, making her chest ache. Daddy and Momma gone. She was alone. They had no other relatives. Her thoughts stuttered to a stop and her mind shouted, "You are an orphan!"

A bird screeched.

She jolted at the sound. There was more to worry about than being alone. She had to protect her parents. She'd heard birds pecked at the eyes of dead animals. She didn't want that to happen to Daddy.

She raised off her mom. Her shirt felt cold and wet on her chest.

A glance down caused a nasty taste in her mouth. She shoved her jacket off and ripped her bloody shirt over her head, throwing it away from her.

Kitree grabbed a sweatshirt out of her pack and pulled that and her jacket back on. Without looking at momma, she hauled a sleeping bag out to her dad. She covered him with the unzipped bag, kissing his forehead before hiding his face. His face was so still, so calm. If not for the unseeing eyes and still chest, she'd think he was watching the clouds for shapes. A game they'd played many times. Anguish sucked the air from her lungs. She'd never hear his voice again or play any games with him. Tears burned, but she held them back.

She scrambled to her feet and returned to the tent to cover momma with another sleeping bag. Kissing her mom's forehead, she vowed to find the person who took her family away.

There was only one thing she could do. Find a ranger station without being seen and find justice for her parents.

Kitree rolled up her sleeping bag without looking at the one that covered her mom. She didn't want to think about leaving her parents. But leaving was the only way to find the person who'd killed them.

She dumped everything out of her mom's backpack and shoved the sleeping bag and as much food as she could carry along with her pocket guide and wildflower book into her mom's pack. Her mom's sky-blue rain slicker lay on the floor beside the clothing Kitree had dumped out. She added that to the pack and found all three of their water bottles. Filling the bottles with the water momma had boiled that morning for their hike out of here, tears trickled down her cheeks.

They should all be going home. Dad to his job, her to see her friends, and Momma to her volunteer things. Kitree blinked hard. That life wouldn't happen.

She swiped at the tears to look for the water purifying drops. She slid the small bottle into a side pocket on the pack.

Kitree shouldered the pack. The straps were out wider than her shoulders. She dug through Momma's belongings and used one of her bandanas to tie the straps together in front of her chest. The map sat open on the floor. They'd all three checked the course they had planned to take that morning. Daddy's bold line going along the east fork trail wouldn't work. She glanced at the trails and decided the best way to avoid the killer was to go west from the lake and over the mountain.

She walked out of the tent without looking down at Momma under the sleeping bag. Tears weren't going to get her to a ranger station and help.

A quick glance at Daddy's body under his sleeping bag blurred her vison with tears.

She hoped someone found them before the wild animals did. "I love you Momma and Daddy, and I'm going to make sure someone pays for this."

With a grieving heart and a determination to find the man who killed her parents, she set out to carry out her mom's wishes. No trail. Tell a ranger.

«»«»«»

If you liked this prologue, ask your local library or book store to order, *Mouse Trail Ends* book 2in the Gabriel Hawke series for you.

About the Book

Thank you for reading book one of the Gabriel Hawke Novels. If you enjoyed the book, please leave a review. It's the best way to thank an author.

Continue investigating and tracking with Hawke in book 2, Mouse Trail Ends.

As I stated in the beginning. I grew up in Wallowa County and have always been amazed by its beauty, history, and ruralness. Many say Alaska is the last frontier but there are so many communities in the western states that are nearly as rural as Alaska. After doing a ride-along with a Fish and Wildlife State Trooper in Wallowa County, I knew this was where I had to set this new series.

Paty

About the Author

Paty Jager is an award-winning author of 32 novels, 10 novellas, and numerous anthologies of murder mystery and western romance. All her work has Western or Native American elements in them along with hints of humor and engaging characters. Paty and her husband raise alfalfa hay in rural eastern Oregon. Riding horses and battling rattlesnakes, she not only writes the western lifestyle, she lives it.

You can follow her at any of these places:

Website: http://www.patyjager.net

Blog: http://www.patyjager.blogspot.com

FB Page: https://www.facebook.com/PatyJagerAuthor/

Pinterest: https://www.pinterest.com/patyjag/

Twitter: https://twitter.com/patyjag

Thank you for purchasing this Windtree Press publication. For other books of the heart, please visit our website at www.windtreepress.com.

For questions or more information contact us at info@windtreepress.com.

Windtree Press
www.windtreepress.com

Hillsboro, OR 97124

CPSIA information can be obtained
at www.ICGtesting.com
Printed in the USA
BVHW031259281021
620186BV00018B/207